HAVEN ASCENDANT

ROBERT M. KERNS

Knightsfall Press

Published by Knightsfall Press
PO Box 280
Mineral Wells, WV 26150
https://www.knightsfallpress.com

ABOUT THIS BOOK

Nothing is ever easy...

Tensions rise as the Coalition pursues its war of conquest. Who will be their next target?

The Provisional Parliament in the old Commonwealth sinks deeper into fascism as people flee their worlds in droves. Those fleeing head straight for Beta Magellan.

Only time will tell when Cole must face the next major choice: get involved in the war or let it pass him and Beta Magellan by.

Which will he choose?

Read Now to find out!

TYPOS

Typos and little slips in grammar are the bane of any author. Unfortunately, they are almost impossible to eradicate completely. I can show you many traditionally published books—twenty years old and more—that have a 'whoopsie' here and there.

That being said, if you find a typo or something that seems to be an error in grammar, please do not hesitate to contact me at typos@knightsfallpress.com.

I will periodically collate any emails and produce updated PDF and eBook files, and I'll make an announcement in my monthly newsletter when the updates have been published.

DRAMATIS PERSONAE

- Cole: Bartholomew James Coleson is the heir to the immensely wealthy Coleson Trust; indeed, some star systems compare their GDP to estimates of the Trust's worth as a metric of economic growth and achievement. The source of this wealth is his family's ownership of Coleson Interstellar Engineering (CIE), the company that owns and maintains the interstellar jump gate network used for transit between star systems, and he is captain/owner of the battle-carrier *Haven*.
- Srexx: Srexxilan is the self-aware AI inhabiting the computer cluster aboard the battle-carrier *Haven*.
- Sasha: Sasha Thyrray is the middle child and oldest daughter of Paol and Mira Thyrray. She is the first officer aboard the battle-carrier *Haven*.
- Harlon: Colonel Harlon Hanson commands the marines aboard the battle-carrier *Haven*.
- Emily: Commander Emily Vance is the daughter of Sevrin Vance and the commander-air-group (CAG) aboard the battle-carrier *Haven*.
- Sev: Sevrin Vance is the second child and oldest son of Carl

and Lindsay Vance in Tristan's Gate. He is Cole's Director of System Infrastructure.

- Painter: Julianna Painter is the former owner/captain of the freighter *Beauchamp*. She is now Cole's Director of Everything Else; if it's not related to the actual construction process of re-building Beta Magellan (which is Sev's responsibility), it falls under Painter's aegis.
- Garrett: Garrett is Cole's oldest friend. He found Cole shortly after the massacre of Beta Magellan and raised him until Cole was ready to go out on his own. Garrett now serves as Cole's spymaster...er, that is...Director of Intelligence.

CHAPTER ONE

In Transit to the Oriolis Jump Gate
The Freighter *Jezebel's Hope*
Zeta Creoris System, Aurelian Commonwealth
14 June 3003, 10:57 GST

"It's no good, Captain," the comms tech announced. "The jamming is too strong."

Captain Adrienne Narvou did her best not to sigh. It was looking like this would be her last run...ever. With eleven successful refugee runs to Tristan's Gate already in the log, she came back for another, but it seemed her luck had finally run out. A destroyer and two frigates pursued her freighter, repeating orders to heave to and prepare to be boarded. She had a good head start, so she might make the jump gate, but it was just a matter of time at this point. Her pursuers surely sent word ahead to the new Oriolis garrison.

"Contacts!" the sensor tech announced, his voice anxious. "Multiple contacts dead ahead at five light-minutes!"

The best civilian sensors on the market had a range of one light-day with any kind of resolution, and Narvou hadn't been able to afford even fourth-best the last time she took her ship in for a refit. The sensors aboard *Jezebel's Hope* exceeded the minimum requirements to be space worthy but not by much. Fortunately, even though five light-minutes sounded really close, it was still almost thirty minutes away at one-fifth-light.

"Show me the plot," Narvou said.

The viewscreen activated, displaying over thirty ship codes. The new ships were arranged in a rough line-abreast formation, creating a wall between her and the jump gate. As Narvou examined the plot, the computer began adding data to the ship codes as the comms system communicated transponders. Fifteen frigates. Ten destroyers. Six cruisers. Three battleships. And one dreadnought.

Narvou's focus flicked back to the ships pursuing her. *Hounds for the hunters.*

Narvou wracked her mind for what she knew of her passengers, trying to figure out why in the stars the Provisional Parliament would dispatch a dreadnought battlegroup for her dinky, old freighter. As far as she knew, none of her refugees were special; they were farmers, artisans, factory workers. Okay...there were a couple scientists, but they had assured her they were minor faculty at a system university.

"Captain! Message broadcast! It's coming from the dreadnought," the comms tech announced. "I can't believe they're overpowering the jamming at this range."

"Play it," Narvou said.

The bridge speakers came alive. "May I have your attention, please? I am Admiral Jennings Trask—"

Narvou's concentration on the message evaporated. One of her passengers *must* have lied to her. Jennings Trask was a legend among the spacer community, widely whispered to be the next Chief of Naval Operations for the Commonwealth. Having almost more decorations than places to put them on his uniform, Admiral Jennings Trask was the officer the Commonwealth sent to solve the unsolvable.

Cheers from her people pulled Narvou from her anxiety-riddled musings, and she blinked as she realized she had no idea why her people were celebrating.

"Play that back," Narvou said, hoping the cheers were related to the message.

"Aye, Captain," the comms tech said.

The speakers once more carried Trask's voice. "May I have your attention, please? I am Admiral Jennings Trask. Task Force 42-Bravo, you are executing illegal orders. I advise you to stand down and withdraw, or we will defend the freighter with all necessary force."

A high-pitched wail erupted, and the sensor tech almost screamed, "Missile launch! Three hundred—that is, three-zero-zero—birds incoming! They're locked on and are homing!"

Narvou watched the dots representing the missiles on the plot as her mind ran the probabilities. The ships of the former Commonwealth used two types of missiles: energy-signature and transponder tracking, and IR-profile tracking. The IR sensor packages were older and cheaper; when the civil war broke out, the Commonwealth had been phasing them out. There was a chance that those three hundred missiles were IR trackers...at least some of them.

"Helm, turn off the Attitude Control System," Narvou said, "and kill the engines. I want us to drift. Comms, kill the transponder and signal the engine room: stop all heat radiation possible. I want to be a hole in the night."

Sparing a glance at the plot, Narvou saw a mass of dots fast approaching her ship from her pursuers. Just as she looked up, though, she saw a throng of frigate and destroyer data codes leap forward from Trask's line of battle. The larger ships were slower to show their movement, but the cruisers, battleships, and dreadnought were moving as well.

The next minutes were the longest of Narvou's life. The wall of missiles bore down on her defenseless freighter as Trask's destroyers and frigates raced to reach her in time. There was no chance the battleships and dreadnought—with their massive missile defense—would make it, so everything depended on the smaller, fleeter ships.

Collision alarms shrieked throughout the ship, some destroyers' and frigates' passage so close they triggered the warning. Narvou's anger spiked at such reckless ship handling, but then she understood what they'd done. By passing so close to the freighter in such a tight formation, those specific destroyers and frigates tried to fool the incoming missiles into locking onto them instead.

Dots appeared around each destroyer and frigate, followed shortly by her sensor tech announcing, "Trask's ships are firing interceptors."

The missiles still bored in toward the freighter, and Narvou realized why the gambit had failed: the missiles' IFF. Trask's ships must have been marked as 'friendly' by the missiles' targeting firmware.

The red dots representing the closing missiles began vanishing in puffs of pixelated destruction as interceptors took them out. Narvou watched the count. Two-fifty. Two hundred. One-fifty. The interceptors were taking a toll, but *Jezebel's Hope* wasn't a warship with combat-grade shields and armor; her shields were just enough to protect against micrometeorites. One missile—just one—would see to her well enough.

"Trask's ships are engaging the missiles with point defense," the sensor tech announced.

The count now started dropping at a much greater rate. Almost in the blink of an eye, the count went from one-twenty-five down to twenty-five, but the destroyers and frigates passed out of range of the missiles, their vectors carrying them beyond the reach of their missile defense.

Narvou took a deep breath as she attempted to settle her mind. Twenty-five missiles. It was a death sentence. She started to apologize to her people for bringing them into this, but her sensor tech's exclamation stopped her.

"Holy shit!" the tech shouted.

"What is it?" Narvou asked.

The sensor tech swiveled to face her, a huge grin spreading across his young face. "The dreadnought is pulling a *Haven*!"

Narvou blinked at the non-sequitur. Yes...*Haven* was also something of a legend among the spacer community by now, but she couldn't think of a specific maneuver that could be called 'a *Haven*.'

Her sensor tech saw she wasn't following, so he swiveled back to his console, saying, "Here...look."

He reconfigured the plot on the forward viewscreen, and Narvou gaped at the new data. Trask's flagship had moved into an escort position *behind* her freighter, rotating so that the ship itself served as a massive wall between the freighter and the incoming missiles. The dreadnought was just far enough away that it wouldn't trigger the freighter's collision alarms.

It wasn't long before the dreadnought moved out of its defensive position, and the freighter's computer could update the plot from the sensor feeds. While serving as a shield, the dreadnought's radiation had been so strong the freighter's sensors couldn't read anything behind them *but* the dreadnought. The first thing Narvou saw was that Trask's destroyers and frigates raced to re-join the formation. The second was that there was no sign of the hostile task force.

"Captain, we're being hailed," the comms tech announced. "It's Admiral Trask."

"Put him on," Narvou replied.

The forward viewscreen switched from the plot to a view of an older gentleman in the jumpsuit Aurelian spacers wore aboard-ship.

"Captain," Trask said, "how do you and your people fare?"

"Very well," Narvou answered. "Thank you for defending us, Admiral. What happened to the task force?"

Silence extended for a moment before Trask said, "Unfortunately, they would not see reason. The ships under my command defended themselves when the task force fired on them."

A heavy weight settled in the pit of Narvou's stomach. There'd be no coming back to the Commonwealth now...not after being involved in the destruction of a task force.

"I see. I'm sorry."

"As are we," Trask replied. "What is your destination?"

"I was planning on taking the refugees aboard to Tristan's Gate," Narvou said, "but I'm not sure if we can make it that far. We have to cross five more systems just to leave Coalition space."

"If I may," Trask said, "I would argue it's unwise, even if you could make it. Tristan's Gate doesn't have sufficient defenses if the Coalition follows."

"Where would you suggest we go, then?"

"There's only one safe harbor for any of us now: Beta Magellan."

CHAPTER TWO

Citadel Station
  Beta Magellan System
  14 July 3003, 09:23 GST

Citadel Station was the name chosen for the new station upon its completion; it led Beta Magellan IV in its flight around the star at the planet's L5 LaGrange point, and the Coleson Clanhold trailing along at L4 was now an empty shell. Several people suggested making the old clanhold into a museum, but Cole wasn't sure about that. The new Hall of Remembrance down on the planet was enough of a museum for his taste.

Cole grinned as he looked out the viewport of the station's shuttle. Sev piloted. Painter sat in the seat behind Sev. They were touring the completed shipyard, starting with the civilian bays. Every bay held ships in various states of construction.

"How are we doing for raw material?" Cole asked.

"In all truth?" Painter asked before sighing. "We're keeping ahead of demand, but just barely. If we weren't recycling the military ships for raw material to use in their replacements, we'd have supply shortfalls.

It will be better, the more mining ships we build...but that's more of a long-term solution than a short-term bandage."

Cole nodded. "How about advertising for shipping-container loads of anything freighters want to deliver? We did it in Tristan's Gate and Centauri. I don't want random people cruising through Beta Magellan until we've built our defenses, but they could deliver the containers to Gateway."

It hadn't taken very long for the system that linked to Beta Magellan to become known as Gateway. The original name was on a star chart somewhere, but those associated with Cole and the revitalization of Beta Magellan never bothered with any name but Gateway.

Painter nodded. "We haven't done it yet. Someone brought it up in a meeting not too long ago, but it looked to be a morale issue for several of the mining teams."

Cole blinked and swiveled to face her. "What? A morale issue? Seriously?"

"Yes," Painter replied. "Several of the mining teams felt that it was the teams' collective responsibility to ensure you had the raw material you needed for your operations. If they were doing their jobs, you shouldn't *need* to buy regolith or whatever from anywhere else."

Cole sighed. "That's just stupid. We have...what...nine mining teams right now?"

"Eleven, actually. We replaced the last two traditional mining ships with Gyv'Rathi designs just about a month ago."

"Okay, eleven mining teams," Cole conceded. "If they worked every hour of every day, could they provide enough raw material to support all our construction programs...even leaving aside the fact that trying to do so would probably be a death sentence?"

Painter shook her head. "No, but they don't seem to recognize that. Plus, I think some of them that are new to mining are afraid they'll lose their jobs; many of them are refugees and recent arrivals at that. The veteran miners are taking them under their wings, so to speak, but the newbies seem the most driven to prove themselves."

Cole sighed. He knew what needed to be done, but he didn't like it. He didn't like that it would take the miners out of commission for the better part of three days, maybe five.

"Okay," he said. "Tell them I want to call an assembly of the mining teams. But I'm not going to call it until we have a five-day supply of feedstock for the recyclers. I'll pay double overtime rates for anyone who puts in the extra hours without safety violations. Once we have that buffer, call everyone in. I want to have a word with them."

By now, the shuttle drifted above the military construction bays, specifically the slips for frigates. Citadel Station had thirty construction bays each for frigates and destroyers, fifteen for cruisers, and twenty more bays that Cole assumed were for battle-carriers. Twenty battle-carrier construction bays seemed a bit much, by Cole's estimation, but he'd taken a strictly hands-off approach to the system's infrastructure design.

"About half the frigate and destroyer bays are finalizing the last of the Oriolis Fifty-Seven," Sev said. "We're starting to recycle the ships we claimed or bought after the first battle of Tristan's Gate, and once we recycle those, we'll move on to our ships from the *second* battle of Tristan's Gate. The ships that didn't go into forming *Haven*'s carrier battlegroup are patrolling the systems we've claimed, especially those with active mining operations. Yes...the mining ships do carry weapons, but a decent pirate fleet could still swarm them."

Cole grinned at the reminder that he had his carrier battlegroup. He wasn't sure he *needed* a carrier battlegroup, per se, but he'd wanted one ever since he'd processed just what *Haven* was. The thought took him back to watching ancient movies with his grandfather that featured carriers and carrier groups, fictional military films or documentaries.

"I have a meeting later today with Sasha and Admiral Sato," Cole said. "They want to discuss where this navy we're building fits into everything...and then, there's the inevitable meeting with Paol. Yes, I want Beta Magellan to have a system of laws and governance, but why does it all have to be so boring?"

Sev chuckled. "Just think what it would be like without those laws and governance. You can survive a little boredom if it protects your citizens in the long run, right?"

Cole laughed. "Yeah. I suppose I can. So, want to tell me why you built twenty construction bays for battle-carriers?"

Sev's expression was unreadable. "Wait till you see them. Then, you tell me."

Cole frowned. That response didn't really make a whole lot of sense, but he'd see soon enough.

The shuttle was most of the way through the fifteen cruiser bays when the furthest ten bays appeared on the sensor feed. They were *massive*—way too massive for battle-carriers—and inactive. Cole blinked as he stared at the sensor feed, his mind locked. His jaw worked as if he were trying to speak, but no sound came.

"Dreadnought bays?" Cole said at last. "You built *ten* dreadnought bays? I can't imagine circumstances where one star system would need one dreadnought, let alone ten. A fleet of battle-carriers would allow me to conquer Human space. Dreadnoughts would just add insult to the injury."

Sev shrugged. "We discussed it, and I felt it was better to have them and not need them than need them and not have them. You're correct. Right now, we don't *need* them, but it's impossible to predict what operational requirements you might find yourself facing. I'd like to think I've come to know you fairly well over the last year and the months before your trip to Centauri. You seem intent on defending people, especially those who would have trouble defending themselves, and the day might come when you're faced with a threat that *requires* building dreadnoughts. You have no idea how much I hope I'm wrong, but I wouldn't be doing my job as your Head of System Infrastructure if I didn't consider the possibility."

Cole nodded. "You make a very good point. Thank you for looking out for me."

Sev chuckled. "It's one of the many reasons you pay me."

"How are we for the jump gate defenses?" Cole asked.

"They're coming along nicely," Sev replied. "Citadel Station also doubles as a defensive emplacement for the planet, and by the time we're finished, Beta Magellan will be one of the most heavily defended systems in known space."

"Good. Once the system defenses are in place here, start moving the construction teams out into the space we've claimed. In addition to the system patrols, I want all of the jump gates in systems we control to have defenses in place."

"You know," Painter said, "there are some who would say fortifying the jump gates will lead to escalation between other star powers."

Cole chuckled. "They're welcome to build system defenses around the jump gates; I don't care about that. Honestly, it makes perfect sense to do so. They'd just better be sure they don't try to control who uses them; the jump gates aren't theirs to control."

Coleson Interstellar Engineering had a reputation for the most ironclad, draconian legal contracts in known space. The penalties associated with breaking the contracts or violating their terms were such that the offender would be better off committing suicide than trying to survive them. Even worse, the contracts spelled out in no uncertain terms a level of corporate warfare CIE would levy against whoever committed the breach of contract that would make hostile takeovers look downright friendly. In the almost three-quarters of a millennium the company had existed, no one had chosen to test the contracts.

Cole nodded, gazing out the viewport as they passed over the inactive dreadnought bays, saying, "You and your people have done well, Sev. I appreciate you, and please ensure all of your people know I appreciate them, too. We should probably be getting back, so Sasha and Admiral Sato can have their time with me."

"You make that sound like they're going to torture you or something," Painter said, grinning.

"I have a sneaking suspicion they're going to come at me again about formally organizing something like a Department or Ministry of Defense, and they're not wrong. I just don't want us to get bloated with all kinds of bureaucracy. I want Beta Magellan's government to be as light and agile and flexible as possible." Cole's voice trailed off for a moment as he swiveled around to face Painter. "Have you given any thought to my promise of building you a new freighter?"

Painter nodded. "I have, and honestly, I've come to enjoy my job more than I enjoyed being a freighter rat. The piece of bridge bulkhead you insisted I save from the *Beauchamp*? It's now a plaque that lists the freighter's name and years of operation, and it hangs on the bulkhead of my office. It's right above another plaque that has my grandfather's and father's picture with an abridged history of the freighter. I'm happy where I am, and I'm grateful you gave me the opportunity. Who knows if I'd ever have found this if you hadn't saved us from that frigate?"

"Well, you're very welcome," Cole replied. "I know I certainly could not have accomplished everything I have without you and Sev and everyone else supporting me. I don't ever want to forget all the contributions people have made to my goals."

Sev chuckled, saying, "Don't worry. We won't let you." Painter broke out in laughter.

CHAPTER THREE

Cole's Office
  Citadel Station
  14 July 3003, 11:00 GST

Cole welcomed Sasha and Himari Sato into his workplace. Like his office aboard *Haven*, the space was spartan at best. No decorations adorned the walls, nor did any personal effects color the space. It was a place of work, of pursuing goals. And besides, there was always the chance Cole would one day meet with someone who didn't work for him, so there was no reason to give such an outsider any insight into his psychology.

"Let me guess," Cole said, once social preliminaries were satisfied. "You want to discuss a Ministry of Defense."

"You don't have to sound so defeatist about it," Sasha replied. "It's not like you don't agree with us."

Cole nodded. "You're right. I do agree with you. I said that very thing to Sev and Painter while they were showing me the shipyard. You also know my objections. I do not want a government so inflated and bureaucratic that it cannot respond effectively to sudden concerns or threats. Some governments on Old Earth—before the jump gates—were so locked into their bureaucracy that they couldn't keep pace with technological improvements. I will not have that. Yes...I want training facilities for new spacers. Yes...I want the ISA's proficiencies and ratings incorporated into our promotion and compensation schedules. Yes...I want the families of any spacer or soldier who dies or is disabled to be taken care of. The problem is how we do it in a streamlined, flexible system. Get with Paol. Heh...pull in anyone you want for the discussion; I don't care. Just find a way to do it without creating a convoluted military-industrial complex like what was so prevalent back on Old Earth."

"There are rumors that you're considering taking *Haven* off on another trip," Sato replied. "Will you be available for us to present any ideas we develop?"

Cole grinned. "That's the beauty of the quantum comms network. I could be in Zurich, and the comms lag would only be fifteen seconds or so...if that."

"Very well," Sato replied, adding one nod. "There is another matter I'm reticent to discuss, but I have reason to believe you will encounter it soon enough elsewhere."

"Oh?" Cole asked. "That sounds rather ominous."

Sato's expression quirked toward an almost-rueful smile. "Yes. It could very well be. A number of forward-thinking people have come to me, asking if you have any children or when you plan to have them."

Sasha jerked her head around to stare at Sato, her eyes hard and her mouth ajar.

Cole blinked. When Cole spoke, his tone carried a harshness most uncommon, especially with those he considered his friends, "Excuse me? What business is it of theirs? My life is mine alone."

If Sato felt any concern about Cole's tone, she didn't show it. "No, Cole, it isn't...not anymore. CIE alone is an empire all on its own. Step back and consider what we're building here in Beta Magellan. You personally own the system, the *entire* system. What happens to it, to all the people living here, when you die...especially if you die without an heir? What happens to CIE? This is something you need to be considering, and you need to deal with it *soon*, whatever course you choose."

"And just what am I supposed to do about it?" Cole asked. "Announce I'm seeking a wife and invite anyone who wishes to apply to present themselves before me? Just who—or what—do you think I am?"

Sato sighed. "I think you are a young man who might just be woefully unaware of the vast influence he has, and that influence is both increasing and spreading. It's already common knowledge throughout this part of the galaxy that anyone who wants to be safe from all the upheaval right now should make for Beta Magellan. Why? Because of you and what you're building. Yes...*Haven* and Srexx and the schematics he kept are *how* you're building, but the fact remains that *you* are driving it. None of this would be here if you hadn't chosen to pursue this goal, and planning for what happens to it once you're dead is part of your responsibility. You owe it to all the people depending on you to have a plan and to publicize that plan."

Cole sighed and leaned back against his chair. "Well...this certainly isn't how I expected this meeting to go."

"I don't imagine it was," Sato replied. "One downside to all you're doing is that you've been the most eligible bachelor in Human space since you accepted your inheritance as the Coleson Heir. I don't know if that has truly worked its way through the minds of the unmarried women in Beta Magellan, but when it does...well...I'm very conflicted. I don't know whether to stay and watch or flee the system to avoid the mass of women who will descend upon you."

"*That* thought isn't comforting at all," Cole replied.

"The way I see it, your only reprieve is that you're not truly accessible. StationNet's directory doesn't register your comms code, so outside of someone seeing you, there's no way to know exactly where you are. And if you are planning on taking *Haven* out on some kind of excursion, any interested parties will just have to pine away for you."

Cole scoffed. "You make an excellent case for taking *Haven* on some kind of excursion."

Sato's expression quirked into a small, neutral smile. "Just don't leave without setting up some kind of chain of command for the system's defenses. I have no reason to believe we'll be attacked anytime soon, but if we are, having no clear lines of command would be disastrous."

Cole nodded, sighing heavily before he asked, "Do you have any more bad news for me?"

"No," Sato replied, shaking her head. "I think we've covered all of it."

"Well, thank you for your time and concern," Cole said. "If you'll forgive me, I have a lunch appointment."

Sato nodded once and rose, Sasha standing with her. Cole also stood, shaking their hands, before Sato and Sasha walked to the office's door. By the time they reached the door, Cole's focus was already elsewhere, or he might have noticed Sasha directing an unsettled look his way before she followed Sato out of the office.

———

The station's commercial levels held a number of restaurants in addition to all the other businesses. These restaurants ran the gamut of styles, from the seedy places certain spacers preferred to upscale establishments even the most aristocratic person would appreciate. One such enterprise was the Sinking Ship, a mid-range restaurant featuring maritime décor from the ancient Age of Sail in Old Earth's distant past. Aside from its excellent menu, the Sinking Ship prided itself on providing an undisturbed experience for its customers. While there was a general level of background noise, anyone raising their voice enough to impact other diners' experiences received a warning from their server, with a second offense resulting in the manager asking the offender to leave and not return until they could achieve behavior more in line with the intended ambiance. One would expect the Sinking Ship to go out of business with such a policy, but it was uncommon to find the place without at least three-quarters of their seating occupied.

Motion near his table attracted Cole's attention, and he looked up to see his lunch guest standing in front of him. Cole grinned and stood, extending his hand in welcome. Amelia Obrist accepted the handshake, and Cole gestured for her to sit.

"So...have you enjoyed your explorations of the station?" Cole asked.

"I have," Amelia replied. "It's far busier than I expected. I even visited the freight docks, and I was very surprised that they didn't have the dodgy, unsafe ambiance so common anywhere else."

Cole grinned. "We don't have much of a criminal element yet. Everyone in the system *wants* to be here, and there are—frankly— more jobs than there are people. Until that changes, I highly doubt we'll have much crime. I know I've said this at least twice, but thank you for accepting my offer. Leland Graf called me a few names the last time I was in Zurich, but he also complimented me on my choice. He said I couldn't have found a better person to take over as Chief Financial Officer of CIE."

"That was very kind of him," Amelia remarked, blushing just enough for Cole to notice. "I'm looking forward to the job. I understand the company has been without a CFO since its relocation from Centauri?"

Cole nodded. "Yes. I'm afraid I had to implement some personnel cuts. I consider myself a very open-minded individual, but I simply cannot countenance people trying to kill me or steal my family's company."

"No, I can't imagine anyone who would," Amelia replied.

"After we finish lunch, we have a board meeting, where I'll announce and introduce you. Everyone should be on their best behavior—today and in the future—but if anyone gives you any problems whatsoever, I want to know about it."

Amelia sat for a moment or two before she shook her head. "No. No, I don't think so. 'Running to daddy' every time someone gets out of line will only serve to undermine my authority, and I don't think it would do yours any favors either. Besides, I'm no stranger to establishing myself. Anything egregious, of course, I'll tell you...but unless whatever it is presents a physical threat to me, my coworkers, or the company, I'll handle it."

"Have you met Garrett yet?" Cole asked.

"Yes, I have," Amelia replied. "Nice enough fellow, and he gave me a list of comms codes to record in my implant and then destroy. He called it 'insurance.'"

Cole chuckled. "He would call it something like that. For right now, Beta Magellan is not open to anyone who hasn't been vetted by Kiksaliks. Eventually, that may change, and there's nothing saying someone couldn't go on vacation outside the system and be compromised. Those comms codes give you a recourse, in case worse comes to worst."

Their server materialized out of the crowd, asking, "Are you ready to order?"

Cole looked to Amelia, and she nodded. Cole gestured for her to proceed, and after the server departed, conversation turned to less weighty matters.

CHAPTER FOUR

Conference Room
   Citadel Station
   14 July 3003, 13:00 GST

Cole led Amelia Obrist into the conference room and held back what he was sure would've been a very gloating smile. The executive board of CIE awaited him, with an empty seat or two. He'd brought the C-level executives of CIE to heel back in Centauri, and ever since, not one of them had been late for a meeting Cole himself attended.

Cole stopped at the head of the table and, gesturing for Amelia to sit at his left, assumed his seat. CEO Jefferds and the rest of the executives ran down the right-side of the table from Cole's perspective, and Cole nodded in acknowledgement.

"I'd like to thank everyone for coming," Cole said, his way of calling the meeting to order. He didn't hold to all the pomp and circumstance claptrap, either. "The first order of business is to introduce you to Amelia Obrist, the new Chief Financial Officer for the company. I poached her from Credit Suisse, and I've been called some names for doing so."

Cole waited for everyone at the table to bid Amelia welcome and directed his attention to CEO Jefferds, saying, "And how goes the deployment of the quantum comms nodes?"

Jefferds nodded once and said, "It's going well, all told. The comms nodes have been added to every jump gate within one hundred light-years. I'm afraid we had to give those techs heading toward Coalition space hazard pay and war-time rates, but the roll-out continues."

Cole nodded. The Coalition evolved out of the old Aurelian Commonwealth (under the so-called 'Provisional' Parliament), the Carnelian Bloc, the Sirius Imperium, and the Eridani Corporation. Cole wasn't exactly sure *who* the dominant players were in that convoluted relationship, and Garrett worked to obtain that intelligence... among other information.

"That's fine," Cole replied. "Ensure our people know we will take care of their families if the Coalition decides to do something stupid, and if that does indeed happen, I will personally see to the Coalition's education on why it should *never* happen again."

Heads bobbed in nods around the conference table. Each of them had seen *Haven*...and the ships coming out of Citadel's shipyard.

"So, what's next?" Cole asked.

The rest of the meeting progressed as an informative—yet thoroughly boring—status update on CIE and its various projects or initiatives. Cole felt his mind starting to wander at various points, but he gamely rallied to focus (mostly) on whomever was speaking at the time.

At the end of the meeting, Cole stood to leave when Jefferds said, "Sir, would you have a moment?"

"Of course, Jefferds," Cole replied, resuming his seat. "What do you need?"

Jefferds watched the rest of the executives file out of the conference room before turning back to look at Cole. He took a breath and said, "Sir, forgive me. This is not easy for me. A number of the executives have expressed concern that you do not have an heir."

Cole sighed. "Not this again." He rubbed his face with his hands and leaned back against his chair.

"Sir, I—"

Cole held up his hand to forestall Jefferds, saying, "Admiral Sato already gave me the lecture this morning. I don't have a solution right this moment, but I promised her I'd think on it."

"Very well, sir," Jefferds replied. "It's just that we really do not wish to return to the bank managing the Coleson Trust. It was a very... stressful...time."

Cole's thoughts flicked back to the period he thought of as the 'Jax' years and chuckled. "Yes, Jefferds, it was. Is there anything else?"

"No, sir, and thank you."

"You're welcome. If you need me, find me." That said, Cole pushed to his feet and left the conference room.

———

Talia stepped into her sister's apartment on Citadel Station and held back a sigh. Sasha sat on the sofa, legs curled under her as she clutched a throw pillow to her chest. Her expression was a blank stare.

"Hey, Soosh," Talia said, "you okay?"

Sasha jerked and looked at her. "Oh, Tallie...I'm sorry. I thought we weren't meeting until dinner."

"I thought we were, too, Soosh. I came looking for you after you were forty-five minutes late."

Sasha blanched. "Forty-five minutes? Tallie, I'm sorry."

Talia shrugged. "It's all right. I just wanted to make sure you're okay. You were giving the decking a thousand-yard stare."

Sasha sighed. "It's out there, now, Tallie. Sato just blurted it out there like it was nothing."

"Uhm...she just blurted what out there?" Talia asked. "I'm not sure I know what we're discussing."

"She told Cole he needed an heir, which presumably means he needs a wife."

Ah. So, that's it. Talia walked over to sit in a chair facing her sister. "And you're afraid someone else will get him."

"No, of course not. I—"

"Soosh, don't you think this has gone on long enough? You were ready to murder Scarlett when she came aboard *Haven*, and you still grit your teeth when you see her sometimes. No matter what you tell *everyone else*, you need to be honest with yourself at least. So, you might as well 'fess up. Just when did you fall for your captain?"

Sasha jerked again and gave Talia a fierce glare. "I have not..." The ire faded from her gaze, and she took a deep shuddering breath, releasing it as a heavy sigh. "I'm sorry, Tallie. I...I don't know, really. I still remember what it felt like—the icy claws in my chest—when I heard them shout Cole was down at that station in Iota Ceti. That means it happened before then, right?"

Talia shrugged, breaking into a grin. "How am I supposed to know? How much time for dating do you think I've had as a med student and resident? Besides, I think a lot of my peers were intimidated by the family name."

"Yeah...boys are weird like that. Over three thousand years, and they're *still* fighting that patriarchal, alpha-man urge. You've had genetics classes; do you ever think it'll go away?"

"Hard to say," Talia replied, "but you're evading the subject."

"That used to work, you know," Sasha retorted, just above a mutter.

"Still evading, Soosh..."

Sasha shot a grimace her way. "Fine, fine. Like I said, I don't know, and it would never work anyway."

"Why not?"

"Well, for one thing, I'm his first officer. Officers aren't supposed to fraternize with people under their command, and I *really* don't like the idea of being anywhere other than *Haven*. I'm not sure Cole would listen to anyone else when he gets one of those harebrained ideas."

"Harlon and Emily don't show any interest in moving on. They could keep an eye on him for you."

"Yeah, but would Cole listen to them? I mean really *listen*? Harlon talks it up how he was the one to talk Cole out of doing any more 'Lone Marine' nonsense. But, Tallie...it wasn't him."

"It wasn't?"

Sasha shook her head. "It was blindingly apparent to everyone in the conversation that Cole just wasn't listening...not to Harlon or

Emily. All three of us were there. They finally got frustrated and walked out. After they left, *I* talked him out of it."

"Really? How?"

"I asked him what would happen to us—you and me specifically—if he left the ship and got himself killed. I asked him what would happen to Srexx. That's when he backed off from going, Tallie. That's what stopped him." Sasha sighed. "Harlon and Emily came to me and asked what had happened after Cole told them he'd step back. I didn't want to go into specifics, so I told them I didn't stop talking until he saw reason."

Talia nodded. "Okay. That makes me wonder if maybe he doesn't have feelings for you, too."

Sasha shook her head. "I'm not going there, Tallie. I'm just not."

"Okay, Soosh. Okay. I'll let it go for now, but you need to do something about it. The day will come when it will be too late, and how will you feel then?"

Without waiting for her sister to reply, Talia stood and left the apartment.

CHAPTER FIVE

Cole's Apartment
Citadel Station
14 July 3003, 17:45 GST

Garrett moved to the second armchair and turned it to face Cole straight-on. The spymaster leaned back and cracked his knuckles before draping his arms over the sides of the chair and resting his left ankle on his right knee. Cole wasn't expecting a visit from Garrett that evening, especially not at such an odd time. But Garrett always had marched to his own beat. That was one of the reasons Cole enjoyed the friendship.

"I suppose if we were more formal about this," Garrett said, "the conversation we're about to have would be termed 'System Security Briefing' or some such. But bureaucrats always spend too much time naming and classifying things in my view, so we're just going to talk. That okay with you?"

Cole grinned. "When has talking with you ever not been okay with me? Besides, I owe you a lot, Garrett. For that alone, my door will *always* be open to you, no questions asked."

"You should be careful before making statements like that...could get you into trouble," Garrett replied with half a grin. "Anyway. So, the short of it is that things are a mess out there. A one-hundred-percent, messed-up-beyond-all-recognition mess. The Coalition is still focused on bringing order to the chaos that is the corpse of the Common-wealth, and it's anyone's guess as to how successful they're being. I think everyone is just sort of waiting to see which way they jump once they've finished...or give up. The Duchy of Musilar is still fighting the good fight, though I don't know how. They must've turned their entire GDP over to defense efforts, because they're burning through ships like there's no tomorrow."

"Why don't they just back out and sue for peace?" Cole asked.

Garrett shrugged. "Who knows? Ego, maybe. It's possible things have reached the point in the Duchy that the Duke will lose his throne if he admits he should never have entered the war in the first place. No one likes a quitter, but no one's overly fond of losing, either. I suppose there's always the chance the Duke's hoping to rally others to the cause, but if you consider only conventional forces, the Coalition is the dominant power in the region right now. There are even whispers they may be looking to invade Zurich somewhere down the line."

Cole chuckled. "They may *try*, but they won't succeed."

"Don't be too sure of that," Garrett replied. "For all its wealth, the Zurich Defense Force couldn't stand up to a fleet the size of the Oriolis Fifty-Seven, and the Coalition can easily field such a fleet for an invasion." Garrett's voice trailed off as he looked at Cole. His expression shifted to one of shrewd appraisal. "What do you know that I don't, Cole?"

"Zurich and Beta Magellan have entered into a mutual defense treaty," Cole said. "They've heard the same whispers you have, and the Banking Commission and System Leadership used Leland to start the conversation about halfway through June. Both parties agreed to keep the treaty a secret."

Garrett blinked. "Damn. None of my people heard *anything* about that, Cole. How in the stars did you keep it so hushed?"

"For one thing, we held the discussions in Zurich. Paol and I went there under the cover of studying their civil government. Well...we took *Haven*. Srexx had his usual fun and couldn't find any data indicating they were negotiating in bad faith, and the Kiksaliks concurred. That's why I've also been pushing our 'adopted' ships through the shipyard. I want to be ready if the Coalition does something that requires *an education*." A thought struck Cole's mind, and he closed his eyes and sighed. "Damn."

"What?" Garrett asked.

"Sev was right," Cole said. "If I take *Haven* and its battlegroup out to deliver chastisement, I'll want to leave Beta Magellan with the strongest possible defense. I'll have to talk to Painter and Sato about our personnel capabilities, but I want the Beta Magellan system picket to be based on a dreadnought. One dreadnought, four battle-carriers... and I'm not sure from there on. We'll use *Haven*'s strike group as the model for system pickets in our uninhabited systems."

Garrett sat there for a second before he pursed his lips. "That's a serious Home Fleet you're planning, Cole."

"Do you disagree?"

Garrett shook his head, slowly at first. "No...no, I don't. I saw the massacre, too. I don't want this system ever to face that again. You're going to have a difficult time keeping that building project secret."

"I'm not even going to try," Cole replied. "I won't advertise it, but word will get out eventually anyway. Between the dreadnought battlegroup and the system forts, anyone who comes here looking for a fight will have a tough time of it."

"What was that line from an ancient movie your grandfather liked?" Garrett asked, grinning. "'I feel pity for anyone who comes here looking for trouble?'"

Cole grinned. "Yeah...something like that."

Cole took a moment to record a reminder in his implant to speak with Sev, Painter, and Sato about the new project. He was sure they'd simply love the extra work.

"Anything else happening out there?" Cole asked.

"Not really. The Coalition is going to be a problem, Cole, and they might be a problem sooner rather than later."

Cole nodded. "I know. Believe me, I know, but I don't want to take us to war until we're ready."

"That's the thing," Garrett replied. "No one is ever ready for war, not even the people who start them."

"I can't leave my people undefended, then. How's that?"

Garrett nodded once. "Better. You also need to consider what they'll think about going to war. Pretty much everyone here *is* here because they wanted a safe place from the fighting. Have you considered their reaction to the idea that you'll be diving into the mess?"

"But what kind of people are we if we turn a blind eye to what the Coalition is doing? How can we sit here protected and safe while people are brutalized because others have power over them? Evil triumphs through the inaction of Good, Garrett. I'm hoping someone else will step in...or that the Coalition falls apart. I don't *want* to go to war. But I can't shake the feeling that the day will come when I have no choice if I want to be someone my family would be proud of."

Garrett opened his mouth to reply, but the overhead speakers chirped.

"Cole?" Srexx asked.

"Yes, Srexx?"

"We have received a priority signal from Gateway. A massive Commonwealth fleet just arrived."

"Damn. Okay. Thanks for telling me." Cole's voice trailed off as he processed what Srexx said. "Wait...did you say a *Commonwealth* fleet?"

"That is what the signal specifies, Cole. Ninety-eight ships broadcasting a transponder identifying them as Aurelian Commonwealth Navy. Five freighters accompany them as well, but they appear to be under escort and not pursuit."

"Okay. I'll issue recall orders from here, buddy. Would you please send an acknowledgement to Gateway for me?"

"Of course, Cole."

"Thanks, Srexx."

The speakers chirped again, and Cole shifted his attention to Garrett. "Didn't you tell me that all the Commonwealth ships were squawking Coalition transponders now?"

"Yes. I haven't received any reports of Commonwealth Navy transponders for weeks."

Cole frowned as both he and Garrett stood. "I suppose it's possible they didn't get the memo. I'd better get out there and see what they want."

CHAPTER SIX

Bridge, Battle-Carrier *Haven*
    Citadel Station
    14 July 3003, 18:45 GST

Cole stepped onto *Haven*'s bridge for the first time in what felt like forever; in all truth, it had only been about a month. The ship was on Gamma Shift, and a person occupied every station, going about their business bringing the ship back to full readiness. Looking from the aft stations to the helm, Cole smiled as he approached the command chair.

Sasha looked over her shoulder at the sound of the port hatch cycling and vacated the command chair at Cole's approach, announcing, "Captain on the bridge!"

Cole gave her a flat look as she moved to the starboard side of the command chair, and she winked, making a mark in the air with her left index finger as if she were keeping score. Even after all the time they'd worked together, they still waged a silent war on just how formally military *Haven* would be. Cole took in the grins of the people at various stations around the bridge and smiled as he sat in the command chair.

"It's good to be home," Cole said. "I have the conn."

"All decks already reported ready to depart," Sasha said. "The rest of the battlegroup is holding station thirty light-minutes outside near-station space, awaiting our arrival."

Cole nodded. "Comms, signal traffic control we are departing, and file a flight plan for the Gateway jump gate. We'll pick up the rest of the battlegroup on the way."

"Traffic control signals 'clear to depart' and 'safe travels,' sir," the comms tech replied.

Cole nodded once. "Well, I think that's our cue. Helm, take us out."

"Aye, sir," the spacer at the helm said. "Undocking now."

The helmsman took *Haven* through a slower version of Cole's 'flip and roll' maneuver, bringing the massive ship to face away from its docking slip. Increasing power to the sublight engines, the battle-carrier then left near-station space.

"We are clear and free to navigate, sir," the spacer announced.

"Put us on a rendezvous course for the battlegroup," Cole replied. "Comms, signal the battlegroup that we're on the way."

One hour and fifteen minutes later, *Haven* took its place at the center of the battlegroup's travel formation, and the entire group powered up to half-lightspeed on a course for the Gateway jump gate.

"I'm very glad the ships accepted the jump engines," Cole said as he leaned back against the command chair.

Sasha nodded. "You and me both. Otherwise, the trip to Gateway would take...what...two days?"

"It's only twelve light-years," Cole countered with a shrug. "I don't think it'd take quite two days. Maybe forty-two hours?"

"Still, that's a long time when the jump gates would allow the transit to be near-instantaneous. It's nice to have the best of both worlds."

. . .

At half-lightspeed, the battlegroup traversed the seventy AUs to the Gateway jump gate in just a bit less than nineteen hours and thirty minutes. The battlegroup shifted into a line-astern formation and—one by one—made the jump to Gateway.

———

Beta Magellan Jump Gate
  Gateway System
  15 July 3003, 14:35 GST

In Gateway, a new station occupied a position thirty light-minutes outside the traffic lanes for the Beta Magellan jump gate; Sev and his people had started construction once Citadel Station neared habitability. Nowhere close to competing with Citadel Station in size or scope, Babylon Station served as a commerce and diplomatic hub for anyone wanting to do business with Beta Magellan. Beyond its role as a marketplace and embassy, it also served as a processing center for incoming refugees fleeing Coalition space.

Gateway's system picket held position one light-hour outside Babylon's near-station space, on a heading toward the Commonwealth fleet. Once the battlegroup shifted back into its travel formation—basically a globe of ships with *Haven* in the center—Cole hailed the picket's cruiser, whose captain doubled as senior officer for the picket.

Commander Jonathan Giles smiled when the comms-call connected, saying, "Hello, sir, and welcome to Gateway."

Cole returned the smile and nodded once. "Thank you. I understand we have some guests. What have they been doing?"

"Not a thing, sir," Giles replied. "After they arrived, they moved outside the designated travel lanes to and from the jump gate and have just been holding position. There was some light comms chatter between the ships, but it was just traffic-control-type stuff, mostly formation and maneuvering orders."

"Have they moved on any shipping or anything like that?" Cole asked.

Giles shook his head. "No, sir. They're just sitting about a light-hour off the primary space lanes."

"Very well," Cole replied. "Feel free to resume your patrol. We'll take it from here."

"Aye, sir. Giles out."

"Helm, plot an intercept course with the Commonwealth ships," Cole said. "Plan for three-quarters-light for the transit, with a reduction to two-tenths-light once the comms lag isn't atrocious. Once you have the course, pass it to Comms for distribution to the fleet. Weaps, let's bring up the battlegroup TacNet, too."

A chorus of "Aye, sir," came back to Cole as they began carrying out his orders.

Less than five minutes later, the spacer at the tactical station announced, "Battlegroup TacNet online, sir!"

"Thank you, Weaps," Cole replied.

"Battlegroup reports ready to maneuver, sir," the comms tech announced.

Cole nodded. "Thank you, Comms. Helm, take us out. Sensors, what can you tell us about our guests?"

The sensors tech soon replied, "Sir, there are ninety-eight warships arrayed in two lines-abreast of forty-nine ships, with the five freighters between the two lines. The lower line contains a dreadnought, twelve battleships, twenty-five cruisers, and eleven destroyers. The upper line contains nineteen destroyers and thirty frigates. None of the warships appear to have any defensive or weapons systems online or even on standby. One of the freighters matches sensor data for *Jezebel's Hope*, a freighter known for refugee runs; our records indicate she's made eleven successful runs into the former Commonwealth."

Cole leaned back against the command chair, considering the tech's report. Whoever they were, they weren't acting hostile. They'd been sitting there for just over a day, and several merchant ships had already passed by them without incident.

"Srexx?" Cole asked.

"Yes, Cole?"

"What's your evaluation?"

Srexx didn't respond for about fifteen seconds. Then, he said, "At this point, Cole, there is insufficient evidence to classify those ships as hostile. They have not behaved in a manner consistent with other Coalition ships; indeed, they do not even identify themselves as *being* Coalition ships, if one bases their identity off their transponders.

"In terms of a threat assessment, I calculate the warships present a minimum of a moderate threat to this battlegroup. I regret that I cannot be more specific; there are a number of variables that cannot be quantified, such as the intentions of the commanders. While the range is still sufficient that pin-point resolution from the sensors is not possible, we are close enough for me to evaluate that these ships are representative of their respective classes as of the beginning of the Commonwealth Civil War. As the range decreases, I will be able to ascertain what modifications—if any—have been made to them."

Cole nodded, saying, "Thanks, buddy. Now, what does your intuition tell you?"

"Cole, as I have stated a number of times since we first met, I do not possess 'intuition' in the manner you reference. That being said, I calculate a sixty-two-percent probability that they are here to talk."

Cole smiled. "Okay, buddy. I appreciate your thoughts. Weaps, the moment they start charging weapons or shields, sound battle-stations. Don't wait for my order."

"Aye, sir," the weapons tech replied.

Cole nodded and looked up to Sasha, who still stood at his side. "Well...I guess all we can do now is wait."

———

Flag Bridge
Dreadnought *ACS Indomitable*
15 July 3003, 18:15 GST

Admiral Jennings Trask entered the flag bridge and waved away the traditional announcement of 'Admiral on deck.' He approached the massive holo-table that was state-of-the-art for Commonwealth ships, standing at his chief of staff's right side.

"He's here, sir," Commander Tucker said, "and he's not alone."

Trask directed his attention to the holo-table, eyeing the data-codes that were approaching his formation at three-quarters the speed of light. The data-codes indicated a standard travel formation for a task group of that size, but Trask felt a twinge of unease as his eyes settled on the massive dot at the formation's center.

"What do you think, Jake?" Trask asked, his voice almost a whisper.

"I really hope he's in the mood to talk, sir," Commander Tucker replied, his voice equally quiet. "We have no data whatsoever on the ships traveling with him, and what we do know about *Haven*...well, I know I don't want to fight them."

"Everything we know of Coleson says he doesn't fire first," Trask said. "Yes, we're in his territory, but we can't exactly shout from the next system over. Well, I suppose we *could* have sent a message from Alpha Anubis, but we would've been inviting attack as we traded messages back and forth. Any Coalition forces pursuing us wouldn't dare enter his territory, and I'd rather not risk any more of my people in combat than necessary." Trask sighed. "All we can do is wait, now."

———

At a range of one light-hour, Cole ordered the battlegroup to reduce speed to a quarter-light. At thirty light-minutes, Cole ordered the battlegroup to hold position at fifteen light-minutes, relative to the Commonwealth fleet.

"All ships report holding station," the comms tech replied.

"Record a message for transmission, please," Cole said.

"You're on, sir," the comms tech replied.

Cole gave his best welcoming smile as he said, "Hello. I am Bartholomew James Coleson, commanding the *Haven* battlegroup. I welcome you to the system and ask your intentions. Coleson out."

Not quite a minute later, the comms tech announced, "Message ready for transmit, sir."

"Send it," Cole responded.

"Well, we'll know what they say in a little over thirty minutes,"

Sasha said, leading her statement with a sigh. "I wish they had quantum comms gear. We could've done this from Beta Magellan."

"I wouldn't have, even if it had been possible," Cole said. "If they turned out to be hostile, we would've been horribly out of position. I think someone might be a tad impatient."

Sasha grimaced. "You're not wrong, and there's no guarantee they'll fire off a response as soon as they receive our hail."

Cole grinned, shrugging.

———

Trask smiled after viewing Coleson's hail. It was good to know the intelligence on Coleson was accurate, in this at least. He eyed his chief of staff, saying, "Thoughts, Jake?"

"I won't lie, sir; I'm focused on the word 'battlegroup.' They haven't raised shields yet, but it doesn't really matter. Our sensors can't penetrate the hulls of those ships. The computer is having fits trying to classify the ships around *Haven*, but given the differences in their physical dimensions, I think we're looking at their version of cruisers, destroyers, and frigates. We've picked out four ships we're assuming to be frigates whose hull contours don't quite match the other similarly sized ships, but we have no idea what that means."

"Very well," Trask said. "Comms, record for transmission, please."

"Ready, sir," the comms officer replied.

"I am Admiral Jennings Trask, and I thank you for your welcome to Gateway. The freighters we escort carry a full complement of refugees. The ships under my command were in the process of leaving Coalition space when we encountered the freighters, and after discussion with our ships' companies, we have decided to ask if you're still hiring. The Provisional Parliament—acting in the name of the Coalition—shows no signs of reigning in their cruelties, and we cannot in good conscience continue to serve them. We look forward to your response. Trask out."

"On the chip, sir," the comms tech announced.

"Send it," Trask replied.

———

"Message coming in, sir," the comms tech announced.

Cole nodded. "Put it on the forward viewscreen, please."

"Aye, sir."

Not even five seconds later, the viewscreen activated, and the bridge crew watched Admiral Trask's message. When the admiral identified himself, Sasha gasped, her left hand flying up to cover her mouth.

At the conclusion of the message, Cole swiveled to face his first officer, saying, "You certainly reacted to the admiral's identity. Do you know him?"

Sasha shook her head. "Only by reputation. Admiral Jennings Trask is...well...he is the ideal for every officer desiring flag rank. If *he* is leaving the Commonwealth, it's far worse than we've realized. He'd never turn his back on the Commonwealth, not unless he felt he had no other choice."

Cole nodded. "Okay...I need to think about this. The least we can do is offer them shore leave privileges at Babylon until we figure this out. Comms, my compliments to Captain Vasquez; please, alert him that our guests are not hostile and I'll be offering them shore leave privileges at his station."

The comms tech replied, "Aye, sir."

Cole sat in silence, his mind swirling around the idea that ninety-eight ships had come asking for a place with him. After a few seconds, he forced those thoughts away and adopted a non-expression, saying, "Comms, record for transmission, please."

"You're live, sir."

"Admiral Trask, I am very glad I'm not a betting man. If you'll forgive me for being frank, I need to consider your request, and at some point, we'll probably need to discuss it in person. That being said, I have no intention of being a poor host, and I offer the hospitality of Babylon Station for shore leave privileges. If you accept, please include your desired cruising speed to the station. Coleson out."

The comms tech added a five-second fade-in and fade-out to the message before announcing, "Ready to transmit, sir."

"Send it," Cole replied.

. . .

Thirty minutes later, the *Haven* battlegroup performed a synchronized 'flip and roll' to orient on Babylon Station and led Trask's ships into the system at a quarter-lightspeed. The transit would take sixteen hours. Cole asked Sasha to schedule a meeting in the bridge briefing room at zero-seven-hundred, inviting Yeleth, Harlon, Emily, and Garrett. That task complete, Cole left the bridge in search of his bed.

CHAPTER SEVEN

In Transit to Babylon Station
  Gateway System
  16 July 3003, 06:45 GST

Cole entered the bridge briefing room and took his customary seat. He'd been awake since zero-five-hundred, and he still grappled with the proper response to Trask's message. On one side, he didn't want to turn anyone away who sought someplace safe to live, and Beta Magellan certainly wouldn't run out of space on the two habitable planets anytime soon. On the other hand, though, Cole couldn't help but feel there was a line somewhere on just how many ships he could accept before the Provisional Parliament became a bit irate; just what they'd do to express their discontent, Cole didn't know, but he'd never been one to poke the bear just for the sake of poking the bear.

The hatch opening interrupted Cole's thoughts, and he watched Sasha, Yeleth, Harlon, Emily, and Garrett file into the briefing room. Garrett sat at the far end of the table, opposite Cole...*his* customary seat. The others assumed their seats, and Cole nodded his welcome to them.

"Morning, everyone," Cole said. "I'm sure by now you're well aware of why I asked for this meeting, so I'd like to begin by showing you the message that started all this."

Cole asked *Haven* to play Admiral Trask's first message, and a hologram appeared over the conference table. Everyone sat in silence as the message played and looked to Cole once it finished.

"So, that's where we are," Cole resumed. "I won't lie; I'm torn between saying 'yes' and sending him on his way. I'm honestly having problems getting past the crews of ninety-eight ships all wanting to flee the former Commonwealth and join us. Beyond that, losing ninety-eight ships would have to hurt. So...thoughts?"

"I think," Garrett said, "the first step is to determine just how many of his people want to join us. That will give us an idea on the scope of the situation. Beyond that, another concern you haven't raised is financial; can we *afford* paying all these people?"

Cole shrugged. "I've never publicized my finances, but I've not tried to keep them secret either. Without losing ourselves to a discussion of numbers, trust me when I say I'm nowhere close to my expenses outstripping my income, and as I work with Paol Thyrray to transition those people who want to have their own businesses away from being employees, my expenses will decrease. None of my concerns stem from my financial situation."

Harlon smiled and shook his head. Emily grinned. It was easy to forget that they sat at a table with the richest person in Human space; until Cole had started funneling his trust fund into Haven Enterprises and Beta Magellan, the interest alone was greater than the GDP of several star systems.

"It has to be bad back home if Admiral Trask has decided to leave," Sasha said. "I mentioned this last night when the message first arrived. Trask is *the* role model for naval spacers in the Commonwealth; everyone who aspires to flag rank would love to have him as their mentor. I...I just can't imagine what the Provisional Parliament has done to make him lose hope in them."

"He would be an asset to us, then?" Yeleth asked.

Sasha, Harlon, and Emily all nodded.

"He's the best flag officer the Commonwealth has," Emily said. "Much like Sato was one of the best for the Solars, if not *the* best."

Harlon looked to Cole, asking, "Is Babylon Station ready for what they're about to receive?"

Cole shrugged. "I gave Vasquez fair warning before I offered Trask shore leave for his crew. So...thoughts? Recommendations?"

"They have impoverished their country and enriched ours," Sasha said. "I say we welcome them and start cycling the ships through the Citadel shipyard as soon as time and resources allow. They don't really have anywhere else to go, and if we turn them away, the Provisional Parliament will try to hunt them down."

"Agreed," Harlon said.

"Yes," Emily added.

Cole looked to Yeleth, saying, "Your thoughts, Yeleth?"

"I, too, think we should welcome these people. Do you intend to evaluate them with Kiksaliks?"

Cole nodded. "Oh, yes. I wouldn't have it any other way. Garrett, would you like to add anything else?"

Garrett maintained his silence but shook his head, declining further comment.

"Very well," Cole said. "When we arrive at Babylon Station, I'll invite Admiral Trask and a few of his people aboard for a meeting. Once they've been vetted by Kiksaliks, we'll proceed. Any questions?"

No one spoke, and Cole nodded one more time, saying, "All right then. Thank you for your time and thoughts."

Cole stood, prompting the others to do the same, and left the briefing room.

———

At eleven-twenty-seven hours, they arrived at Babylon Station and began the rotation of providing Trask's ships shore leave. Only those ships whose companies were on shore leave docked at the station, as all ninety-eight ships docking would leave Babylon critically short of docking ports or slips for the routine traffic scheduled over the next several days. All that remained was the conference with Admiral Trask.

. . .

Cole spent quite some time deciding how he wanted to handle the conference with Admiral Trask, and as the first ships docked at Babylon Station, he smiled as a thought came to the forefront of his mind.

"Jenkins, hail *Indomitable*, please," Cole said, "and ask for Admiral Trask on my behalf."

"Aye, Cap," Jenkins replied.

Cole looked at Sasha and winked, making his own mark in the air.

"I have Admiral Trask for you, Cap," Jenkins announced.

"Onscreen, please," Cole said.

The forward viewscreen activated, displaying an image of Admiral Jennings Trask. Both he and Cole smiled at the same time, as Cole said, "Admiral Trask, thank you for taking my call. I'd like to invite you and six of your people aboard *Haven* to discuss matters over lunch."

"Thank you, Mr. Coleson, and I'm happy to accept. May I inquire as to the uniform of the day?"

Cole grinned. "Please, sir, call me Cole, and ship-suits are fine with me. I'd much prefer an informal conversation with a side of food than a formal dress mess."

Admiral Trask's lips quirked in something that might have become a smile, if a smile had been permitted. Then, he nodded once. "Very well, Cole. When should we arrive?"

"How does twelve-thirty sound?" Cole replied.

"It sounds perfect, thank you."

Cole nodded once. "Excellent. We'll bring your shuttle onto our flight deck, and I'll have someone on hand to offer our hospitality to your pilot, if she or he won't be dining with us. I look forward to our conversation, sir. Cole out."

At twelve-fifteen, the shuttle bearing Admiral Trask and six of his people landed on the flight deck at the position specified by *Haven*'s Flight Control. The position just happened to be close to the aft cargo lift; Cole didn't want to bruise anyone's dignity by inflicting the transit shafts on them right away.

Red—the massive Igthon who'd been with Cole since Iota Ceti—greeted Admiral Trask and his party as they disembarked the shuttle, then dismissed the spacer standing beside him when he saw the pilot was to remain with Track. From there, Red conducted Trask and his people to the captain's private dining room on the mess deck.

———

Cole stood with Sasha, Yeleth, Harlon, Emily, Garrett, and Wixil just inside the hatch to the captain's private dining room. In truth, it probably should've been a formal dress mess, given the ambiance of the dining room, but that had never been Cole's style. That hadn't stopped the stewards from laying out the better dinnerware with the ship's crest on it, though. It wasn't the fine china and crystal glasses that would be used for a true formal dinner, but it certainly wasn't the dinnerware in the dining halls, either.

Cole smiled as he regarded Wixil while they waited. He remembered the shy young Ghrexel he'd met in Pyllesc a little over four years ago and felt a surge of pride at how far she'd come. He made a mental note to ask Yeleth if her people had any kind of ceremony marking one's transition to adulthood just as the hatch irised open to admit Admiral Trask and his party.

"Welcome aboard *Haven*, Admiral," Cole said, taking a half-step forward and extended his hand.

Trask approached Cole and accepted the handshake as his people filed into the dining room behind him, saying, "Thank you, Mr. Coleson. You have a truly remarkable ship."

"I thought we were past the 'Mr. Coleson' bit. Please, call me Cole, and allow me to introduce my people. I'm sure you all recognize Commander Sasha Thyrray, my first officer. Yeleth is Ship's Purser. Colonel Harlon Hanson commands the ships' marines, and Commander Emily Vance commands the ship's flight crew. The gentleman is Garrett, my oldest friend, and beside him is Wixil. Wixil is the Alpha Shift helm officer."

Trask greeted each person as Cole introduced him or her, shaking hands.

"Well, if I may return the favor," Trask said, "this is my chief of staff, Commander Jacob Tucker; my flag captain, Captain Carl Jackson; my staff intelligence officer, Commander Victoria Brown; *Indomitable*'s Sergeant-at-Arms, Chief Petty Officer Alexandra McKee; Spacer-First-Class Kayla White, an Engineering rating; and Spacer-Third-Class Arthur Gaines. From what Captain Jackson tells me, Mr. Gaines hasn't specialized yet, as he just promoted out of Spacer-Recruit on the journey here."

Cole moved down the line, shaking each person's hand as Trask introduced him or her and reiterating his welcome. When Trask introduced Spacer-Third Gaines, the young man's cheeks colored a bright red at all the attention.

Cole smiled as he approached him and, as he shook Gaines's hand, said, "Congratulations on your promotion, Mr. Gaines, and welcome."

Spacer-Third Gaines jerked a nervous nod as Cole stepped away and led his people to the side of the table where they'd face the hatch. The table had seven chairs on either side, and Cole walked to the center chair on his side. Trask mirrored him, and he and Cole left their people to sort out their seating order on their own. The last person hadn't even made contact with his seat when the hatch irised open once more to admit two stewards carrying menu tablets. The stewards passed out the menus and took drink orders.

Once the stewards were on their way, Cole looked to Trask and said, "So, Admiral, how many of your people want to join you in coming to work with us?"

"All of them," Trask replied. "That's why I extended your invitation to CPO McKee, Spacer-First White, and Spacer-Third Gaines. I wanted to ensure as many of us were represented as possible."

"That's impressive," Cole replied.

"If I may, sir," CPO McKee said, "it's true. Every single one of us are fed up with what the Provisional Parliament has done to the Commonwealth. We have no interest in serving the Coalition."

Cole nodded. "Some would say resignation would be the proper course in such a situation, instead of effectively stealing billions of

Commonwealth hardware and—for lack of a better term—defecting to me."

"The Coalition rewards those who resign with imprisonment at best," Commander Brown said, "and execution at worst. I'm not sure what the inciting event was, but the Coalition has turned into a nightmare of tyranny unlike anything since Humanity expanded from Old Earth."

The conversation faded as the stewards returned to deliver their drinks.

Cole took a healthy swallow of his iced tea and said, "So, before this goes any further, I want to be very clear about something. All of my people have passed an interview and vetting process, and I use Kiksaliks to verify honesty. Everyone you see at this table has done so. The process grew out of my desire to ensure no one came aboard *Haven* in the early days who might pose a threat to Sasha or Talia Thyrray. Since then, I have continued the practice, because it removes any question of why someone is here. Every person aboard your ships must pass this vetting to earn a place with us, and anyone who objects to this is welcome to hop a freighter out of the system. Do you wish to proceed?"

Trask looked to each of his people, and each person nodded. After polling each of his people, Trask returned his attention to Cole, saying, "Yes, we do."

"Very well. Sorting all this out will require several days, I'm sure. I wanted to settle that matter before the food arrived, because I didn't want anyone to be anxious about whether I'd say no while we ate. I don't want to give anyone indigestion."

CHAPTER EIGHT

Over the next two weeks, the personnel aboard Babylon Station worked their way through both the crews of the Commonwealth warships and the freighters' passengers. After Admiral Trask told Cole the story of how he and his people ended up with the first freighter, *Jezebel's Hope*, Cole invited Captain Narvou aboard *Haven*.

Cole looked up as the hatch irised open and smiled when Sasha led Captain Narvou into the bridge briefing room. Even though Cole had never met her before, he couldn't help but feel she looked a little shell-shocked, and he suspected the transit shafts were to blame.

"Captain Narvou," Cole said as he stood and extended his hand, "thank you for coming aboard. Would you like refreshments or a meal?"

"No, thank you, sir," Narvou replied. "I had just finished eating when your invitation arrived. I do appreciate the offer, though."

Cole returned to the seat at the corner of the table (just to the left of his normal place) as Captain Narvou chose the next seat. Sasha walked around the table to sit directly across from the freighter captain.

"So, Admiral Trask told me how he met you," Cole said.

Narvou smiled. "Remind me to send the bridge and sensor logs of that meeting to you, sir. I think you'll enjoy it."

Cole blinked. "May I ask why?"

"At one point during the incident, my sensor tech said, 'Holy shit! He's pulling a *Haven*!'"

Cole's expression shifted to neutral as he wracked his brain for what might be considered 'pulling a *Haven*,' and when a thought came to mind, the grin erupted once again. "Put his ship between yours and weapons' fire, did he?"

Narvou nodded. "The radiation from his dreadnought was so strong, it was all we could see on our scopes until he backed off. Well, it might not have been if our sensor suite was better."

"I understand that. Those large warships radiate like a star when they're at battle-stations," Cole replied.

"Forgive me, sir, but I doubt you invited me aboard to discuss how I came to meet Admiral Trask."

Cole shook his head. "Not as such, no. Captain, you have something of a reputation for being a refugee runner, and I just wanted to be sure you're aware your ship now has a bounty on it throughout Coalition space for your involvement in the destruction of their task force."

"The bounty surprises me a bit," Narvou admitted, "but I knew I couldn't go back to the former Commonwealth after Trask's ships demolished the destroyer and frigate."

"Well, if it's any consolation," Cole countered, "the bounty on Trask is absolutely obscene. It's almost as high as Sasha's bounty. So, what do you plan to do now?"

Narvou took a breath and released it as a heavy sigh. "I don't really know, sir. Helping refugees reach safety is really all I want to do, and I can't do that now. I'm not even sure I should fly the *Hope* out of here; with that bounty, I may not be safe anywhere."

"You have options, Captain," Cole said. "I'll find a place for you if you'd like to work for me."

Narvou nodded. "Thank you, sir. May I think about it?"

"Naturally," Cole replied. "The last thing I want is for you to feel like I'm twisting your arm into a decision. I'm not hurting for personnel, not even close, but I'll find a place for someone who's done as much as you have."

"What about my people?" Narvou asked.

"I'll find a place for them, too," Cole said.

Narvou nodded again. "Okay. I'll take it to them and see what everyone says. They're enjoying the hospitality of Babylon Station right now, except for a brow watch. We were on that ship by ourselves for a long time."

"Yeah...it's always nice to see bulkheads that aren't your own," Cole replied. "I even splurge every now and then and visit an actual planet."

Cole grinned when Narvou broke out in giggles.

"Thank you for coming, Captain," Cole said after the giggles ended. "Would you like a tour of the ship?"

"Oh, no, sir, but I appreciate the offer. A second trip in those transit shafts will be quite enough, thank you."

Cole looked to Sasha. "Why don't you return her to the flight deck via the cargo lifts? That might be better."

Sasha nodded. "I probably should've brought her here that way as well, but I'm so used to them now, I never considered it."

Cole stood, prompting the ladies to do likewise, and extended his hand once more as he said, "Captain, don't forget about my offer. Think it over, and discuss it with your people. Even if it's not right away, you have a place with me should you ever decide to accept it."

Narvou gave Cole a respectful handshake. "Thank you, sir. It was great meeting you."

Sasha escorted Captain Narvou out. Cole watched them go and took a half-step toward the hatch when it irised back open to admit Garrett. He smiled at seeing Cole.

"Ah, there you are," Garrett said. "I've been looking for you."

Cole grinned. "Dare I ask why?"

"You're not going to believe the results from vetting Trask's people," Garrett said as he moved to a chair at the conference table and sat.

Cole returned to a chair and sat as well, leaning back against it. "Okay, lay it on me."

"Every ship had at least one covert agent aboard. One frigate had thirty, and every single one of them thought they were the only one aboard."

Cole blinked. "Seriously? None of them knew about any of the others?"

Garrett shook his head. "Not according to the Kiksaliks. It was almost funny, really. We're up to around one-hundred-fifty covert agents, but we still have two or three ships' complements to get through. I imagine the final count will be a bit higher. We should finish by the end of the week—early next week at the latest—and we'll hire one of the freighters that visits Babylon Station to ship them out. Have you alerted Sev to all the work you have for him?"

"Yeah," Cole said. "He's looking forward to using their dreadnought to provide raw materials for our first new dreadnought. If that's the case, it looks like our first dreadnought will end up being named *Indomitable*. I'm not sure that's the name I would've chosen, but ehh... whatever works."

"After we vet them, we debrief them," Garrett continued, "and Cole, it's worse than we thought in the former Commonwealth. Way worse. A part of me wants to pull all of my people *out* of there, just to keep them safe. I won't, because we need the intel, but I'm definitely increasing their hazard pay. A spacer from one of the frigates watched Station Security execute a child for stealing food, Cole...shot the poor kid dead right in front of the market stand."

Cole took a deep breath and released it as a slow sigh. "Something's going to have to be done."

"Maybe so, but we're the only ones who could do it," Garrett replied. "With the inclusion of the Eridani Corporation and the Sirius Imperium, the Coalition now fields the largest fleet in known space. They even beat out the Solars, Cole. They may not be the most advanced, but after a certain point, quantity is a quality all its own."

Cole sighed again. "Why can't these idiots just stop?"

"Cole, eventually, the brutality and abuse of power becomes part of the culture. It becomes 'just the way things are.' People will try to escape it, but very, very few will try to fight it. Speaking of that, you should also know those five freighters held a bit of a surprise for us, too."

Cole closed his eyes and fought back a groan. "I'm almost afraid to ask."

"Five emissaries," Garrett said, "one aboard each ship and from five different systems: Oriolis, Spark, Eta Anubis, Epsilon Anubis, and Iota Anubis. They represent resistance movements from each of their systems, and they all want to talk to you. Oh, and you should also know the rep from Epsilon Anubis is a double agent."

Cole blinked. "What?"

Garrett nodded. "That's what the Kiksalik told me, anyway. I haven't singled her out yet, but I thought you should know going into any conversation that she's really working for the Provisional Parliament. Her orders are to obtain as accurate a picture of resistance forces and locations as possible before reporting back to a local handler...whereupon I imagine whoever she names will disappear in the dead of night. Considering how blatantly these people appear to operate, they may not even wait for night. The only upside to the whole situation is that she doesn't have any hidden suicide devices; apparently, the resistance screens for that sort of thing, since the Provisional Parliament has used it in the past."

"Every stormfront needs a silver lining," Cole said. "So, how do we handle it?"

Garrett shrugged. "The way I see it, we have four options: try to turn her, Mushroom Protocol, expose and arrest her, or just kill her. The thing is, though, I'm not confident she can be turned. The way the Kiksalik described her mind to me, I think she's a true believer. Oh...and I wouldn't turn her over to the resistance people, either. Some of those folks can be a bit brutal themselves, no matter what high ideals they claim. She'd probably have to suffer through some mistreatment before she died, and there's no guarantee her death would be all that quick."

Cole grimaced. "I've never liked the thought of torture. It doesn't achieve anything, and it's utterly barbaric."

"You're preaching to the choir, Cole," Garrett agreed.

"Damn," Cole said, sighing once more. "What a mess." Cole sat in silence as he considered the situation. An idea emerged, and the more he thought about it, the more he liked it. "What the heck. Garrett, please bring her here with Red. I'm going to talk with her. Tell Red before you get her that I want him standing right behind her chair... just in case she turns violent."

Garrett frowned. "Are you sure about this?"

Cole shrugged. "What's the worst that can happen?"

Now, Garrett sighed, shaking his head as he left the briefing room.

———

Garrett only required about forty minutes to return with the spy, and Cole didn't bother to stand as a host and greet her when Garrett delivered her. He had taken the time, though, to remove most of the chairs from around the conference table, leaving three. Cole sat in one. Another faced him from about eight feet away, and the third was on the far side of the table.

"Take a seat," Cole said, pointing to the chair facing him, while Garrett walked around the table to sit in the remaining chair.

"Is this how you treat all your guests?" the woman asked.

"No, just the spies," Cole replied and nodded toward the chair. "Sit."

She didn't move, so Red took steps. Placing his massive left hand on her shoulder, he marched her to the chair and plunked her into it.

"What is this?" she asked, her voice almost a growl. "I'm no spy."

"Let's not waste time with pointless denials," Cole said, snapping his fingers.

Garrett activated the room's holo display, showing a picture of the woman and various information. He said, "In contrast to the name you gave your interviewer, you are—in truth—Greta Castillian. You were born on Caledonia and were recruited into the Commonwealth Intelligence Service right out of college. I will admit we don't have your personnel file, but that's only because we haven't visited Aurelius lately. The last time we were there, we weren't exactly looking for Aurelian deep cover operatives."

"So, Greta," Cole continued, "the jig—as they say—is up. Your mission is over, and how this conversation goes will determine what happens to you. If you continue to assert your cover story, I suppose

I'll have no other option than to turn you over to the other emissaries with everything we know about you and leave them to decide your fate."

Greta moved. She didn't telegraph her intent. Her facial expression never changed. But she didn't consider the Igthon behind her. Greta wasn't even halfway out of her seat before Red's hand clamped onto her shoulder, his thumb and forefinger encircling her throat. She grimaced as Red's claws dug into her flesh as he pushed her back into the chair.

"That wasn't smart," Cole said, hiding a grin.

"I suppose you're going to torture me now," Greta hissed. "You're no better than those traitors you support."

Cole shook his head. "I don't torture people, Greta. You realize what will happen to the innocent people whose trust you've gained, once you file your report? You know what will happen, right?"

"Those traitors deserve their fate," Greta said, her expression shifting into a snarl. "How dare they turn their backs on the Provisional Parliament!"

"And what of the children? Do they deserve to die beside their parents?"

"Nits make lice, Coleson. If Lindrick had been more on the ball, you wouldn't be interfering now."

"I see," Cole replied and looked to Garrett. "Your thoughts?"

"I've been reviewing the interviewers' report in my mind, and I'm honestly having difficulty finding any redeeming qualities. What kind of response are you thinking?"

Cole sighed. "I'm trying to talk myself out of spacing her."

Garrett leaned back against his seat. "You have reams and reams of legal precedent on your side for doing so and, quite frankly, considerable ethical justification. I suppose we could imprison her or set her to hard labor, but we'd still have to feed her. I'm not sure she's worth the resources of keeping her alive. We already have the identities of her contacts in Epsilon Anubis; there's not much more she can tell us."

"What are your thoughts about this?" Cole asked, looking back to Greta.

"I accepted this assignment fully expecting to die for the Coalition. Do what you will."

"Process her into the brig, for now," Cole said. "I want to consider the matter for a day or two."

Red pulled Greta out of her seat and pushed her out of the briefing room.

Cole sat staring at the vacant seat in silence for several moments before turning to Garrett, saying, "Well...she was a real piece of work, wasn't she?"

"I'll be honest," Garrett replied. "Her comment about the children sealed her fate in my eyes. If I had met her out somewhere, she'd already be dead. From the Provisional Parliament's perspective, though, it makes a certain amount of morbid sense. If they didn't kill the children, those children would probably grow up to become resistance fighters. But killing children doesn't win them any friends, so it's a failure in the long run anyway."

Cole shook his head and suppressed an urge to shudder. "Okay. Let's get out of here." With that, Cole pushed himself to his feet and led Garrett out of the briefing room.

CHAPTER NINE

Conference Room
  Babylon Station
  Gateway System
  2 August 3003, 09:30 GST

Cole stepped through the hatch and scanned the conference room. It wasn't a large space like the bridge briefing room aboard *Haven*. The conference table was at most fifteen feet long, and there was just enough space around the table to allow for easy walking and movement without making the room feel claustrophobic.

Cole removed all but nine of the chairs around the conference table. As he was moving the final chair outside the conference room, stewards arrived with three cooled carafes of water. They placed the carafes at the quarter, half, and three-quarter points on the conference table, then placed glasses for each chair still remaining at the table, four on the emissaries' side and five on Cole's.

Cole moved to one of the room's corners and turned to look across the table at a diagonal. The setup looked good. Cole nodded.

"Thank you for your time," Cole said, addressing the stewards who stood by the open hatch. "Where should we put the extra chairs?"

"There's another conference room across the corridor that isn't scheduled to be used today," one of the stewards replied. "We can put the extra chairs there until you've finished your meeting."

"Excellent," Cole replied.

The stewards moved to do so, and Cole enjoyed their surprise when Cole moved two chairs himself. As they left the vacant conference room, Cole and the lead steward looked each other in the eyes and nodded in unison. She seemed to appreciate how Cole 'led from the front.'

Cole expressed his thanks to the stewards once again, shaking each of their hands, before returning to the conference room where he would await his friends and guests.

Sasha and Garrett arrived first. Yeleth and Red arrived next. Cole sat in the center of the five seats, Sasha to his right and Yeleth to his left. Garrett sat to Sasha's right. The final seat on Cole's side was for Juliana Painter, who had come out to Gateway to meet the emissaries and now escorted them to the conference room. Red took up a standing position in the corner opposite the hatch and over Cole's left shoulder.

When the hatch irised open to admit the four remaining emissaries, led by Painter, Cole and his friends stood. Cole gestured to the unoccupied seats as Painter moved to hers. When Cole resumed his seat, everyone else sat as well. Cole hid his amusement at that.

"Thank you for meeting with me, and help yourselves to water as you like," Cole said. "I am Bartholomew James Coleson. To my right is Sasha Thyrray, and beyond her is Garrett. To my left is Yeleth, and you already know Juliana Painter. Before we get into why you requested this meeting, I have an uncomfortable item that must be addressed. I'm sure you've noticed that one of your number is missing. The young lady from Epsilon Anubis is, in fact, a covert agent informing on your resistance organizations to the Provisional Parliament."

"You lie," the gentleman from Spark said, his voice a growl as he moved to rise.

Red took one step forward and growled. All four emissaries paled.

Cole looked the gentleman from Spark right in his eyes, saying, "No one likes to be called a liar, sir, especially when they are not. If you are unable to maintain a civil tone and behavior, my friend will escort you out, and I make no promises that he'll be gentle. Do you understand?"

The gentleman from Spark jerked a nod.

"I didn't hear you, sir," Cole said.

The man's eyes flicked to Red for less than a heartbeat before he said, "I understand."

Cole smiled. It did not touch his eyes. "Excellent. Let us proceed. The spy is currently enjoying the hospitality of *Haven*'s brig while I decide on a course of action. Now...what business brings you here?"

The woman from Oriolis cleared her throat and asked, "How do you know we're not spies, too?"

"I won't discuss my vetting process or intelligence network," Cole replied. "Suffice it to say, I am confident each of you is who you claim to be."

The four emissaries looked to one another for a moment before the woman from Oriolis spoke again. "As you already seem to know, we represent the resistance organizations on our respective worlds. Our organizations have voted to appeal to you for assistance in liberating our systems, and we have further voted to appeal to join you."

Cole blinked. "Join me? Would you care to clarify that, please?"

"Each of our systems were members of the Aurelian Commonwealth. Within that system, we enjoyed a number of benefits—system defense beyond what we're able to provide ourselves, preferred trading status, and many others. Since the Provisional Parliament has signed on as one of the founding entities of the Coalition, our traditional freedoms and reasons for being members of the Commonwealth no longer exist.

"Liberating our systems is a short-term goal. None of our systems possesses the manpower or infrastructure to defend ourselves from the might of the Coalition. In order for our systems to thrive and prosper long-term, we must replace what we had with the Commonwealth, and we believe a federation of star systems based around your ideals would be an excellent starting point."

It took all of Cole's experience and willpower not to gape at the emissaries.

"Let me make sure I understand what you're saying," Cole said. "Beyond obtaining my assistance in liberating your systems, you want Beta Magellan to join a...successor state to the Commonwealth?"

"No," the gentleman from Iota Anubis said. "We want Beta Magellan—and you—to lead it."

Cole leaned back against his seat. He wondered if he looked as gobsmacked as he felt. Silence reigned in the conference room as Cole processed what he'd just heard.

"Why not Paol Thyrray?" Cole asked at last. "He has far more knowledge and experience at being a statesman."

The four emissaries glanced at Sasha. The woman from Oriolis spoke.

"You are correct. The Thyrrays of Aurelius are excellent statesmen, and Paol represents his family well. Unfortunately, the time for Thyrray primacy is past. We have nothing against him providing counsel and wisdom, but our people believe it is time for a new voice, a new vision. And our people think that new voice should come from the man who would use his own ship to shelter life pods."

Cole chuckled. "Admiral Trask did that; well, he sheltered a freighter with his dreadnought. Why not get him to do this?"

"You did it first," the emissary from Spark countered, "and you've provided safe homes and employment for every refugee that has passed your vetting process."

The lady from Oriolis nodded, adding, "When you first arrived on the scene, people joined you because of Sasha and Talia Thyrray. You have since developed a reputation of your own, and now, people want to join you because of *you*."

"How do you know I'm not some closet despot," Cole asked, "just waiting to unleash my tyranny on the galaxy?"

A soft half-smile curled one side of her mouth as the woman from Oriolis replied, "Your actions tell the galaxy what kind of man you are, Mr. Coleson, and those actions are not tyrannical or despotic."

Cole sighed. "I need time to think about this. My knee-jerk reaction is to say 'no.' I'm not even sure I have the ground forces to help you liberate your planets, and quite frankly, I don't even want to *think* about where your other proposal would lead."

"We do not need military assistance to liberate our planets, Mr. Coleson," the woman from Oriolis countered. "Our resistance organizations have that well in hand. What we lack is a means to liberate and hold the *system*."

Cole's mind flitted to the rather impressive collection of ships that awaited processing in the Citadel Shipyard and nodded. "I might be able to help with that, true enough, but I need to consult with a few of my associates to see just what our naval force levels are."

"And you want to discuss our second item with a number of your associates," the woman from Oriolis said, smiling.

Cole chuckled. "Well, yeah. That's a direction I've never contemplated, and right this moment, I'm not comfortable with it at all. I can promise you this much; I will give the matter reasoned, unbiased thought."

"That is all we can ask," the lady from Oriolis replied. "Thank you for your time, Mr. Coleson, and we look forward to hearing from you."

The emissary from Oriolis stood, prompting her associates to stand with her. Cole stood, and his friends did likewise. The emissaries turned to leave, and the hatch opened to reveal the lead steward from the group who delivered the carafes of water. The steward offered to guide the emissaries back to their quarters, and Cole nodded his acceptance.

As soon as the hatch irised closed, Cole returned to his seat, though 'collapsed into it' might have been a better description, and allowed his expression to mirror how shell-shocked he felt.

"What am I supposed to feel about that?" Cole asked, speaking after a considerable silence.

"I'd think you'd partly feel flattered," Painter offered. "It's not every day people come to you and say, 'we want to form a new federation and want you to lead it.'"

Cole shuddered. "I don't even feel like I have a handle on running Beta Magellan. How am I supposed to run a federation of six systems?"

"If you do this," Garrett said after a chuckle, "and expect it will stay at just six systems..."

"Yeah, I know. If we do this, I'd be a fool to think it would sit at just six systems. Oh...and you heard that, right? There's no such thing as 'if *I* do this.' All the success I've had has been one-hundred-percent because of you and everyone else who has signed on with me. I'm not about to agree to that federation business unless all of you are with me."

"We're already with you, Cole," Sasha countered. "Where you lead, we'll follow."

A chorus of "hear, hear" rose from the table, with Garrett's lone exception of "Damn right."

Cole sighed. "Let's go back to *Haven*. Harlon and Emily are there, and we can use the briefing room systems to conference in Sev, Paol, and Sato from Beta Magellan."

––––––––

As Cole and his associates returned to *Haven*, a small ship docked at Babylon Station. It was a courier-class vessel, sized to transport small-volume top-value cargo at high speeds. Its pilot and sole occupant exited the ship and passed through Babylon's customs station without incident, but his identity triggered an alert notifying Station Security that one of the names provided by Cole had just passed through Customs.

The name was one of the several aliases used by Qeecir's lieutenant. Qeecir controlled most of the crime in the nearby unclaimed space, operating out of the Baldur system. He sent his lieutenant to investigate the possibility that Jax Theedlow wasn't dead, and, if that were true, to discover the fate of the *Howling Monkey* and Qeecir's three thousand kilograms of precious metals, then return with Jax to Baldur for a...discussion.

––––––––

Cole led his friends into the bridge briefing room. Just returning to *Haven* made Cole feel better, more relaxed, and he almost regretted calling the conference. Cole assumed his customary seat, and the others slid into seats down either side of the table.

The overhead speakers chirped, broadcasting Jenkins's voice from the bridge, "Cap, I have that conference call you wanted."

"Thank you, Jenkins. Send it to the briefing room, please," Cole replied.

The speakers gave a double chirp as three holographic forms appeared as if they sat in chairs further down the table. Cole smiled. No matter how much he thought he was used to Gyv'Rathi technology, it still amazed him at times.

"Thank you all for coming," Cole said, calling the meeting to order. "I just met with the emissaries from four systems across the border in old Commonwealth space. They asked us for two things. One, they want military assistance in liberating their systems from the forces of the Provisional Parliament. They specifically stated that their respective resistance groups could handle the inhabited worlds; they're only asking for naval forces to establish space superiority. The second thing they asked is far more unsettling to me on a personal level. They want to form a new federation to serve as a successor state to the Commonwealth, and they want Beta Magellan—and me specifically—to lead it. I'm not expecting we'll reach a decision on this right now."

"Well, I for one think it's an excellent idea," Paol Thyrray said, "and beyond that, I understand why they didn't approach me about it. There needs to be *something* to fill the void of the Commonwealth, especially if we start helping systems liberate themselves. If we only help them long enough to gain their independence and sovereignty, there's nothing keeping the Coalition from returning with more warships and troop transports."

Sato nodded, too. "Paol makes excellent points. I also think establishing a successor state is a worthy goal, and while I may be a bit biased, I cannot think of a better system or person to lead a fledgling state than Beta Magellan and you, Cole."

Heads physically present at the table began to nod, much to Cole's chagrin.

"I won't lie," Harlon said. "The whole idea of Beta Magellan being at the center of some new federation caught me totally off-guard, but the more I think about it, the more I like the idea. Yes, we could stand back and leave those systems to their plans for a successor state, but everyone here knows just how long that would last without a capable defense. We're the best defense in Human space; of course, they want us to join them. The rumors of new offensives from the Coalition are becoming increasingly common, and I personally don't think it will be too long before we hear of them moving against one of the nearby neutral systems, maybe even one we've befriended."

"All right," Cole said. "Let's make this official. Raise a hand if you think the federation idea is something worth pursuing."

Every person in the conference—including those attending from Beta Magellan—but Cole raised a hand, even Red from where he stood in the corner.

"Well, damn," Cole said and sighed. "I was hoping at least one of you would talk the rest out of it."

CHAPTER TEN

Captain's Day-Cabin, *Haven*
   2 August 3003, 21:37 GST

Cole peeled back the covers on the bed and resisted the urge to grin. It had been a long day, and all he wanted to do was sleep.

The overhead speakers chirped, broadcasting, "Bridge to Captain."

So close... Cole sighed and took the three steps to the comms panel, tapping the command to accept the call.

"Cole here. What do you need?"

"You have a call from Commander Vincent, sir."

Cole blinked and wracked his mind. Who was Commander Vincent, and why would he be calling? The only Commander Vincent that came to mind was Commander *James* Vincent, commanding the Charr system picket, the next system anti-spinward toward the old Commonwealth.

"Is that James Vincent out of Charr?" Cole asked.

"Yes, sir," the bridge officer of the deck replied.

"Okay. Send the call to the day-cabin, please."

Within moments, a prompt appeared in Cole's field of vision asking where Cole wanted to receive the incoming comms call. Cole selected the viewscreen on the bulkhead of the sitting room area and routed the audio through the day-cabin's speakers. The viewscreen immediately activated and displayed an image of a man with salt-and-pepper hair and vibrant green eyes.

"Apologies for calling so late, sir," Commander Vincent said, "but I thought you'd want to know we have a situation."

Cole chuckled. "It's been that kind of day. Lay it on me."

"A task force of thirty-five ships just arrived through the Sapphire jump gate, and they're squawking Coalition transponders. They broadcast this message."

Vincent nodded to someone off-screen, and the viewscreen blinked to display a young man in a ship-suit in the Coalition's colors.

"Attention," the young man said, "I am Captain Neville Irving. We have credible intelligence that you are harboring mutineers, led by Jennings Trask, and we demand you hand them over to us and return the Coalition property they stole. You have ten hours to respond."

The viewscreen blinked back to a view of Commander Vincent.

Cole chuckled. "I didn't know you were harboring mutineers in Charr, Commander. Where are you hiding them?"

"You found me out, sir. They're crammed in my closet."

Smiling, Cole said, "Okay. Reply that you've forwarded his message to the relevant authority, and you're expecting a response within twenty-four hours."

Vincent nodded. "Yes, sir. May I ask what that response will be?"

Cole grinned. "I have the *Haven* battlegroup in Gateway. I figured we'd come out to Charr and say hello."

"Why do I have the feeling it's not going to go well for them?" Vincent asked, adding his own grin to the mix.

"That depends entirely on how much sense that Neville fellow has. If he turns belligerent on you, fall back to the Gateway jump gate and let me know."

"Aye, sir," Vincent replied. "We'll be waiting for you."

"Thanks for the call, Commander," Cole said. "I appreciate it."

Vincent nodded once, then ended the call.

Cole stood in silence a moment, marveling at the quantum communications technology. Charr was fifteen light-years from Gateway, but you never would've known it based on the quality of the call. After a few more seconds lost in thought, Cole shook himself and accessed his implant, choosing the comms function and selecting the bridge as the recipient of the call. Cole chose the day-cabin's speakers for the audio.

Moments later, the overhead speakers chirped and broadcast, "Bridge, Officer of the Deck."

"How many people does the battlegroup have over on Babylon?" Cole asked.

"Uhm...well, I can't speak for the other ships in the battlegroup, but all of our people are aboard."

Cole almost sighed. "Have comms signal a general recall order for all battlegroup personnel. We depart for Charr in two hours. Log the orders so that Delta shift is aware of it."

"Aye, sir," the young man replied.

"Thank you. Cole out."

Cole turned back to his bed and smiled, saying, "*Haven*, kill the lights."

"The ship's lighting is not a life-form that can be killed, Cole-Captain," the ship's computer immediately replied. "Please, clarify your request."

Cole heaved a sigh as he walked to his bed. It almost felt like the ship's computer was messing with him. "*Haven*, turn off the day-cabin lights."

The day-cabin went dark.

———

Charr System
3 August 3003, 13:57 GST

Cole entered the bridge and walked toward the command chair. Mazzi looked over her shoulder and stood, saying, "Captain on the bridge!"

"I have the conn," Cole replied as he stopped. "*Haven*, bring up the tactical plot, please. Show near-space out to...one light-hour."

The tactical plot appeared, hovering in the air and centered between the command chair and the helm. Thirty-five data codes hovered in a cluster just far enough off the transit lane to the jump gate to keep from impeding traffic. The *Haven* battlegroup approached the formation at fifteen percent of lightspeed and arrayed in a standard travel formation, with the Charr system picket moving off to resume its patrol.

"Sensors," Cole said, "what do we have?"

"Thirty-five ships squawking Coalition transponders, sir," the sensors tech replied. "I'm reading one battleship, six cruisers, eight destroyers, ten frigates, and ten corvettes. Presumably, the battleship is the flagship."

Cole's eyes flicked over the tactical plot, taking in the Coalition formation. They weren't in a combat formation Cole recognized, but he'd restricted his studies and training to the material available in the ISA's courseware.

"Okay. Weaps, bring the ship to alert status, and activate TacNet. Comms, what's the comms lag now?"

The technician at the weapons station sounded off an, "Aye, sir," and condition lights throughout the ship began flashing amber; after thirty seconds, they would revert to steady.

Cole turned to look at the comms station as Sasha entered through the starboard hatch. The technician there keyed a couple commands.

"We should be down to about twenty minutes' lag, sir," the comms tech said.

Cole frowned. "Might as well send a message by bird. Fine. Hide the tactical plot, and record for transmission, please."

The tactical plot disappeared as Cole turned to face the video pickup. When the comms tech gave him the go-ahead, Cole began, "Greetings. My name is Bartholomew James Coleson. I have reviewed your message regarding Jennings Trask, and as the old saying goes, I'm disinclined to acquiesce to your request. Furthermore, given our credible intelligence of the abuses levied against the formerly free citizens of what is now Coalition space, you may regard this as our formal notice that Coalition vessels of *any* kind are not welcome in any system claimed by Beta Magellan. You have one hour to light off your drives and turn toward the jump gate back to Coalition space, or we will interpret your presence as hostile. That is all."

Not more than fifteen seconds later, the comms tech said, "Ready to transmit, sir."

"Send it on full broadcast, no encryption," Cole replied as he sat in the command chair. He looked to Sasha, who had stopped a respectful distance off his right elbow, and asked, "Thoughts?"

Sasha angled her head to the left just a bit, saying, "Well, if they weren't spoiling for a fight when they arrived, they will be now."

Cole shrugged. "Circumstances are already building toward a confrontation between us and the Coalition. Sure...I could smile, nod, and make nice to stave off that confrontation for a while, but they're killing people, Sasha." Cole glanced at the time in his implant. "It's going to be at least twenty minutes before we see any reaction. You hungry? I skipped lunch."

"I can hold the fort here, sir, and call you when something happens," Sasha replied.

"Yeah...you're probably right. I'll just send an order to the mess deck and ask some eager soul to run it up to the office."

Twenty-five minutes later, Cole returned to the bridge just in time to hear the report of the Coalition ships' reaction.

"They're charging weapons," the sensor tech reported.

"I have the conn," Cole said as Sasha vacated the command chair. "Sound battle-stations." Klaxons started blaring throughout the ship as the condition lights shifted from solid amber to flashing red. "Flight ops, my compliments to the CAG, and instruct her to launch fighters with orders to engage the frigates and corvettes. Weaps, pick a corvette, and designate it as 'Do Not Engage' for the battlegroup; someone needs to take the message home that they're not welcome here."

Sasha turned toward the starboard hatch, saying, "I'm going to the auxiliary bridge," as she fast-walked to the hatch.

Cole gave an answering nod that Sasha probably didn't see as his eyes flicked over the tactical plot. "Comms, signal combat formation Gamma-Three to the battlegroup, please."

"Aye, sir," the comms tech replied.

The Alpha shift bridge crew started filtering through the hatches, hustling to assume their duty stations for combat. Wixil smiled as she walked past Cole and took over the helm.

"Message coming in," Jenkins said, having taken over from the Beta shift comms tech.

"Put it up," Cole said.

The forward viewscreen activated to show Captain Neville Irving. Cole smiled upon seeing the man's jaw clenched, red creeping up his neck.

"Mr. Coleson, the Coalition is not accustomed to caring what some tin god in a backwater system says. You *will* turn over Jennings Trask, his personnel, and the ships he stole, or we will wipe your pathetic excuse of a population from the face of the galaxy. I have been authorized to use lethal force."

The silence was palpable as everyone looked to Cole. Everyone aboard now knew he'd survived the massacre of Beta Magellan, and most were aware of his conviction that such would *never* happen again.

"Record for transmission, please," Cole said, his voice flat and unemotional.

"Ready, Cap," Jenkins replied.

"Mister Irving," Cole said, "Beta Magellan has already suffered one massacre, and I tell you now that your little task force has insufficient strength to capture and hold this star system, let alone wipe all signs of life from Beta Magellan. If you have even a modicum of good sense, you will flee like the cur you are. Anyone who chooses to fight will be a cloud of expanding atoms when I leave this system. This moment— this moment right here—is where you choose whether you live or die. Choose well."

Jenkins soon reported, "Ready to transmit."

"Send it as a wide-beam broadcast."

Mere seconds later, Jenkins said, "It's sent, Cap."

"Thank you, Jenkins," Cole replied, his eyes locked on the tactical plot.

"Cole?" The bridge speakers broadcast Srexx's voice.

"Yeah, buddy?" Cole asked.

"I am downloading the Coalition fleet's computer storage media. May I ask you to refrain from destroying them for approximately fifteen-point-seven-three-nine-five minutes?"

Cole grinned. "Sorry, buddy. The best I can give you is fifteen-point-seven-two minutes."

"I shall endeavor to expedite...oh. That was a joke, was it not?"

More than one person around the bridge chuckled along with Cole as he said, "Yes, it was. I won't start the fight, so when we start destroying ships depends on them."

"They must shoot first?" Srexx asked.

Cole nodded. "That's right. It's a matter of principle with me that I never fire first."

"One moment..."

Everyone on the bridge—even Cole—shared a look or two between one another during the ensuing silence.

"There," Srexx said, at last. "I believe I have addressed the issue."

"Okay," Cole said. "Mind if I ask what you did?"

"I do not mind at all."

Cole waited a few seconds before he sighed, then said, "Okay, Srexx...what did you do?"

"I wiped the software command relays between all weapons control stations and the weapons themselves. Those devices held no interest to me, and the resulting delays in repairing their fire control systems will allow me to complete my download."

"Wait," Haskell at Sensors said. "Does he mean they can't fire any of their weapons right now?"

"Yes," Srexx replied. "I thought that was what I said."

"What about local control of the gun turrets?" Mazzi asked from the weapons station.

"According to the respective computers," Srexx said, "the gun turrets do not possess local controls."

Cole fought to suppress a chuckle as he asked, "Anyone want to guess on how long it will be before we start seeing ships with hard-wired relays for weapons controls? They got rid of the software controls for ejecting the cores pretty fast after Caernarvon."

"I'd guess it depends on who examines the logs of the corvette we send back," Mazzi replied. "I don't think we have sufficient information to make any guesses, but you can be certain there'll be a book running on it soon."

"You would've thought they'd have those relays hard-lined already, though," Haskell said. "Too much can go wrong with software."

"You are indeed correct, Mister Haskell," Srexx replied. "A lot can go wrong."

Something about Srexx's tone and phrasing drew Cole's attention.

"Srexx, buddy, what are you doing?"

"I am going behind the repair parties and re-wiping the relays they have already restored."

Cole closed his eyes and allowed himself a moment of sympathy for the poor souls responsible for damage control on those ships.

"That's...almost cruel, Srexx," Cole said.

"I'm still downloading the data in their storage media," Srexx replied. "It has been several cycles since I have encountered new data, so why should I allow the Coalition commander's inaccurate assessment of his own competence to impede my download?"

"To say nothing of saving their lives, right, buddy?"

"Admittedly, Cole, I do not devote many compute cycles to those who intend our people harm. If they surrender before we destroy them, then I shall re-evaluate the number of compute cycles they deserve at that time."

Srexx lapsed into silence, and the bridge crew waited. Cole almost felt like he should step the ship down to alert status instead of battle-stations, but he didn't know if Srexx would stop re-wiping those relays without warning. In the end, he needn't have worried.

After what seemed like an almost interminable silence, Srexx said,

"I have completed my download, Cole. Would you like me to stop wiping the software relays?"

Cole nodded. "Yeah, you probably should. Let's see if they want to start this after all."

Thirty minutes passed. Then, Jenkins announced, "Message incoming, Cap. It's from one of the Coalition cruisers."

Cole frowned, shrugging. "Why not? Put it on."

The viewscreen activated to display a woman with faint lines around her eyes and wisps of gray lacing her dark hair.

"Mr. Coleson, I am Commander Rosalind Briggs. Captain Irving has suffered an unfortunate...malady...and regrettably is no longer able to command this task force. With your permission, we will depart your system and send a message buoy back to Coalition space with your communications that Coalition forces are not welcome in your territory.

"Captain Irving was a recent *political* appointee with little experience in fleet—or even ship—command, and we'd rather not die in a pointless confrontation. We await your response."

Cole turned the idea over in his mind. He didn't want to bathe his battlegroup in lives and ship debris, but he knew without a doubt the day would come when he had no choice in that. Still, he felt he should make certain they understood the score.

"How long would it take them to reach the jump gate, Wixil?" Cole asked.

The young Ghrexel's hands flew over the helm controls for a moment or three before she replied, "Assuming a speed of two-tenths-light, they'll reach the jump gate in a little over three hours."

"Jenkins, record for transmission, please," Cole said.

"Ready, Cap."

"Commander Briggs, I grant you your reprieve. I did not come to this system looking for a fight, but you need to understand something. I don't care where you go or what you do, but if you begin preying on systems we call 'friend,' you won't survive our next meeting. Make sure your people understand that. You have four hours from the receipt of this message to get your ships out of my system. Coleson out."

Twenty minutes later, the Coalition ships pivoted almost in unison and lit off their drives on a speed course for the jump gate. *Haven* and her battlegroup held station and watched them leave, serving as a silent warning not to deviate from the plan.

Three hours and thirty-five minutes after Cole sent his message, the last Coalition ship transitioned through the jump gate. Cole ordered a stand-down from battle-stations and a return to Babylon Station in Gateway.

CHAPTER ELEVEN

Babylon Station
  Gateway System
  4 August 3003, 09:17 GST

Sasha entered the café on the station's concourse and smiled at the pleasant aroma filling the space. Unlike Cole but like so many others aboard *Haven*, Sasha loved a good cup of coffee, and this café had the reputation of brewing the best cups this side of Old Earth. She chose a table for one (or perhaps two if they were very friendly) and placed her back to the wall. The server took her order, and she browsed news stories on her tablet while she waited.

A shadow moved in front of her, and Sasha looked up to see a man she didn't know standing over her. Without invitation, he pulled out the chair opposite Sasha and sat.

"I'm sorry," Sasha said. "I'm not here to meet with anyone."

"I know," the man said, "but you see, Sasha Thyrray, you have information I want, and I would like to offer you the opportunity to provide that information in a manner that leaves you unharmed."

Sasha lifted one eyebrow in an ages-old expression. "Is that so? Just what information do you want?"

"The whereabouts of Jax Theedlow."

Sasha maintained her facial expression, saying, "I've never met anyone by that name."

"Odd," the man replied, removing a small pad from a pocket on his jacket. He activated it to display a picture of Sasha, Yeleth, Harlon, and Emily walking with Cole through the concourse outside; Sasha guessed it was taken when Cole came aboard the station to meet the refugee emissaries. "You're walking beside him in this image."

Sasha accessed her implant and sent a broadcast to all similar implants that she needed any available security personnel near the café to arrive with haste.

"So, you're saying the man in the foreground of this photo is this Jax Theedlow you're trying to locate?" Sasha asked to buy herself time. "Why do you want him?"

"He disappeared with property that did not belong to him but was entrusted to his care. I have been charged with finding him and returning him to my employer for an explanation. It would go better for you if you cooperated with me."

Movement at the door drew Sasha's attention, and she saw a collection of *Haven*'s marines she knew from the gym enter the café. They scanned the room in short order and started making their way to her.

"Really, Miss Thyrray," the man said, just as the marines were nearing arms' reach. "I don't know what you expect to achieve by trying to imply there's someone behind me, but it's not going to work. I'd rather not employ more *invasive* methods to get what I want. It's always so messy."

"This guy bothering you, Commander?" the lead marine asked as she stopped less than two feet from the back of the man's chair.

The man froze, his eyes flicking side to side as if trying to see behind him without turning his head. Sasha gave him a slight smile that held no mirth just as the server brought her coffee. She accepted the cup, thanking the server, and took a sip. The café lived up to the hype; it was an excellent brew. Sasha savored another sip before she placed the cup on the table.

"To my mind," Sasha said, "very few people could be looking for Jax Theedlow, and none of them are individuals I'd invite to a social affair. I suppose I could threaten you like you did me, but to be honest, I'm not in the mood." Sasha directed her attention to the marine standing right behind the man. "Take him to *Haven*. Put him in the brig, and alert Garrett that he was threatening me for information about Jax Theedlow."

"Aye, ma'am," the marine replied and shifted her eyes down to the back of the man's head. "Are you going to come along quietly, or will we have to subdue you?"

The man stood, starting to turn around as he said, "I'm not above beating some sense into a—" He stopped speaking when he saw just how many marines awaited him.

"Yeah," the female marine said, "that's what I thought. Let's go, tough guy."

Sasha enjoyed another sip of her coffee as she watched the marines lead the man out of the café. She took a moment to send another message that her security situation was resolved before going back to the headlines on her tablet.

———

Cole's Quarters
    Battle-Carrier *Haven*
    Gateway System
    5 August 3003, 18:56 GST

When the hatch chime sounded, Cole looked up from his tablet to view the corridor video on the large viewscreen. He saw Garrett standing outside and smiled, instructing the hatch to open via his implant. The hatch irised open, and Cole stood to receive his oldest friend.

"What brings you around at this time of the evening?" Cole asked, shaking hands with Garrett.

"Sasha went fishing yesterday and came back with a rather nice haul. I've been processing it, shall we say, and thought you might want to know about it."

Cole frowned, gesturing for Garrett to sit as he resumed his own seat. "I didn't know Sasha fished, and I'm pretty sure there aren't any planets in the system with large bodies of water, let alone life-bearing bodies of water."

Garrett grinned. "Well, in all truth, the fish came to her. He tried threatening her for information, and she sent an implant broadcast for any available security personnel to come to her location." Garrett could see Cole was growing impatient, so he cut to the chase. "Vince Comstock."

Cole's only perceptible reaction was a slight tightening around his eyes and fresh tension in his jaw.

"Yeah, my thoughts exactly," Garrett replied. "I've spent several hours with him since he started enjoying our hospitality, and I have assembled a rather impressive collection of information. He's been Qeecir's primary lieutenant now for the better part of five years, Cole; he knows that slimy lizard's whole operation, and he's told me everything. He even knows the location of Qeecir's secret mine. It's an unclaimed system that's never been surveyed, two jumps core-ward from Baldur."

"How did it end up with jump gates without being surveyed, especially so close to Commonwealth space?" Cole asked.

Garrett shrugged. "Beats me, but it did. The system doesn't even have a name on the official register, just a catalog number. The lack of a survey might have something to do with the system being part of a seldom-used route to Caernarvon from Baldur, but that's pure speculation on my part."

"So, what else did Mr. Comstock have to say?"

Garrett smiled. "Qeecir is very unhappy with you. It seems he's more distraught over the disappearance of the *Howling Monkey* than the loss of all that metal. I can understand that, I suppose. His mining system seems to have an abundance of the stuff, but he only has so many ships, especially ships with no active warrants."

Cole grinned. "It's so unfortunate I've inconvenienced Qeecir, Garrett. Oh, whatever shall I do?"

"Yeah, I can tell you're all broken up about it," Garrett replied, chuckling. "Seriously, though, this isn't something that will go away. We're going to have to deal with Qeecir...and probably sooner rather than later."

"You're right," Cole replied. "Schedule a conference call for tomorrow morning. I'd like Sato, Sev, and Paol to attend from Beta Magellan, plus the usual suspects here. Is Painter still aboard Babylon?"

"No," Garrett said. "She returned to Beta Magellan shortly after we left for Charr."

"Make sure she's in the conference, too."

Garrett nodded and stood. "I'll see you in the morning, then."

—————

The next morning, Cole entered the briefing room and found Sasha, Yeleth, Garrett, Harlon, and Emily already waiting for him. Even those conferenced in from Beta Magellan sat at the table in holographic form.

Cole found his seat and scanned the faces before him, asking, "I'm not late, am I?"

"No," Sasha said. "We're just early."

"Oh. Good. I hate being late," Cole replied. "Garrett, you're the reason we're here. Care to start?"

Garrett nodded once and launched into a quick briefing to ensure everyone was up to speed on the situation at hand.

"So, this guy is Qeecir's lieutenant?" Harlon asked once Garrett finished his presentation.

Garrett nodded. "He's been the number-two guy in Qeecir's operation for the past five years."

"Does it strike anyone else as a little odd that Qeecir would send his lieutenant on an op like this?" Harlon asked.

Cole shook his head. "It's not odd to me. Qeecir always used Vince for tasks where he needed a fast, beneficial resolution. There's a reason he's Qeecir's right hand, as it were."

"Is there any chance of achieving a reasonable resolution with this Qeecir?" Sato asked. "Can she or he or it be reasoned with?"

Cole shrugged. "It's difficult to say. Qeecir is one of the major crime figures in the region. He and Bosil control all sorts of criminal enterprises from the fringe of our territory core-ward past the former Commonwealth and spinward almost all the way to the Asiatic Concordat. Truth be told, it would probably give his other pilots ideas if he didn't deal harshly with me for scrapping his ship and stealing his metal."

"And his base of operations is the Baldur system?" Sato asked.

Cole nodded. "Yes. He runs the station Baldur's Gate like a tyrant. All the shipping in and around Baldur needs his good graces, so the people have problems finding transport away from the system."

"Then, we should annex Baldur and remove Qeecir as a threat before he causes us more problems," Sato replied. "Has he come to the attention of any system authorities?"

"Oh, yes," Garrett answered. "Like Vince, Qeecir has warrants in several systems and even a nice bounty in one or two. The problem is that no one wants to front the cost required to get him out of there, and it wouldn't be long before someone moved in to take his place."

"Not if we annex the system and leave a system picket, marine force, and a governor to establish a proper system government," Paol replied. "It'll take time to shift the system culture away from criminal enterprises, don't get me wrong, but that's the most viable long-term solution."

Sato nodded. So did Sasha and Harlon.

"If I understand the local star charts," Yeleth said, "Baldur is the next system core-ward from our claimed territory. If we do nothing, how long will it be before the criminals of Baldur make trouble for our miners and freighters? Yes, our miners are protected by system pickets, and our freighters are better armed than some destroyers, but that's beside the point. We shouldn't allow a threat to our people to exist."

"There are a great many threats to our people, Yeleth," Cole replied. "Where do we draw the line before we turn into something like the Coalition?"

"You both make good points," Sasha said. "Everyone who knows you, Cole, understands that this is a threat that must be faced. The refugees—especially the emissaries—might not. I personally think we should annex Baldur sooner rather than later and put someone in charge who can transition the system away from being a criminal hub, but we have to approach it very carefully. If we just go ahead with this, people may start whispering that we're no better than the Coalition."

Cole nodded, saying, "You're right, Sasha. I don't think there's any other way to handle this than full disclosure. Painter, reach out to the people in Beta Magellan, and schedule a time where a broad cross-section of the population can be in the Grand Hall aboard Citadel Station. We'll ask the emissaries to come with us and enjoy a front row seat, and we'll also broadcast the assembly to every system claimed by Beta Magellan. I think it's time to tell the story of Jax Theedlow."

CHAPTER TWELVE

Grand Hall Assembly Venue
  Citadel Station
  Beta Magellan
  10 August 3003, 09:30 GST

The Grand Hall was nothing more than a massive space with a stage and stadium-style seating built to a massive scale. It could seat upwards of five thousand people with a modicum of comfort and almost double that if the occupants were willing to be friendly. Between the exceptional acoustics and the audio system, a person could deliver a speech from the stage with no concerns about being heard by the people in the farthest row.

A single podium stood in the center of the stage. A person filled every seat, an accurate cross-section of the entire population of Beta Magellan, and true to Cole's word, holo-cameras recorded the stage to broadcast the event across the quantum comms network to every system claimed by Beta Magellan.

The murmur of quiet conversation between those present was an undercurrent of white noise throughout the hall, everyone waiting to learn why they'd been asked to be here or be watching.

At nine-thirty on the dot, Cole strode onto the stage and stood at the podium. He looked out over the assembled crowd and smiled.

"Good morning," Cole said. "I want to thank you for coming or choosing to view this via the broadcast. Many of you know me, or at least know of me. I'm Cole. That's who I am, but my name is Bartholomew James Coleson. I didn't ask you here today to discuss my name or who I am. I need to tell you about Jax Theedlow."

Cole watched the people in the audience share looks among each other at the non sequitur. Their curiosity was writ large across their expressions. Who was Jax Theedlow, and why did he warrant Cole's attention?

"In 2986," Cole resumed his presentation, "I lost my family in the massacre of this system. It was an organized, orchestrated attack, and rather than risk whoever it was coming after me again, I hid. I spent thirteen years in hiding, working on the fringe of Human space. During that time, I used the name Jax Theedlow." Cole watched their reactions as he connected the dots for them. "I did all kinds of work during those years, but what I loved most was piloting. I ended up piloting freighters on the fringe of society while I built a stash to disappear. Jax Theedlow died the day I met Srexx, but now, Qeecir is looking for Jax. Qeecir poses no threat to me or any of us, but he could harm those who trade with us or those who desire to start over here.

"Why is this important? Well, Qeecir rules his criminal empire from the station Baldur's Gate in the Baldur system, and both Himari Sato and Harlon Hanson have advised me that I should annex Baldur and eliminate Qeecir. Qeecir isn't going away, and the rules criminals live by won't allow him to let bygones be bygones. As long as he's out there and in power, he will try to be a thorn in our side. The thing is, I wanted to discuss this with you. I wanted you to understand what is happening, and I wanted you to know I'm not building the next Coalition. So, you tell me how you think Qeecir should be handled. What do you think we should do?"

Cole turned and indicated the large screen hanging behind him, where a Net address appeared.

"Use this site to tell me your thoughts on the situation. Do we ignore Qeecir? Do we proceed as Sato and Harlon have advised and annex Baldur? Is there a better way we haven't thought of? Yes, I technically own the system, but Beta Magellan is as much your home now as it is mine. You have as big a stake in what we're trying to build as I do, if not more, and I feel you should have a say in how we handle this situation. The site will be available for input for twenty-four hours. At one second after twenty-four hours, the site will lock out further input. I look forward to reading what you have to say. Thank you for your time."

Cole turned and strode off the stage, leaving a stunned silence filling the hall in his wake.

The next day, the results of Cole's impromptu poll spoke volumes. Of the 1,524,521 people who claimed Beta Magellan citizenship, 914,713 people cast a vote on how to handle the Qeecir problem. Eighty-five-point-seven-nine percent of those voted to annex Baldur and eliminate Qeecir as a threat.

———

Cole leaned back against his seat in the bridge briefing room. Sasha, Yeleth, Harlon, Emily, and Garrett sat with him. Holograms of Admiral Sato, Painter, and Sev occupied seats further down the table.

"Well, you have your mandate," Sasha said. "How do you want to do this?"

Cole sighed. "It's going to be a mess, no matter how we do it. Since Baldur and the mining system are technically unclaimed systems, we can claim them, but I don't want to do that until we've dealt with Qeecir and his organization. Srexx?"

"Yes, Cole?"

"I'm going to be relying on you for a list of all personnel in Qeecir's organization," Cole said. "He is obsessive about notes and personnel records, so once you have those files, we should be able to identify everyone working for him. Heh...you might even find a picture of a younger me in there."

"Of course, Cole," Srexx said. "I will need time to peruse the station's computer and copy its data, and Qeecir being alerted to our efforts might complicate matters."

Cole nodded. "I know, buddy, which is why the next part of my plan is going to cause a major argument."

"And just what *is* the next part of your plan?" Harlon asked.

"We take Vince Comstock's ship with us, and I fly it into Baldur's Gate...alone. *Haven*, the battlegroup, and the system pickets will maintain full stealth close enough for Srexx to plunder the station's computers. Emily and Harlon, you'll prep fighters and assault shuttles for an assault on the station, and I'll keep Qeecir distracted until Srexx has what we need."

Silence ruled. Everyone stared at Cole.

"I...do not like your plan, Cole," Srexx said. "I have insufficient data to calculate true probabilities, but my initial evaluation is that your proposal places you in considerable danger, possibly extreme danger."

"*Thank* you, Srexx," Sasha remarked, her voice carrying an edge to it. "Have you considered the possibility that Qeecir might just shoot you out of hand? If you die, Cole, *everything* we're building here collapses."

Scanning the expressions directed at him, Cole saw that everyone else agreed with Sasha and Srexx. He sighed.

"Look, I get it, and I appreciate your concern. I don't think it's wise to storm the station, though. That would give Qeecir or one of his top people plenty of time to purge their data. We need him distracted. We need him believing he's in control as long as possible, until we have everything we need to eliminate his organization once and for all. I don't see how we can do that without having all his attention focused on me. Yeah, his guard might still be up while he's focused on me, but he won't be thinking about protecting his data. He'll be focused on the *Howling Monkey* and, once I tell him what I did, the ten-thousand kilograms of precious metals I stole from him across four years or so."

"There's just one hole in your plan," Harlon said. "Won't he wonder why you've returned? Won't he question you flying into Baldur in his lieutenant's ship?"

"May I offer a modification to your plan?" Srexx asked.

"I'll always listen, Srexx," Cole replied. "I'll always listen to any of you."

The briefing room hatch irised open to reveal Scarlett.

"Srexx said I needed to be here?" Scarlett said.

"I agree with Colonel Hanson," Srexx said, "that the likelihood of Qeecir seeing through your ruse is potentially quite high. The modification I would suggest is that Scarlett resume her role of Red Pattel and deliver you to Qeecir after she witnesses you killing Vince Comstock. Between the medical staff and my own efforts, she should be able to provide a medical report that will prove Mister Comstock's death beyond all doubt."

Scarlett's eyes widened for a moment before her expression hardened. "You have Vince Comstock? Why fake his death at all? I'll happily gut that toad from crotch to sternum."

"That sounds like you two have a history," Cole said.

"I've always said there are different classes of criminals, Cole," Scarlett replied, "and Vince goes out of his way to harm people even when there's no need for it. That said, I don't like trying to fool Qeecir into thinking I've captured Cole. I think that has as much chance of going bad as Cole just walking in there alone. Why don't we go in there together? It'll put Qeecir off balance, having to face something he expects—which is Cole—and something he doesn't—me. Knowing that vile lizard, having him off balance is your best shot."

Cole gestured for Scarlett to join them at the table, which she did. Then, he looked to everyone else, asking, "Thoughts?"

"It would give you limited backup on-site," Harlon said, "and I like the idea of having Qeecir off balance. Since you called him a lizard, Scarlett, I'm guessing he's a Thurian?"

Scarlett nodded. "The smaller genome, not one of the massive warriors. I always heard he decided to pursue an alternative career rather than try to excel in his caste back home."

"Well, that's something at least," Harlon replied. "A Thurian warrior in a blood rage is not something I'd want to face."

"They're not as tough as you'd think," Cole countered.

Everyone turned to stare at Cole.

"What?" Cole asked. "If you can get one to open his mouth, just toss a plasma grenade down his throat. The hide's tough enough to keep most of the blast inside, but be sure to avoid the mouth, nose, eyes, and...well...rear."

"That sounds suspiciously like personal experience," Sasha said.

Cole shrugged but said nothing.

"How soon can we have system pickets for Baldur and the mining system?" Sasha asked.

"Reinforced system pickets," Cole added. "I want there to be enough ships to run down pirates or criminals who try to separate on multiple vectors."

"When are you looking to move on Baldur?" Sev asked. "If it's soon, we'll have to pull ships from existing tasking and replace them once we recycle Trask's fleet."

"What systems can we pull from without compromising them?" Cole asked.

"You're looking at it the wrong way," Sato said. "All of our system claims are publicly registered in addition to claim buoys placed at all the jump gates in the systems. I don't recommend pulling ships from the pickets near the old Commonwealth, simply as a matter of prudence, but those systems more than two jumps away from our borders don't really need pickets. No one in their right mind is going to start a war with us."

"How many system pickets do you feel we could pull?" Cole asked.

Sato manipulated controls outside the video pickup of the hologram system, and a star chart of Beta Magellan's space appeared above the conference room. "We currently claim these systems. The border systems and the systems one jump in from the border need pickets, not to mention Gateway and Beta Magellan itself. That leaves us these nine systems that currently have pickets but are far enough from the border that the pickets aren't really needed."

"Those systems have the standard pickets?" Cole asked.

Sato nodded. "Yes, they do."

"That's...some serious firepower," Cole said, his eyes flicking across the star chart. "Okay. Pull 'em. Pick a rally point in Gateway, and the battlegroup will meet them there. Sev, I want you to focus on getting Trask's ships recycled as fast as possible. We'll be moving on those five systems that sent emissaries to us eventually, and I'd prefer not to reduce the forces 'back home,' as it were, to achieve our objectives in those systems."

"I'll have an estimate to completion for you when you return from the Qeecir operation," Sev replied.

"About the emissaries from those Coalition systems in the old Commonwealth," Sato said, "have you reached a decision about their proposal?"

Cole sighed. "Yeah, I have. As much as I might prefer otherwise, I agree that there needs to be some kind of stabilizing influence in this region of space. It certainly isn't the Coalition, and so far, none of the independent worlds seem to be organizing anything. I'd just as soon stick to our own situation and leave the rest of the galaxy to itself, but I can't abide the Coalition slaughtering innocents. I don't want that leaving this conversation yet, though. There's a long way to go from where we are right now to announcing that, and I don't feel we're anywhere near ready."

Everyone nodded, and Cole couldn't miss their smiles. He could see they were glad he decided to accept their advice to proceed with founding a successor state to the former Commonwealth.

Cole allowed the silence to extend for several moments before he tapped the table with both palms and said, "Okay. If there's nothing else at this time, I'll take the battlegroup back to Gateway and bring Vince's ship aboard *Haven*. Once the pickets from those nine systems have gathered, we'll all head out for Baldur. Let's get to it, people."

That said, Cole put actions to his words and pushed back from the table, standing and leaving the briefing room.

CHAPTER THIRTEEN

Near-Station Space, Babylon Station
Gateway System
12 August 3003, 07:35 GST

Haven and her battlegroup floated in the void, just outside the traffic patterns surrounding Babylon Station. Vince Comstock's courier-class ship was already sitting on the flight deck, courtesy of a pilot who 'won' the job during Emily's daily flight-crew briefing. It seemed all that remained was waiting for the nine system pickets to arrive.

Cole entered his office and sat at his desk. A thought had just struck him, and he wanted to discuss it with Painter and Paol. Accessing the comms function of his workstation, he typed up a quick text message that asked Painter to arrange a conference call with Paol whenever she and the statesman had a spare minute or three. He chose the quantum comms network as the transmission medium and fired off the message. He didn't even have time to close the comms function before an 'Incoming Call' alert appeared.

Cole blinked and accepted the call. A small hologram showing Painter and Paol sitting together appeared, hovering above the desk's surface.

"Morning, sir," Painter said. "Paol and I were discussing other matters when your message arrived, and we saw no reason to make you wait. What's on your mind?"

"A couple things...basically, the government of Beta Magellan," Cole replied. "Where are we with that, Paol?"

Paol cleared his throat. "Well...honestly...I'm still working on the constitution. The basic body of laws was very straightforward, and as you know, I submitted those for your approval quite some time ago. Until we have an actual government, those laws will be enforced by marines under the authority of Colonel Hanson; it's not perfect, but it works for now.

"Your insistence that Beta Magellan's government be as a light and agile as possible and with limited bureaucracy is proving the most challenging aspect to writing the system's constitution. I've been studying historical examples, and I've cribbed quite a bit from Thomas Jefferson and the democracies of the ancient Greek city-states. At the time, true democracy wasn't practical in those city-states for a variety of reasons, but with our quantum comms network and a few tweaks, I think we might make it workable—at least a modification of it, anyway."

Cole nodded. "Okay. I'll continue to leave the matter in your hands, and when it comes time to write the charter for that federation the emissaries want us to build, that will probably end up being all you as well. If you feel you're underpaid or understaffed, let me know, so we can discuss it. So, aside from all that, I have two ideas I think we need to start working on sooner rather than later: a Ministry or Department or Whatever of Research and a Ministry or Department or Whatever of Defense.

"My main concern is that we form a cadre of researchers to take the knowledge and technology present in Srexx's archives and start building on that. I can't imagine the Gyv'Rathi stopped their technological advancement after they exiled Srexx, so we need to start ours. We have an enormous tech advantage right now, and I want to keep it for as long as we can.

"As far as the Whatever of Defense, I think we should focus on the Navy and Marines at this time. We need an academy and training facilities. Involve Sato in that. Heh…I'll have Srexx forward whatever training curricula he swiped from the Commonwealth and Solars. Something tells me he didn't just walk away with the cookie jar; I'm betting he has the whole pantry. I'm thinking this will be in the conceptual stages for quite a while. After all, we just received a major influx of spacers and marines that I don't think any of us were expecting, but it's something we should have in place *before* we actually need it. Any questions?"

Paol and Painter looked to one another before looking back to Cole and shaking their heads.

"No," Painter replied, "I think we're good here. I'll start working up recruiting lists for scientists and engineers."

Cole nodded. "Thanks. Oh…and you might want to work up a consideration of folding CIE into Beta Magellan's research department, maybe a sub-branch or something. Beta Magellan will always be a direct holding of the Coleson line, so there's no reason not to do that unless you find something. Just something to consider. Thank you. Cole out."

The hologram above his desk vanished as Cole closed the call. A quick series of commands brought up the system scan and showed him the system pickets hadn't arrived yet, and Cole leaned back in his seat as he considered what he should do next.

———

Courier-Class Ship
  Baldur System
  21 August 07:15 GST

Cole stretched and looked at the pile on the adjacent bunk. The gun belt, holster, and fighting knife were three pieces of his past Cole never expected to need again. Well, the holster wasn't the one he used to carry as Jax, and neither was the pistol it held. Srexx had refused to allow the courier ship to leave the flight deck unless Cole agreed to a sidearm that was the best the available Gyv'Rathi tech could provide, and he provided a holster and multiple charge packs to go with it. Cole wasn't too surprised to see Scarlett wearing the same holster and kit, either.

In many ways, the courier reminded Cole of the *Courageous Sloth*, the ship where he'd been an apprentice pilot and met Scarlett while she was still Red Pattel, the Pirate Lord of Sector 82. There was a cockpit, three passenger quarters, a galley, and a space the ship plans called a cargo hold which was really more of a storage closet with a high-security door. Unfortunately, the so-called cargo hold hadn't contained any goodies when Cole checked upon boarding for the first time...for old time's sake.

Cole entered the cockpit and sat at the pilot's console. Scarlett occupied the co-pilot's seat and smiled as Cole entered.

"Morning, sleepy-head," Scarlett said, adding a suggestive wink to her smile.

"Morning, Scarlett," Cole replied. "How are we doing?"

Scarlett made a show of consulting the co-pilot's console before she spoke. "We're a couple hours in-system from the Bounty jump gate. I've calculated a flight path for the sole station in the system, Baldur's Gate, which will ensure we don't arrive until the fleet is here. We're proceeding along that flight path at a sedate one-tenth-lightspeed, and we have no contacts on the scope at this time."

Cole nodded. "Wow. Thanks."

Scarlett leaned back against her seat, her playful demeanor returning as she turned to look at Cole. "So, do you ever think back to when we met and wonder what it would've been like if you had stayed with me?"

"Honestly?" Cole asked, swiveling his seat to face her.

"Well, yeah...of course, honestly."

"Nope," Cole replied without missing a beat. "But keep in mind, Scarlett, I am not—nor have I ever been—the kind of person who'd consider piracy a viable life choice. That's not to say I haven't thought of you from time to time down through the years. You've always been very attractive physically, and you're a much more attractive person now that you've decided to leave Red Pattel behind."

"Then why haven't you taken me up on any of my offers?" Scarlett asked. "Not to put too fine a point on it, Cole, but there have been times I've done everything short of holding up a flashing neon sign that I'm yours for the taking. I've had a devil of a time figuring out whether you're playing hard to get or just oblivious."

"Sorry about that," Cole said. "When you first came aboard *Haven*, I couldn't be sure whether it was genuine interest—or at least genuine boredom—or extreme gratitude for saving your life. Then, later on, you worked for me. It always seemed...wrong, somehow...to date people who worked for me. Too much of a captive audience, I guess; I'd never know whether someone said 'yes' out of true interest or fear for her job."

Scarlett somehow managed to lean even further back in her seat, adopting an appraising expression as she asked, "So, that's why you've never pursued Sasha?"

Cole blinked. "Sasha? Why would I pursue Sasha?"

Now, it was Scarlett's turn to blink. "You *have* looked at your first officer, right? Aside from that, I'm pretty sure she's head-over-heels for you."

Cole's jaw literally dropped as he leaned forward. "Seriously? What makes you say that?"

"Well, for one thing, do you remember how she always glared daggers at me when I first came aboard *Haven*? It didn't start until you and I began spending time together. She either saw us or heard about it and probably drew the wrong conclusion. It wasn't until we made it back to Beta Magellan without anything ever happening between us that she started treating me halfway civil."

Cole relaxed against his seat, leaning back as he directed a blank stare at the decking. After several moments, he heaved a sigh. "Well, this complicates matters. I almost wish you hadn't told me."

Now, it was Scarlett's turn to blink. "Excuse me? One of the most eligible and desirable women in Beta Magellan is seriously into you, and you wish I hadn't told you? Care to explain that?"

"You said it yourself. She's my first officer, Scarlett," Cole said. "I can't...that is...what kind of example would I be setting for my people if I started a relationship with my first officer? And just think of what kind of trouble I'd be in if it went sour. Talk about a mess." A sudden thought occurred to Cole, and he jerked his head up to face Scarlett. "Is that why she declined command of a cruiser?"

Scarlett shrugged. "Beats me. We're not exactly best friends, but it wouldn't surprise me. Sometimes, we take the best we can get when it looks like we can't have what—or who—we want."

"If you're right, I'd think the last place she'd want to be is *Haven's* first officer," Cole countered. "If she really does feel the way you think she does, wouldn't her current placement just be a slow torture?"

"Hey...at least she sees you every day. She gets to hear you laugh, see you smile. It could be a lot worse."

Cole closed his eyes and shook his head as if to clear it. "Damn, Scarlett. I'm not going to be able to get this out of my head. Why did you tell me?"

"You're facing a pretty big decision about the whole family thing," Scarlett replied. "I just wanted to be sure you were aware of all your options and didn't end up making a colossal mistake."

"You know about everyone getting on my case about the lack of an heir?"

Scarlett shrugged. "It's pretty obvious if you stop to think about it. Just don't rush into anything...and be sure to look at your options from every angle."

Cole sighed again and shook his head once more. "You know, you could've waited until *after* the mission to tell me."

"There's no guarantee we'd have the time. You're pretty much a captive audience right now, tiger." Scarlett punctuated her statement with another playful wink.

Cole fought the urge to sigh again. It was going to be an even longer trip to Baldur's Gate than he first thought.

CHAPTER FOURTEEN

Baldur's Gate
  Baldur System
  22 August 3003, 22:57 GST

The courier approached near-station space for Baldur's Gate. There was no sign of *Haven* or any of the ships that traveled with her, but Cole had a message from Sasha saying they were in position. It was time to go see an old 'friend.'

"So, you haven't really discussed the plan for when we get in there," Scarlett said as Cole input the commands to take the courier into its docking bay.

Cole chuckled. "Nope...I have not. If I had brought it up in the meeting, someone—possibly multiple someones—would've argued about it. It would've been this big thing that served no purpose."

"So what *are* we going to do when we get to Qeecir?" Scarlett asked.

"Does he know you as Red Pattel?"

Scarlett shrugged. "I'm sure he knew *of* Red Pattel, but to the best of my knowledge, we've never met."

Cole turned that over in his head for a moment as he checked the docking progress. Finally, he said, "Okay. Don't mention Red Pattel at all, unless somebody else does first. Qeecir won't disarm us or search us or anything like that. He's an arrogant lizard that way, and it's going to be his downfall. Your job is to watch my back. Qeecir and I will have a little back-and-forth; there may be a little excitement, and then, we'll call in the marines."

"This has to be one of the vaguest plans I've ever heard," Scarlett said. "If I didn't know better, I'd say you didn't trust me."

Cole shook his head. "It's nothing like that. I just have a very specific reason for doing it this way, so just this once, I need you to trust me. You'll understand on the other end of this, I promise."

Scarlett gave Cole a sidelong look as he brought the courier into its docking bay; she didn't like the undertone she was picking up in Cole's voice, but she owed him her life. She chose her side back in Centauri. The ship was small enough that it didn't need an external airlock, and within minutes, Cole had the landing struts extended and was bringing the tiny ship into the bay. Even after three years since he'd touched helm controls, Cole's mastery of piloting showed. There was hardly a *thump* as the courier settled onto its landing struts, and it took Scarlett a moment to realize they'd landed in the docking bay.

"Damn, Cole," Scarlett said as she stood to leave the cockpit, "you're smooth. I don't think *I* could've landed her that smooth."

Cole grinned, and for a moment, his face and entire demeanor made Scarlett think of a giddy boy, overjoyed at doing what he loved most.

"I hardly ever get to pilot anything anymore," Cole said as he stood. "It's nice to know I still have the touch."

"You could get a small runabout, you know," Scarlett said, leading the way out of the cockpit. "I mean, you own one of the largest ship-yards in known space. I'm sure it wouldn't be *that* difficult to get some-thing built."

"You are absolutely right. I *could* do that, but if I did, what about Srexx?"

Scarlett blinked at the apparent non sequitur. "What about him?"

"I'm his first friend, Scarlett. The people who built that ship left him entombed in what was a planet at the time, because they found out Srexx achieved full sentience. And I promised him we'd see the galaxy together. What would he think—how would he feel—if I asked Sev to build me a runabout? Sure...I could be overthinking the situation, but he's done so much for us—for all of us—that the last thing I want is to hurt him in any way."

"You sure you're not just afraid of him going all 'kill the organics?'" Scarlett lifted an eyebrow to punctuate her question.

Cole chuckled. "I'm not afraid of my friends, Scarlett. If I were, then they wouldn't be friends."

Cole stepped past Scarlett and led the way out of the courier.

———

Scanning the corridor around him, Cole decided that the station hadn't really changed all that much in the four years (plus or minus) since he'd been aboard. Unlike most stations, the corridor's surfaces seemed to carry a coat of grime, and the air carried a scent Cole wasn't sure should be there. He knew it wasn't in the air on the more-maintained stations like The Gate in Tristan's Gate, any of Zurich's stations, or any of his stations.

Cole and Scarlett soon entered the station's main concourse, and Cole couldn't help but focus on the people moving through the space. No one looked up. There were no smiles. On Citadel Station, the main concourse often had groups of children running, playing, and laughing; here, there were none. And every hundred feet or so, at least one armed pirate wearing Qeecir's colors stood in silent watch.

"I'd forgotten how bleak it was here," Cole remarked, his voice little more than a whisper.

Scarlett nodded. "It's bad. I can't remember the last time I saw a station that had security forces carrying lethal weapons."

"Spoiled you, have we?" Cole asked, adding a slight smile.

"I'm starting to think you have," Scarlett replied, scanning her surroundings as much as she could without turning her head.

. . .

Qeecir operated out of what had once been the largest club on the station. If the place had a name, it had long since been lost to the mists of time. Qeecir used the space as both an office/throne room and market. No guards stood outside at the entrance, but that was normal. Inside, there'd be a small army.

Upon entering, Cole stopped and waited for his eyes to adjust to the darkness. After a few moments, he scanned the space, looking for his quarry. It didn't take long to spot Qeecir; the crime lord of the local region held court in a massive booth at the far-right corner of the room.

Setting off at a steady pace, Cole led Scarlett across the space, dodging the vacant tables that normally held merchants and their wares, until the two reached the booth where Qeecir sat.

Qeecir looked up at Cole's approach, and his expression betrayed nothing of what he thought or felt at seeing Cole after so long a time. Qeecir's scales were an odd shade of blue-green, and Cole saw he still carried the jagged white scar that ran from the crest of his skull to his left jawline.

"Well, well...Jax Theedlow," Qeecir said, the pitch of his voice still hovering around the dividing line between bass and tenor, "it has been a long time. Oh, forgive me. You're Bartholomew Coleson now."

Cole chuckled. "I always was, Qeecir. Jax was just a convenient fiction while I sorted out what I wanted to do with my life."

"And building an empire is what you want to do with your life, then?" Qeecir asked. "I could've helped with that."

"Honestly, Qeecir, I kind of fell into that. My plan at the time I stopped piloting for you was to disappear on a planet somewhere and leave the Coleson heritage behind. But life's like that; plans never survive contact with it."

Qeecir hissed. "'Stopped piloting for me,' is it? You *stole* from me, boy. Did you really think I'd...what is it you Humans say...let bygones be bygones?"

All joviality and mirth vanished from Cole's demeanor in an instant. "Be very, very careful with your next words, Qeecir. I'm thinking the next ninety seconds will determine how this conversation ends."

"Oh? And why is that?" Qeecir asked. "You came into my *lair*, boy, and all by yourself at that. Your belief that you have any control over this situation is grossly inaccurate."

"Claiming that I'm all by myself isn't being fair to Scarlett, here," Cole replied, "but even if she weren't here, just because I'd be all by myself doesn't mean that I'd be alone."

Cole accessed his implant and initiated a call to Srexx.

< *Yes, Cole?* > Cole heard Srexx's voice in his ears as if he stood directly under one of the speakers aboard *Haven*.

"Status?" Cole asked, and Qeecir's eyes narrowed in response.

< *I am ninety-eight percent finished in my download, Cole. I have all personnel records of Qeecir's organization and am now collecting his financial information.* >

"Time to completion?" Cole asked, his eyes never leaving Qeecir.

< *By the time we end this call, I should have a complete copy of all data on the station, even the protected archives Qeecir believes to be severed from the primary datanet.* >

"Thanks, buddy. Would you mind passing a message to Sasha for me?"

< *Of course not, Cole.* >

"Please, tell her I said, 'engage.'"

< *I have just completed my download, Cole, and am passing on your message now.* >

Klaxons erupted throughout the former club as red lights started pulsing. Every guard in the vicinity of Qeecir drew a weapon.

"What is it?" Qeecir shouted. "Why the alarm?"

"A massive fleet just appeared, sir!" A nearby individual who bore the look of a tech geek shouted. "They're broadcasting Beta Magellan transponders!"

Qeecir's eyes pivoted back to Cole. "What is the meaning of this?"

"You would never have cut your losses and left me and mine alone, Qeecir," Cole replied. "Beta Magellan is annexing Baldur and taking over your station. You have a choice: surrender and live out your life on a prison planet somewhere; or do something stupid and not survive the next five minutes."

Just then, the speakers throughout the club (and the station if those present could've heard them) chirped and began broadcasting, "Residents of Baldur's Gate, may I have your attention, please? My name is Sasha Thyrray, and it is my honor to serve as First Officer aboard the battle-carrier *Haven*. My captain, Bartholomew James Coleson, has annexed this system for Beta Magellan, and our marines are executing a forced boarding to secure the station. Please, sequester yourselves in your homes until further notice; we do not intend harm to any civilians, but this is a very fluid, very dangerous situation. If you are out and about, we cannot guarantee your safety. Thank you; that is all."

The speakers chirped again.

"How *dare* you!" Qeecir raged as he leaped to his feet, his clawed hands reaching for Cole as he lunged across the table.

The whine of an energy weapon erupted, and a bright green bolt struck Qeecir square in his chest, burning an inch-and-a-half hole through his torso where his heart once was. The corpse collapsed onto the table, and its momentum carried it off the side to land on its back and stare unblinkingly up at the ceiling. The guards eyed Qeecir's corpse and then looked to one another.

Cole turned to see Scarlett holding her pistol. Her eyes flicked from point to point as she kept her finger on the firing stud.

"Damn, that was a quick draw," Cole said.

A partial smile flicked across her lips as Scarlett replied, "Thanks. Never fired one of these before, though; Srexx really knows his sidearms."

One of the guards closest to the scene lifted his hand.

"Yes, dearie?" Scarlett said.

"I've seen his scales shrug off lasers," the guard said. "What was that?"

"You know," Scarlett replied, her tone conveying consideration and a hint of curiosity, "I'm not really sure. I've been told it's one-shot effective against everything up to collapsed-atom materials like neutronium, though. I don't suppose any of your friends fingering their guns are wearing neutronium body armor, are they?"

The four or five guards who'd been rubbing their fingertips across their sidearm grips blanched and, using slow deliberate movements, moved their hands away from any weapons and lifted them into the air. Before any more guards could duplicate their associates' stance, the entrance to the club collapsed inward, and *Haven* marines charged inside. Scarlett returned her pistol to its holster and smiled at the chatty guard.

"Thank you for asking, dearie," Scarlett said, adding a wink. "You probably saved their lives."

Within what seemed like mere moments, the marines had Qeecir's former guards on their knees and disarmed.

CHAPTER FIFTEEN

Baldur's Gate
  Baldur System
  24 August 3003, 09:23 GST

Cole stood in the remains of the station administration suite, frowning at the sight before him. What should've been a clean, orderly place dedicated to overseeing the day-to-day tasks any station needed to survive was in fact a junk heap. It was a literal junk heap. In his cursory glance alone, Cole identified the pieces of eight different items. He saw the remains of an anti-grav pallet's power generator. In the corner off his right elbow, a magnetic coil from...well, *something*...leaned against the bulkhead. Depleted energy cells, emitter coils, fractured catalyst chambers...the only part of the space that wasn't supporting scrap was the ceiling.

Cole's implant alerted him to an incoming call from Sasha. He accepted and used his link to StationNet to route the call to the compartment's audio system.

At least the station's computer was in tip-top shape. Srexx wouldn't tell him what state it was in when they arrived, but some of the systems people aboard *Haven* assured Cole the station's computer and its accompanying datanet were now pristine.

"Well, the station administration suite is trashed," Cole said by way of a greeting.

"That's not all," Sasha replied, and Cole felt a pit form in his stomach. "Our techs are having a problem tracking that odd smell you reported. They sent images of the environmental systems, and we're now fabricating emergency atmo systems to support the station's population until we can correct the problem. From the looks of it, the whole environmental plant was limping along on the brink of catastrophic failure; what we're hearing is they spent half the day— every day—keeping the system working. And don't even get me started on the algae beds; I'm pretty sure it would be more accurate to call it stagnant pond scum."

Cole closed his eyes and took a deep breath. "So, bottom line...is the station salvageable? Do we need Sev to send out an emergency crew for a temporary station while we build a new one?"

"Our people are still carrying out their engineering evaluation," Sasha replied. "I'm not sure we have a definitive answer on that yet. I have seen Chief Engineer Logan muttering prayers, though; I think we're up to twelve in the last hour."

Cole frowned. "I didn't know Max was all that religious."

"I'm not sure he was...at least not until he started reading reports from the field assessment teams."

Cole blinked, asking, "Do we have the lift capacity to evacuate this station if we need to?"

"I'll have to get back to you on that. We're still working on an accurate nose count. Qeecir apparently had slave pens in the lower levels of the station."

"Okay. I'm not waiting. Send word to Painter. I want every available freighter to re-configure for emergency shelters and head here at maximum speed. What's the status on control of the system?"

"The fighters are back aboard," Sasha answered. "We have complete and total space superiority in this system."

"Well, there's that at least," Cole replied. "I may have to leave

Haven here with you in command of the system and take some ships to Qeecir's mine."

Silence settled onto the comms call.

"Sasha?" Cole asked.

"Might I suggest picking a senior officer as task force commander in your stead?" Sasha asked at last. "The people on the station are starting to come out of their quarters, and they seem to be responding well to your presence and the new laws for the system we published. If you leave now, it may undermine what little progress we've made with the populace."

Cole sighed. "Yeah...I suppose you have a point. Okay then. Split the combined system pickets into two groups: five pickets and four. Make sure the group of five has a reliable, experienced commander, and they'll move on Qeecir's mine. The group of four will serve as a reinforced picket for Baldur. With *Haven* and the battlegroup hovering around the station, let's keep three of the pickets near a jump gate with the last one patrolling the system. Have we canvassed the asteroid fields and planetoids in the system? I don't want anyone left hiding who could create problems later."

"Yes," Sasha replied. "There was a matter involving a few asteroids in the outer field, but that's been resolved. Might I suggest we discuss that later?"

So, there was something about it Sasha didn't want to discuss on an open call. Fair enough.

"That's fine, Sasha," Cole said. "My days of wading through scrap piles are over, though. Let's get some people in here to clear out this space, so the engineers can evaluate it when they arrive."

"Aye, sir," Sasha answered.

A marine approached Cole's left elbow and stood at parade rest a respectful distance away. Cole nodded in greeting to the woman and said, "Sasha, I have a marine at my elbow. I should probably see what that's about. Is there anything else?"

"I think we've covered everything, sir."

"Alrighty. Thanks. Cole out." Cole turned to the newly arrived marine. "And how can I help you today?"

The marine snapped to attention, saying, "Sir! Private First Class

Dorya Leshi reporting. Captain Otecji offers her compliments and asks if you have time to visit the command center, sir. A group of civilians has approached her, claiming to be the council for the station's residents."

Cole nodded. "Good call. I was wondering when we'd see something like this. Lead the way, if you please."

"Sir!" PFC Leshi replied, adding a nod that wasn't *quite* a salute before executing a parade-ground-perfect about-face pivot and striding out of the compartment.

It took a little over ten minutes to reach the command center for the station's occupation force, and make no mistake, circumstances still very much rated the label 'occupation force.' Patrols still found holdouts and pockets of resistance, and Cole was sure it would be a while yet before things truly settled.

The moment Cole stepped into the command center, every marine present snapped to attention. Cole fought the urge to grind his teeth at the display, because he never wanted anything like that for himself, but he paused for a moment and sought out the senior-most present with his eyes and nodded once. That individual—a lieutenant—returned Cole's nod and went back to what he'd been doing when Cole arrived; the rest of the marines followed suit.

PFC Leshi led Cole across the compartment to a hatch. She rapped on the hatch twice with her left hand before keying the controls to open with her right. The moment the hatch started cycling, she pivoted and moved aside.

Cole stepped through the hatch and found himself in a conference room. The five marines in the compartment snapped to attention at Cole's entrance, while a collection of people in ragged and dirty clothes watched from their seats. Cole made eye contact with the woman wearing captain's bars and nodded once; she returned the nod and relaxed, the other marines relaxing with her.

"Sir," the captain said as she stepped around the table to greet him, "I'm Captain Cera Otecji, commanding the security force for the station."

"It's nice to meet you, Captain," Cole replied, offering a handshake that Otecji accepted. "PFC Leshi said you have representatives of the station's residents."

"Yes, sir," Captain Otecji said, turning back to the conference table. "They approached us this morning."

Cole took one step toward the table and the seven occupants who eyed him warily. He nodded in greeting, saying, "Hello. I'm Bartholomew James Coleson. I'm glad you came to us; I was afraid I'd have to put out a call for representatives over the station's public address system."

One of the people—a woman of middle age with a glare in her eye —locked eyes with Cole, asking, "So, just answer me this: what gives you the right to claim our home?"

Cole blinked. "Uhm...that would be interstellar law. This system was listed as unclaimed/unaligned in the System Registry, and there are no records of any potential claim even being filed, let alone finalized claims."

"We've been here far, far longer than you," the woman countered. "Don't you think that gives us the right to this system? After all, pretty much every person on this station was born here...well, the people you haven't locked up, and good riddance to those bastards anyway."

Cole scanned the faces of everyone at the table before returning his gaze to the woman. She was clearly the spokesperson for the group before him and possibly held considerable sway within the station community at large. He had to get this just right, or he'd have a bigger mess on his hands than the station's environmental systems.

Cole took the few steps necessary to reach the chair closest to the speaker. He pulled the chair back from the table and sat, leaning forward toward her and resting his elbows on the chair arms.

"I hear what you're saying and I understand your concerns," Cole said. "Please, believe me when I say I have no intention of being an ass about this. To be completely honest, I was in something of a bind, myself. I knew Qeecir ran this system, and I knew there was nothing I could do to keep him from posing a perennial threat to anyone wanting to trade or visit or what-have-you with Beta Magellan. I also knew there were innocent people in this system, who'd lived here their whole lives. I explained the situation to my people in Beta Magellan and our surrounding systems and laid out our options as I saw them; the majority of votes came back in support of annexing this system and removing Qeecir and his organization as a threat.

"I have two goals for this system: one, ensure that it never again becomes a threat to my people, and two, give everyone here the chance to become 'my people' with all the benefits and responsibilities that entails. I have engineering teams inspecting every inch of this station right now, and they've already made a frighteningly long punch list of repairs and upgrades that need to happen. When they finish their assessment, we'll step back and look at the situation to see whether we should fix this station or build a new one, and no matter which path we choose, the work will be done at no cost to the people of Baldur."

The woman leaned back against her seat and crossed her arms, still giving Cole a moderate glare. "So, you're not going to raise our taxes any?"

"Taxes?" Cole asked.

"Yeah," the woman said. "That lizard taxed us into oblivion. The first time a person didn't pay, his enforcers would deliver a beating, and the person's taxes would go up. The second time, a worse beating and another hike...since the person was a repeat trouble-maker, you see. The third time, well, they'd just kill you and take everything you and your family owned; you'd be lucky if your whole clan didn't go dancing with the stars."

Cole blinked. "Yeah...that's going to end. I have all of Qeecir's financial records, so my people and I will go through them and figure out something. I'm not going to make any promises about Qeecir's finances, but I'll be sure to keep everyone apprised of what gets decided. Now, as for the taxes...I don't tax my citizens; I use the sales tax model, based on a tiered system of goods classification, and I'd like to think our classifications make pretty good sense. The feedback I've received from my citizens in Beta Magellan lead me to believe it's a very fair and balanced system, and I'll be implementing it here once we get everything settled."

"You mean your soldiers won't come to our homes every month

demanding half our income?" another person at the table asked, his voice barely above a whisper.

Cole shifted his attention to the young man, and Cole's heart went out to him when he visibly suppressed a flinch. "He took *half* your monthly income? Seriously?"

The young man's entire demeanor conveyed the impression of a small prey animal ready to bolt, but he jerked a nod without meeting Cole's eyes.

"Damn...that's just wrong. Okay. Pass this on to your fellow residents. I don't know what I'll find in his financial accounts, but whatever *is* there, I'll divide evenly between the residents of the station."

The woman who'd been the speaker for the group gave Cole another glare. "I suppose that includes the slaves, too?"

Cole shook his head. "No. I'll take care of the slaves out of my own funds. I see them as being kind of a special case, anyway, and we have procedures and an infrastructure in place to help them get on their feet after being captive."

"And what do you expect from us for all your generosity?"

"Live your lives, and I'd like for anyone who wants to stay to help me turn Baldur into a place we can all be proud of. Ninety-nine-point-nine-nine percent of Beta Magellan's citizens are former refugees; most are from the former Commonwealth. Each and every one of us knows what it's like to be in a bad situation with no good options for relief. I'd like the residents of the station to become citizens, people who have a stake in the welfare of the system and want to have that stake."

"And just what do you take away from all this, then? If you're not taxing us to death and not claiming any of our people for your own... what's your margin? What's your angle?"

Cole sighed. "I know what it's like to lose everything; I have stood on the street where I grew up, surrounded by blackened husks that used to be my neighbors' homes, and I have helped carry the bodies of my parents and grandparents to graves that I myself helped dig. What's my angle? Lady...'my angle,' as you put it, is doing everything I can to ensure something like that never happens again as far as my authority and influence reach.

"I want to create a place of safety and hope, where people can go about their daily lives doing what they want to do with no fear of tyrants or criminals, or of government trying to be one or the other. It's a lot of work, and anyone who ever said it would be easy is a liar and a fool. But it's the goal I've chosen to make my life's work, and I welcome anyone who wants to help me achieve it.

"Now...if I may, I suggest you gather the residents of the station or converse with them however you do so; pass on what I've said along with the new laws for the station I've published on StationNet. I'll see to it the new tax laws are up there sooner rather than later, too. We'll be here a while until we settle on a plan for the station, so take some time and figure out who wants to be a part of what I want to build here. When you're ready to talk again, somebody here at the command post will be able to find me. Thank you for coming, and if you'll excuse me, I need to get back to work."

Cole nodded once and stood, leaving the conference room.

CHAPTER SIXTEEN

Cole's Day-Cabin, Battle-Carrier *Haven*
    Baldur's Gate, Baldur System
    30 August 3003, 13:23 GST

"Well, well," Scarlett said, her voice almost a purr. "I've finally managed to get inside your...quarters. I suppose that's progress of a sort."

Cole chuckled and shook his head. "You're incorrigible...you know that, right?"

Scarlett gave Cole a half-smile accented with a suggestive wink. "A girl has to maintain her focus and reputation, dearie."

Cole sighed. "So...I have a job offer for you."

"Oh? Do tell."

"I want you to be the System and Station Administrator here," Cole said, "and I want the person in charge of the mining system to report to you as well. You know, we're going to have to think of a better name for that than 'mining system.' I already have Sev working up construction crews; he's thinking he'll have the system defenses in place in about a year, since he doesn't need to crash-build a station... yet...and that's for both systems. After that, I want to investigate the possibility of replacing this station with something better and building a station to replace that refinery in the mining system."

"How about Midas?" Scarlett asked.

Cole blinked. "Midas? I don't follow."

"The name for the mining system," Scarlett answered. "How about Midas?"

"Yeah...that would work," Cole replied. "That would work really well. One second..." Accessing his implant, Cole made a note to record the system's name in the Registry as 'Midas.' "Okay. So, are you interested in the job?"

Scarlett nodded. "Dearie, I'm happy to do whatever you ask." Then, she smiled; it was almost a predatory smile that carried hints of humor and mirth.

Cole grinned. "You just don't give up, do you?"

"I'll make you a promise: I'll give up on the day you say, 'I do.'"

"And just to whom must I say that?"

Scarlett shrugged. "I think that's still a bit undetermined, so I've adopted a 'wait and see' attitude. I'm sure it won't be nearly as fun or interesting as what I'd like to see, though." Scarlett added a wink that said more than her words.

Cole felt his face heat, and Scarlett threw back her head and laughed.

"Gotcha, dearie," she said. "Do you have any idea how long I've been trying to get you to blush? Oh...it doesn't invalidate anything I just said, of course, but it's a victory all the same."

Cole sighed.

"You know," Scarlett said after a few moments of silence, "you never did show me that plan you mentioned coming into Baldur's Gate. I suppose it's a moot point now, but I must say...you sure know how to keep a girl in suspense."

"Oh, yeah...*that* plan," Cole replied. "Uhm...well...I had decided I was just going to walk in there and shoot him. But we started talking; one thing led to another, and you sorted out the situation for me."

"You? Really?" Scarlett almost gaped at Cole. "Do you mean to tell me that the White Knight of Beta Magellan was going to commit cold-blooded murder?"

Cole held Scarlett's gaze for several seconds before he said, "Scarlett, I'll do whatever it takes to protect my people. If that means having a trade treaty with Tristan's Gate, I'll do that. If that means going to war with the Coalition, I'll do that. And if it means burning down a crime lord who never cared about anyone but himself...well... yes, I'll do that, too."

———

Cole scheduled a meeting with the residents of the station and announced that Scarlett O'Donnell would be taking over direct authority in the system in his stead. There was some unease at the change-over, but Scarlett stepped forward and explained that Cole couldn't stay in Baldur for any length of time, having responsibilities in Beta Magellan that he must discharge. Cole was pleased to see how well Scarlett handled the situation and decided he'd made the right decision in naming her as Administrator. Following the meeting, Scarlett walked with Cole to the shuttle bay, where Cole promised a civics team from Paol's side of the house would arrive soon.

With Baldur and Midas secured, Cole returned to *Haven*, and the battlegroup set course for Beta Magellan.

———

Citadel Station
    Beta Magellan
    2 September 3003, 08:17 GST

Cole worked his way through reports on the progress made in Beta Magellan while he'd been in Baldur. For some reason unknown to Cole, his people had chosen to stockpile the reports, instead of sending them to him through the quantum comms network. Cole was about a third of the way through the digital 'stack.'

"Cole?" the speakers broadcast Srexx's voice.

Smiling at the blessed interruption, Cole leaned back in his seat, replying, "Yeah, buddy?"

"I have been working my way through the data from the computers aboard the ships in Trask's fleet, and I have reached a number of conclusions I would like to present. How should I schedule a presentation and request specific attendees?"

Cole grinned. "Well, you could send each of your attendees a message inviting them to the presentation and giving a brief reason you feel the presentation is needed."

"Interesting," Srexx responded. "Is that how you do it?"

"Honestly, no. I tend to call the meetings and tell everyone when they should be there. While I aim to be very polite and considerate in doing so, I don't beat around the bush about it, either."

"Would you please schedule a meeting for me?" Srexx asked. "I am...uncertain...the people I request to attend will do so just to hear my conclusions."

"Okay," Cole replied. "Give me an overview of your conclusions, without duplicating the presentation you want to make."

"People around you—and you yourself—continue to refer to the Commonwealth or former Commonwealth or Provisional Parliament. The data obtained from Trask's computers suggest to me that doing so is erroneous for multiple reasons, the most significant of which being that the Provisional Parliament has been reduced to a figurehead at best. None of the computers contained specific coordinates as to the Coalition's capital, but the data I have consumed leads to the inescapable conclusion that our neighbor is the Coalition and not any remnant of the Aurelian Commonwealth." Srexx paused for a moment. "Cole, the classified communications lead me to conclude that the Coalition is moving into a phase of military expansion; my evaluation is that they will move against an unaligned star system within the next month, and if their first military expansion is successful, I evaluate there is a significant probability they will not stop with their first conquest."

Cole sighed. "Yeah, that's important information. I've never known your analyses to be completely and totally wrong. All right. I'll call a meeting for you to present your findings."

"Thank you, Cole."

The passage of a few hours found Cole arriving in the bridge briefing room. He was the first, but the other attendees were on the way. Srexx requested that Paol, Painter, Sev, Sasha, Yeleth, Red, Harlon, Sato, Emily, Garrett, and Mazzi each attend. That seemed a slightly odd list to Cole, but he trusted his friend.

The others arrived in short order and, once seated, looked to Cole.

"Srexx," Cole said, "we're all here."

"Thank you for attending," Srexx replied. "I have spent the past few weeks examining the data downloaded from the ships in Admiral Trask's task force, and I reached the conclusion that you should be aware of my evaluations."

A holographic star chart appeared, hovering in the space over the conference table. It showed a region centered on Beta Magellan out to a radius of about one thousand light-years. It didn't escape Cole that Beta Magellan and those systems it controlled were highlighted in blue. Neutral or independent systems were colored white, and unclaimed systems were not colored at all. Srexx had chosen red to represent Coalition space, and red blobs marked the star chart much like a child had flicked a brush with red paint at the hologram. The largest blob was the former Commonwealth. The other blobs represented what once were the independent polities of the Carnelian Bloc, Sirius Imperium, and Eridani Corporation.

"As you can see from the star chart, the Coalition controls an impressive amount of space, and with the combination of their respective fleets, the Coalition now fields the largest navy known to exist," Srexx said. "For the next few minutes, I shall endeavor to explain and prove why using the phrase 'the former Commonwealth' is inaccurate and perhaps leads to a willful ignorance of what is happening within Coalition space. For now, I shall refrain from bombarding you with the evidence that led me to my conclusions, but if you should want to evaluate those conclusions, I'm happy to provide all the evidence."

Srexx paused for a moment, and the star chart zoomed in on what once had been the Aurelian Commonwealth. At the very fringe of the star chart, the lower-left of the hologram, one could see some blue from where Beta Magellan 'bordered' the territory.

"Over the past eight months, the Coalition authorities have implemented martial law in all their systems, even those outside this area. Anyone who questions the government or those implementing its directives is imprisoned; consequently, the prison and construction industries are booming, but those are the only facets of the economy experiencing a boom. At the third instance of questioning the government or local authorities, the so-called offender is executed, and the authorities make no distinction between adults and children when it comes to their supposed criminal offenses.

"The Coalition does not have complete supremacy across many of the systems in this view, but while the local populations fight with all they have, they are losing ground. The Coalition's central command anticipates a complete victory across all these systems within another fourteen months. Based on the data I have seen, I calculate that conclusion is erroneous; I predict the Coalition will eradicate all resistance in these contested systems within eight to ten months.

"The Coalition has implemented a massive draft across all its systems, pressing all able-bodied people into military service. Along with this, I have data indicating a massive up-swing in the construction of ships, troop transports, and their associated support vessels. This has led me to conclude that the Coalition is preparing for a massive military offensive. They are already driving back the Duchy of Musilar and the Rigellian Alliance in their pre-existing war, and I posit that they will move against an unaligned system within the next month. I further calculate that the Coalition will move against Tristan's Gate within the next eight to fourteen months and either the Ghrexels or the Igthons within five to seven years. I evaluate that pitting Humans against Ghrexels or Igthons is not wise and a waste of material, but if my calculations are correct, perhaps they know something I do not."

"Srexx, no offense," Harlon said, "but how accurate is your data? Have you considered the possibility that the information you're basing these conclusions on is false?"

"I have indeed accounted for that possibility, Colonel Hanson," Srexx replied. "I found communications in Trask's computers that did not match the information contained in the classified archives. These communications were not classified at all and carried headers indicating they were for public distribution. If I had based my conclusion on those communications alone, I would not consider the situation to be as dire as I have evaluated it is."

"Srexx, would you mind copying me on everything you evaluated for these conclusions?" Garrett asked. "I'd like for me and my people to conduct an independent analysis to confirm your findings."

"Of course, Garrett," Srexx replied. "I find myself gladdened that you wish to conduct such an analysis. I would welcome the conclusion that I have misinterpreted something from a lack of understanding about Humans."

Garrett chuckled. "I'd like to think you have, but I don't think our conclusions will vary that much from yours...except maybe on the numbers side. Our math probably won't have your level of precision."

Just then, the speakers chirped and broadcast Jenkins's voice, "Bridge to Cole."

"Go ahead, Jenkins," Cole replied.

"Cap, we just received a flash message from Captain Vasquez on Babylon Station. A freighter just arrived loaded to the gunwales with refugees; they report that they fled Caernarvon after a massive Coalition fleet entered the system and engaged the SRN task force there. It was almost a Pyrrhic victory, but the Coalition now claims the system. Vasquez says the freighter's navigation and sensor logs corroborate their story."

"Thanks, Jenkins. Cole out."

A weight settled on the shoulders of everyone in the briefing room, manifesting as a stunned silence that was almost palpable. It seemed Srexx's first prediction had already come true. After several moments, those attending started glancing to each other, and soon, everyone turned to Cole.

"What do we do?" Sasha asked, voicing the question everyone present wanted to ask.

For a moment, Cole wanted to hide from the enormity of what was approaching, but that wouldn't achieve anything. He stamped down on that impulse and mentally squared his shoulders.

"The way I see it," Cole replied, "the only thing we can do is start organizing an alliance to oppose the Coalition, but we need to do so *very* quietly. I do not want any potential members of this alliance to expedite being targeted because the Coalition learns what we're doing. Srexx, can you create a logical presentation of your evidence and conclusions and record it on enough data crystals for everyone here?"

"Yes, Cole."

"Good. It will need to be in a data format accessible to people who do not have Gyv'Rathi technology.

"Yes, Cole. If I may add, I already inferred that stipulation."

Cole chuckled. "Sorry, buddy. Sev, your immediate priority is to get the shipyard manufacturing high-speed couriers; I want one for everyone here. Bump any projects you need to make that happen within the next day or two. After that, your immediate priorities are—one—recycling the ships in Trask's fleet as quickly as possible without introducing production errors and—two—the system defenses. Start with our border systems and move in from there. Once Trask's fleet has been recycled, dig into Srexx's archives and find schematics for troop transports and ground forces equipment, like tanks and artillery."

Sev nodded.

"I think our first step is liberating those five systems," Cole said. "Sato, task a series of scout frigates to begin reconnaissance of those systems, and form a war council to start planning the operations. Personally, I think we should aim for a simultaneous assault, but I'll leave that up to you experts. Oh, and don't pick anyone in this room for your war council...unless you mind them being gone for a month or two; I have a prior claim on their time. Is there anything else?" No one spoke. "Right then. Srexx, thank you for bringing this to our attention. Sev and Sato, get started on your respective tasks. I'm taking the battlegroup to Gateway to interview the Caernarvon refugees."

With that, Cole stood and led the way out of the briefing room.

CHAPTER SEVENTEEN

"Cole, may I have a moment?"

Cole was about to reach the bridge hatch when Paol's voice stopped him. He turned and saw the older man fast-walking to catch up.

"Follow me," Cole replied. "I need to get things started for the run to Gateway, but we can talk after."

Paol blinked. "You want me to follow you onto the bridge?"

"Sure," Cole said, adding a shrug. "Have you ever been on the bridge of a starship before?"

"No, I haven't."

Cole grinned. "Come on, then."

Paol jerked a nod and followed Cole into the outer bridge hatch. He froze, though, at the sight of two marines standing at the security check. One wore a normal ship-suit. The other marine stood just behind the first in heavy armor and held a rotary cannon.

"Captain," the marine in the ship-suit said, respecting Cole's preference by nodding once instead of saluting.

"He's with me," Cole said, waving a thumb over his shoulder to indicate Paol.

"Aye, sir," the marine replied. She turned to Paol and said, "You're clear, sir. Follow the captain."

"Thank you," Paol said and hastened to follow Cole.

Cole stepped through the inner hatch and smiled when he saw Mazzi's deputy rise out of the command chair.

"Captain on the bridge!" the officer said, using his announcement voice.

"Keep your seat," Cole said, waving the young man back into the command chair. "I'm just dropping by to issue a couple quick orders. Comms, issue a five-hour recall for all personnel, and signal the battle-group to do so as well. Helm, plot a flight path to Babylon Station in Gateway and transmit orders to the battlegroup that we'll depart seven hours from now."

A chorus of "Aye, sir," echoed back to Cole.

"Thank you," Cole responded and pivoted to find Paol gazing around the bridge, wonder and awe writ large across his expression. Cole smiled. "Want the two-credit tour?"

Paol froze, his expression much like a child caught at the cookie jar. "Uhm...well...yes, if you don't mind."

Cole grinned. "Of course not. Follow me."

Cole proceeded to take Paol to each of the stations, starting with Marine Ops and Flight Ops in the port recess. He spent at most fifteen minutes, because the bridge wasn't really that involved. But...no one could miss Paol's almost-child-like glee at touring the space where his daughter worked.

"And where is Sasha's station?" Paol asked as they completed the circuit.

"Well," Cole replied, "she technically has two. When we're on normal operations, she'll either be in the command chair or that station just behind the starboard recess. When the ship is at battle-stations, Sasha relocates to the auxiliary bridge with the Beta Shift bridge crew."

"And what's the auxiliary bridge like?" Paol asked.

"It's basically a stripped-down version of what you see here, occu-pying about two-thirds the space. Each of the stations there mirror their counterparts here, so the watch-stander in Auxiliary Control can see everything that happens in the event they have to take over control of the ship. Just between us, though, I hope they never need to; that would probably mean rather bad things for me."

"I'm sure," Paol said. "Thank you for this, Cole."

"You're welcome. When we finish with whatever you wanted to discuss, you should call Talia if she's aboard and get her to show you the hospital deck. Let's step across the corridor to my office."

Cole led Paol to his office, taking a moment to greet Akyra and make sure nothing universe-ending was waiting on him. When she said it had been quiet all morning, Cole proceeded into his office with Paol in tow. Gesturing for Paol to choose his seat, Cole slid behind his desk and eased into his own chair.

"So...what's on your mind?" Cole asked.

Paol cleared his throat and said, "I was thinking it might be wise to write up letters of introduction and intent for those people you're planning to send off in the courier ships. It would probably go a long way to making the meetings more efficient."

Cole leaned back against his seat, turning over the matter in his mind. "Okay. I see what you're saying. It could certainly save time, if you or Yeleth or whoever could present a letter when you first ask to schedule a meeting. Assuming the decision-makers read the letter, you guys wouldn't have to spend so much time bringing them up to speed."

"Exactly," Paol replied.

"I like it," Cole said. "You write up the letters and send them to me. If I feel they need any correction, I'll call, and we can hash all that out."

Paol nodded once. "Makes sense. I'll have those for you probably before you reach Gateway."

Cole shrugged. "I don't know that you need to be in such a rush about it. The couriers won't be ready for at least a couple days."

"I realize that," Paol said, adding a mischievous grin. "I'm just anticipating you'll have comments on the wording."

Cole chuckled. "Fair enough. Anything else?"

"No, sir. Thank you for your time." Paol stood, with Cole following suit, and they shook hands.

———

Haven and her battlegroup spent three days at Babylon Station while Garrett and his people interviewed the Caernarvon refugees. Cole spent some of that time visiting with Admiral Trask and the four emissaries; he was very careful during his visit with the emissaries not to give any hint of their preparations in Beta Magellan. When they asked if Cole had given any thought to their idea of a Beta-Magellan-based federation, Cole explained that he was still considering the matter.

Near the end of the third day, Garrett informed Cole that he and his people had completed all their interviews, leaving only analysis and reporting still to do. Garrett hoped to have a preliminary report ready for the group by the time *Haven* returned.

The purpose for their trip to Gateway achieved, Cole ordered the battlegroup back to Beta Magellan.

———

Bridge Briefing Room
    Battle-Carrier *Haven*
    Beta Magellan
    5 September 3003, 09:17 GST

Cole leaned back against his seat as he waited for everyone to arrive. He'd asked the same people to attend that had heard Srexx's presentation, and some were still en route from Citadel Station.

"Cole?" the overhead speakers broadcast Srexx's voice.

"Yeah, buddy?" Cole asked.

A few heartbeats of silence preceded Srexx's next statement, "I want to thank you for arranging the meeting where I presented my conclusions. I appreciate that everyone took my conclusions seriously and consider it a compliment that Garrett wanted his people to check them."

Cole smiled. "Srexx, you're one of us; of course, we're going to take what you say seriously. Just because you can't shake hands with us doesn't lessen or invalidate what you have to say."

"Thank you, Cole. It is...nice...to belong."

"You're welcome, buddy. Say...you need anything?"

"In what respect, Cole?"

Cole sighed. "Well, I don't know, really. I was checking on you. If there was something you wanted or needed to improve your quality of life, I'd try to get it for you."

"Ah." Silence. "I could always use more data to process. My stores of encrypted data are running a little low, and Qeecir's encryption algorithm was a disgrace to data security. It required little more than forty seconds at twenty-five percent utilization to decrypt. We have not encountered any ships from the Duchy of Musilar, Rigellian Alliance, the Ghrexels, Igthons, or Thurians. Encountering ships from any of the non-Human races would be best, as it would give me the opportunity to learn one or more new languages in addition to their encryption methods."

"Well...I think we're going to be invested in the area around Beta Magellan for a little while," Cole replied, suppressing a grin, "but as soon as I can arrange for us to visit the other races, I'll do it. Sound good?"

"Yes, Cole. I appreciate that. It is unfortunate that the Coalition is treating innocents in such a way, and I agree that such conduct needs to cease. I will gladly provide any assistance I can toward that goal."

Cole smiled. "Thanks, buddy. I appreciate it."

Just then, the hatch irised open, allowing the attendees to enter. Cole held his smile as he stood and shook hands with each of them. In short order, everyone was seated.

"Thank you all for coming," Cole said. "Garrett, you said you have some information for us."

"Yes," Garrett replied, "and it's not pretty. We conducted Kiksalik-assisted interviews with the Caernarvon refugees and the freighter crew, not from a standpoint of verifying their information, but rather to tease out real from imagined experiences. In any situation like this, where the witnesses have a chance to sit around talking about what they saw, you'll have a lot of cross-contamination, and fortunately, the

Kiksaliks provide a method for cutting through all that. To be clear, the best information came from the freighter crew and the freighter's computers; Srexx was kind enough to obtain the logs from the freighter for us."

Cole almost asked if someone had obtained permission first but ultimately put the thought aside. Yes, he firmly supported the idea of personal privacy and protection from unreasonable search...but one of his closest friends was a curious AI with exponentially more computing power than anything the Human race had ever devised. Every time Cole brought up the matter, Srexx always countered Cole's argument with the simple statement that the data should be better protected if it was intended to be truly private. Cole saw his point and still sought a good rebuttal.

"From the communications logs, sensor logs, and historical system traffic data," Garrett continued, "we have established a rough timeline for the invasion, at least up to the point that the freighter left Caernarvon. The Coalition forces entered the system through three of the four jump gates and converged on the Solar Republic task force. The Solars made a good showing of themselves, but the Coalition brought just enough ships to the fight that the Solars were destroyed. It is unclear from the data we have if the Coalition forces took any prisoners."

"Once word of this reaches Sol, that will bring the Republic in on the fight, won't it?" Sasha asked.

"I wouldn't bet on it," Sato replied.

Everyone at the table displayed different expressions of shock or disbelief.

"I have a hard time believing that," Cole said. "The Solar Republic has been the teacher in the schoolyard for as long as anyone can remember; they *always* step in when 'the children' start getting out of line."

"Don't expect it this time," Sato countered. "There are people back in Sol and Centauri who communicate with me fairly regularly, and not to put too fine a point on it, what I'm hearing out of the Republic is almost frightening. The Republic government is still in flux and upheaval following your disclosure of the 'Rossignol Files.' Those files and your...direct...handling of the people attacking you and CIE brought quite a lot of the backroom power-mongering into the light, if not all of it, and the average citizen doesn't like what they've seen. In just the three years since your press conference, there have been five public referendums at the Republic level that have gutted the halls of power of almost every elected official with any experience. At the time of the most recent referendum, the incumbent with the longest term of service had twenty-two months in office, and the destabilization has filtered down to the individual member planets as well. That twenty-two-month incumbent—by the way—did not keep her office.

"Yes, the Solar Republic is still the superpower of Human space... well, not counting us...but they're too disorganized right now to make use of it. Honestly, it'll go one of two ways when news of the task force's destruction reaches the Republic: one, it will galvanize the situation, and the people will demand action, leading to a mass of inexperienced policy-makers flailing as they try to learn on the job; or two, the people won't even notice it in their quest for honest politicians and a fully transparent government. Does anyone question which outcome I'm expecting?"

Silence reigned as Sato scanned the faces looking back at her.

"Yeah...that's a little scary," Harlon said, his voice softer than normal.

"Would the disorganization make them a target for the Coalition's expansion?" Garrett asked.

Sato scoffed. "Not if the Coalition has half a brain. It's one thing to pick off a system that was just a trade hub, especially when the value of that trade hub has declined significantly in recent years. If the Coalition leadership is stupid enough to stick their noses into one of the Republic's member systems, they'll get more bitten off than just the nose. The problem, there, is that the Coalition now has the largest fleet in space...heh...well, it did before Trask and his people brought that fleet to us. I haven't seen the classified Coalition numbers, but I do remember the Republic's force levels. The Coalition doesn't outnumber the Republic by *that* much, and the Republic has better tech and better-trained people."

Garrett made eye contact with Cole. "Do the jump gates record the transponders of transiting ships?"

Cole shook his head. "Nope. That's one of the ways CIE maintains its independence and monopoly. They don't track—or care—who uses the gates, as long as they pay their transit fee."

"It would be nice if you could have your people write a firmware patch for the jump gates to watch for Coalition ships," Garrett replied. "That would give us a little bit of advance warning where they're headed."

"Just because CIE does not track transits," Srexx interjected, "does not mean the ships are not tracked at all."

"Explain, please," Garrett said.

"In order for the interstellar comms network to function, there must be routing information for each ship. In short, for the system to send messages, the system must know where the messages need to go. Since the implementation of the quantum comms network, we have access to near-real-time routing data for every ship in known space."

"How 'near' is 'near-real-time,' Srexx?" Garrett asked.

"The jump gates in the furthest reaches of Ghrexel and Igthon space have not been upgraded as yet," Srexx replied, "but across the sphere of Human space, the routing data in the communications hubs receive updates no later than five minutes after a transit."

Smiles or grins broke out around the table.

"And CIE has access to this data?" Sato asked.

"CIE does not," Srexx countered, "but I do."

"Srexx," Cole said, "please start monitoring Coalition fleet movements through the routing tables of the comms networks."

"Yes, Cole. It will require some time to process all routing data currently available. I shall alert you when I am current."

"Okay," Cole remarked. "So, we've established that the odds of a Solar Republic response to the Caernarvon invasion is most likely not coming. The way I see it, we're committed to those five systems. My position is that we'll remain aware of the situation but do nothing beyond that. Now...talk me out of it."

"They were less than friendly when we were there," Sasha said, "but I can kind of understand that. I mean, one ship had just neutralized the battlegroup sent to protect them by the Solar Republic. They *knew* we could've rampaged through the system, and they would've been powerless to stop us. That colors your interactions and approach a bit. I think we should start putting together contingency plans for helping them...not to help *them* as such but more to combat the Coalition."

"I see your point, Sasha," Emily remarked, "but do we know if they even *want* our help? I wasn't aware any of the refugees we interviewed were connected to the Caernarvon government."

"No," Garrett supplied, "none of them were connected to the government beyond a couple people who had worked in a records office somewhere."

"Look," Painter interjected from the far end of the table, "it's all well and good to sit here, shake our heads, and say it's not our business...but the time will come when it *is* our business. Everything I've heard says we will be at war with the Coalition sooner rather than later, and personally, I think we should plan to move on their more recent acquisitions first. Yes...they'll be more heavily defended, because they are—or are near—the front line, so to speak, but those will be the populations most favorably disposed toward fighting the Coalition in my mind."

The conversation faded, and Cole took that to mean everyone with something to say had said it.

Cole tapped on the table with his knuckles, saying, "I appreciate everyone's thoughts. I think it best if we categorize Caernarvon as an evolving situation at present. Let's keep an eye on it but not make it our primary focus. Sev, are the courier ships ready?"

"The last one is completing space trials today," Sev replied. "The others have all checked out."

"Very well. In that view, let's discuss travel assignments. Sev and Harlon, I'd like for both of you to go to Tristan's Gate. Yeleth, you'll go to the Ghrexel homeworld, and Red, you'll visit the Igthons. Painter, I'm asking you to visit the ISA and Zurich leadership; since both are in the same system, it should be fairly straightforward. I think those will do for now, but keep the remaining couriers prepped and ready to go just in case. Are there any questions?"

When the room remained silent after five seconds, Cole nodded once. He stood and led everyone out of the briefing room.

CHAPTER EIGHTEEN

Courier Vessel 47-Alpha
    Zurich System
    11 September 3003, 07:18 GST

Painter looked up from her tablet when the pilot's console played the tone for an incoming message. She stood up from the small table in the equally small galley and walked the necessary steps—no more than ten meters—to arrive in the cockpit. Accessing the console, she saw a text message from Cole.

Slipping into the pilot's seat while still eating her sandwich, Painter keyed the commands to display the text message on the multi-function display where cockpit windows would exist on ancient atmospheric craft.

Hello, Painter,

. . .

If you're reading this, you've arrived in Zurich. Forgive me for being so secretive about this, but it was part of the terms requested by the system leadership in Zurich.

Back in June, Paol and I went to Zurich, telling everyone back home that it was a trip to examine the civics of their government. While that was true in a sense, the actual purpose was to negotiate and enact a mutual defense treaty between Zurich and Beta Magellan. They requested the meeting through an old family friend at the bank and asked if we would be agreeable to the treaty, given the situation with the Coalition.

As far as I know, you are the third person on our side to know about this agreement. Hmmm...better make that fourth, as it's safe to assume Srexx knows everything we know. I ask that you keep the contents of this message to yourself, as it would be classified at the highest levels if we actually had a data classification system. If anyone questions your right to have this knowledge, respond that they are welcome to contact me directly; all relevant parties have my direct comms code.

Find me if you need me.

Sincerely,
*   Cole*

Painter stared at the message on the display, the sandwich in her left hand forgotten. She blinked a couple times as she processed that Cole had concluded a major diplomatic mission with no one the wiser.

The comms system chirped, jerking Painter out of her musings. A cruiser and destroyer with the Zurich SDF approached off her port bow; the cruiser was hailing her.

Painter keyed the commands to accept the hail and put the sandwich out of view as the comms channel came online. Painter found herself looking at a man just a few years older than her.

"Hello, and welcome to Zurich," the man said. "I'm Commander Giles Ivanov. Please, forgive me for asking your purpose in Zurich today."

Painter smiled. "Hello, Commander. I am Julianna Painter, and I've come to Zurich at the request of my employer, Bartholomew James Coleson. I hope to schedule meetings with the ISA and system leadership."

If Painter's purpose in the system surprised Commander Ivanov, he didn't show it. The man merely nodded once, saying, "Very well. We'll transmit your relevant clearances. I hope you enjoy your stay in our system."

"Thank you, Commander," Painter replied. "I appreciate your time."

The comms call ended, and within thirty seconds, the console informed Painter of a data burst received from the courier. She accepted the data burst and keyed the commands to display the contents on the viewscreen. It contained a short bit of text with the courier's hull number and transponder code, followed by an encrypted packet that contained her full clearance to transit the system. For most ships, the hull number and transponder code were burned into chips in the comms system and extremely difficult to change, spoof, or counterfeit.

After satisfying her curiosity about the data burst, Painter set it aside and worked up two letters—one for the ISA and one for the system leadership—in which she stated her desire for a meeting. After reading over it a couple times, she attached the letter of introduction Cole had given her to each letter and fired them off to their respective recipients. Both the ISA and the system leadership had offices in Zurich One, the oldest of the system's stations, which would make things much easier.

———

The next morning, Painter eased into the pilot's seat, coffee in hand, and accessed the comms system. Selecting 'Zurich One Traffic Control' from the list, Painter keyed the command to initiate a call. Within moments, the cockpit's speakers chirped as the call connected.

"Zurich Traffic Control, how may I assist you?" the cockpit's speakers broadcast.

"Hello," Painter replied. "This is Julianna Painter aboard Beta Magellan Courier Forty-Seven-Alpha. I'm calling for clearance to dock."

"One moment please," the traffic controller said.

Painter took another swallow of coffee while she waited.

"I do apologize for the wait, Ambassador," the traffic controller resumed. "We have a priority docking bay for you in the diplomatic section. Do you require any additional services?"

Painter almost dropped her coffee. Ambassador? Now she wished she had actually *read* that letter of introduction before she sent it.

"I don't believe so at this time," Painter answered.

"Very good, ma'am," the traffic controller replied. "As per standard protocol, I have notified Zurich Foreign Ministry of your arrival, and they informed me that a representative will meet you at the docking bay. On behalf of Zurich One, we hope you enjoy your stay."

"Thank you. I'm sure I will."

The speakers chirped once more, signaling the end of the call. Painter took the few moments necessary to locate the transponder for her docking assignment and keyed the commands necessary to activate the autopilot. A prompt came up to grant the station's automated docking control permission to pilot the craft, and Painter accepted.

That task complete, Painter accessed the ship's computer, digging into the system in search of the letter Cole had given her. It didn't take long to find it, and Painter felt a bit light-headed as she read it.

Bartholomew James Coleson
of Beta Magellan
to
The Honorable Leadership of Zurich

My friends:

In these uncertain times, with war spreading throughout the Expansion Zone, I believe the occasion has arrived to establish a more formal relationship between the people of Beta Magellan and Zurich. To that end, I have decided to accredit before your government, Ms. Julianna Adrienne Painter, with the rank of Ambassador Extraordinary and Plenipotentiary.

Ms. Painter has earned an exceptional level of trust, which enables me to make this assertion without concern or reservation. I ask that Ms. Painter be given full credit and credence in all she may communicate on my behalf.

Sincerely and with respect,
 Bartholomew James Coleson

Painter collapsed against the back of her seat, staring at the text on the screen in front of her. A portion of her conscious mind simply refused to process what she was reading. How could she be an ambassador? She was just a freighter captain. Well, *former* freighter captain. What was she now? That question led Painter to consider for the first time in a long while just how much responsibility Cole entrusted to her. The civilian shipping answered to her. She—or her people—oversaw all civilian hiring...all of it across Beta Magellan and all of its territories. She worked with Sev in coordinating crews for all new starship construction. And...that was only just the start of it. Still, she didn't feel like she warranted the title of Ambassador. That was just too much, wasn't it?

A faint shuddering throughout the ship signaled that it was now resting on its landing struts inside the docking bay. Painter keyed the commands to display an external view on the main screens, and she grimaced at seeing the collection of people filing into the docking bay; every single one of them looked 'important.' With a heavy sigh, Painter left the cockpit for her quarters; if she was meeting important people, she probably shouldn't do so in a freighter rat's ship-suit.

. . .

Painter used her implant to retract the boarding ramp and secure the ship as she walked across the docking bay to her welcoming committee. The stray thought that she hoped her visit to Zurich would go better than had Cole's visit to Qeecir almost made her laugh, but she managed to maintain her pleasant non-expression.

A middle-aged man at the front of the group took a couple steps forward as Painter neared them, extending his right hand and saying, "Welcome to Zurich, Your Excellency. I am Nathaniel Vaughn, Under-secretary to the Foreign Minister, and it is a pleasure to make your acquaintance."

"A pleasure, sir," Painter replied, "and thank you for the kind greeting."

"You're very welcome. Zurich knows how to treat her friends. Now, if you will come with us, I shall escort you to your temporary quarters while we sort out the list of potential facilities for your embassy. The Foreign Minister has arranged some time tomorrow for the formal presentation of credentials, and we should be able to schedule a meeting with the leadership within two or three days."

Painter hoped she hid her shock well. A meeting with the system leadership—any system's leadership—within two or three days? They must view Cole and Beta Magellan as very good friends indeed to move with that kind of alacrity. A notification from her implant compounded her suppressed surprise; the ISA would grant her an immediate meeting at a time of her choosing.

Perhaps, this mission to Zurich wouldn't be so bad after all.

———

Painter keyed the command to close the hatch of her temporary quarters and leaned against the bulkhead. At least with the formal presentation of credentials over, she could focus on her real reason for being in Zurich. Using her implant, she sent a message to her ISA contact asking when would be the best time for a meeting; the response was immediate and stated they could be ready at any time. They ended up settling on meeting in an hour, giving Painter time to change and traverse the station to their offices.

The ISA offices in Zurich doubled as both a regional administrative center for the organization as a whole and also the ISA office for Zurich, where spacers could go to test for new ratings or join the organization or search for jobs. Stepping through the hatch into the lobby, Painter found herself in a large open area much like the ISA office in Tristan's Gate. Smiling at the familiarity, she approached the reception desk.

"Good day," Painter said. "I'm Julianna Painter, and I have an appointment with the ISA leadership."

The young man at the desk nodded. "Welcome to the ISA. One moment, please, while I alert the leadership that you've arrived." He keyed a few commands on his workstation, and his eyes went very wide very fast. "Uhm, ma'am...er...Madame Ambassador, please forgive me. Take the lift to your right, and someone will be waiting for you."

"Thank you," Painter replied, adding a nod and what she hoped was a reassuring smile. As she walked the short distance to the indicated lift, she grinned at the young man's reaction; the mischievous side of her could get to like that title Cole sandbagged her with.

The passage of three minutes or so saw Painter entering a rather plush office a couple of levels above the main ISA space. Seven people waited for her, sitting around a curved table. The aide leading Painter indicated an unused chair and offered refreshment—which Painter politely declined—before leaving.

"Madame Ambassador," the woman sitting at the center of the group said, "welcome to the headquarters of the Interstellar Spacers' Association. I am Vera Ghent, Chair of the ISA Commission. Mr. Coleson has been a very good friend to our members, and we look forward to returning the favor. How can we help you?"

"Well, my purpose here today is more in the nature of updating you as representatives of the ISA on our current intelligence regarding the

Coalition. This data crystal contains a presentation about current affairs within the Coalition along with a number of predictions based on the data included. We all know spacers talk to one another and often do a better job of disseminating warnings and advisories than official channels, but Mr. Coleson thought it best to offer a formal notification of what we've learned."

"Of course," Ms. Ghent replied. "We appreciate Beta Magellan looking out for us."

"We're all spacers," Painter said, "and spacers look after their own."

"Hear, hear," a man off to Painter's left vocalized.

"Well," Ms. Ghent resumed, "why don't you give us an overview of the material?"

Painter shifted her position in the seat for greater comfort and started with the abridged presentation. Twenty minutes later, she concluded with Srexx's predictions.

Ms. Ghent spoke first. "Yes, the Coalition's invasion of Caernarvon does argue that they're pursuing a policy of militaristic expansion. Our analysts will have to examine the data before we'll be in a position to agree with your evaluation that they'll move against Tristan's Gate or somewhere similar within six months to a year, but based on what we're seeing it almost seems a foregone conclusion. There have even been quite a few rumors that the Coalition may target Zurich, intending to control interstellar banking."

Painter nodded. "We've heard those same concerns ourselves."

"Thank you for bringing us this information," Ms. Ghent said, "and please thank Mr. Coleson as well."

"I shall do so. If there's nothing else, I'll let you get back to your day."

Ms. Ghent nodded, and Painter stood. She made her goodbyes and left the office.

CHAPTER NINETEEN

Vance Residence
 Tristan's World
 Tristan's Gate System
 15 September 3003, 12:49 GST

Sev and Harlon sat in the great room of Sev's parents' house. Carl and Lindsay Vance and Jed Hanson sat with them. Sev and Harlon had just finished going through the presentation with their families that they hoped to deliver to the system leadership.

"That is an alarming analysis," Jed remarked in his gruff voice. "I don't like it at all. What are those idiots up on The Gate doing about it?"

Sev chuckled. "Isn't your grandson one of 'those idiots'?"

"Nah," Jed replied. "He declined to run again when his term was up. They have an almost all-new pack of fools running the system now. Stone's still the Defense Minister, though; at least that chump of a system president can do one thing right."

"Is the new batch really *that* bad?" Harlon asked.

Lindsay shrugged. "It depends on what you want and what your goals are."

Just then, the doorbell rang several times in quick succession followed by urgent knocking.

"What in the world?" Carl grumbled as he pushed himself to his feet. Not even two minutes later, Carl returned with Defense Minister Stone.

"Minister Stone?" Lindsay asked. "Be welcome in our home, but I must say this is a surprise."

"Thank you for your welcome," Stone replied and looked at Sev and Harlon. "You need to leave...right now."

"What?" Carl asked.

Jed's eyes narrowed into a glare. "What have those damn fools done now?"

"I just left a meeting in which General Trumball successfully convinced President Harker to take possession of your ship," Stone answered, "even after you'd transmitted your letter of credence. The SDF is already mobilizing, and if you don't lift off now—like within the next ten minutes—your ship will be seized. They'll probably hold you for questioning, too."

Sev closed his eyes and shook his head, then resumed his eye contact with Stone as he said, "Have they given *any* thought to what Cole's response will be if they do this? Do they honestly think he'll just roll over and accept this?"

Carl, Lindsay, Jed, and Stone blanched.

"What?" Harlon asked.

"My implant just lost connection with SystemNet," Jed replied. "They must've deployed a jammer."

"They were faster than I anticipated," Stone remarked. "Ambassador Vance, I now declare before you that I fear for my life and the lives of my family. Accordingly, I wish to file a request for asylum with Beta Magellan."

Sev accessed his implant and navigated the menus to send a data burst containing everything he'd just heard in the last ten minutes back to Cole and Srexx via the quantum comms network. Then, he activated his emergency beacon, which also utilized the quantum comms network.

"I just sent a data burst to Cole," Sev said.

"Me, too," Harlon added. "Did you activate your beacon also?"

Sev nodded just as the front and back doors exploded inward. Men and women in the armored uniforms of the Tristan's Gate SDF stormed into the house. Within moments, the residence was secure, and General Trumball strode into the great room. She glared at Stone.

"Well, well...I guess we moved a little too fast for you, didn't we, Mister Stone?" Trumball said and turned to Sev and Harlon. "On the authority vested in me by the System President of Tristan's Gate, I hereby notify you that we are seizing your vessel in the interests of system security and arresting you until such time as you turn over any and all access to and command codes for the vessel. Defense Minister Mattias Stone, I am arresting you on suspicion of disseminating classified information and obstruction of SDF operations. I am authorized to use all necessary force if you resist."

Sev smiled as he stood, saying, "You're too late. He already knows."

Sev, Harlon, Jed, Carl, Lindsay, and Stone all took a small amount of pleasure at seeing General Trumball's jaw slacken just a bit.

Captain's Day-Cabin
Battle-Carrier *Haven*
Beta Magellan
15 September 3003, 13:08 GST

Cole shrugged his shoulders as he rolled his head in a circle. He'd been sitting at his desk in the day-cabin all morning, working through the recertification exams the ISA required for his collection of ratings, and he was a little stiff in the upper half of his body and almost numb in his lower half.

"Cole?" the overhead speakers broadcast Srexx's voice.

"Yeah, buddy...what's up?"

"I have just monitored two data bursts. They are addressed to both of us, and they are from Sev and Harlon. I have also just received notification that they have activated their emergency beacons."

Cole took a deep breath. "Thanks, Srexx. Would you please put the data bursts on the main viewscreen in the cabin?"

Over the next scant minutes, Cole watched the scene involving Defense Minister Stone from both Sev and Harlon's perspectives, and the longer the data bursts played, the harder Cole's glare became.

"If my people have even been *scratched*, Srexx..."

"Cole, if I may, I advise restraining one's emotions until we have more data upon which to base a conclusion and formulate a response. As matters exist now, there is no indication that Sev or Harlon or Defense Minister Stone or anyone else has been harmed. A reasoned, measured response at this juncture might be best."

During Srexx's comments, Cole's anger ebbed. The situation still offended and angered him, but the initial flare-up of emotion had faded.

Cole smiled. "Thanks, buddy. I appreciate your thoughts as always."

"What would you like me to do, Cole?"

"Notify Sato, Sasha, Garrett, Harlon's deputy, Sev's deputy, Painter's deputy, Paol, and Yeleth's deputy that I'm calling an emergency meeting. We'll handle this from a conference room over on Citadel Station. Then, I want you to contact Vasquez and arrange a press conference via comms; I'm going to make sure the Expansion Zone is fully aware of what Tristan's Gate has done, so they understand our response."

"Notifications sent, Cole," Srexx said as Cole stood and headed for the day-cabin hatch, "and I have just sent word to Captain Vazquez as well."

"Thanks, buddy," Cole said as he exited his day-cabin. "I appreciate you."

Cole led Sasha into the conference room aboard Citadel Station to find everyone else waiting. Glances among those already present started circulating around the table when they saw Cole's expression.

"Thank you for attending so quickly," Cole said, assuming his seat at the head of the table. "We have a situation. Srexx, if you would please, play one of the data bursts."

A hologram appeared over the table and played through the five to seven minutes before the Tristan's Gate SDF invaded Carl Vance's house. By the end of the play-through, shock dominated the expressions around the table.

"That's where we stand right now," Cole stated. "I have already notified Captain Vasquez to assemble representatives of all the news agencies on Babylon Station for a press conference via comms. It is a foregone conclusion in my mind that we're going after our people. I would like your thoughts on whether our response stops there."

"Governments have gone to war over less provocation," Paol said, "and I can't imagine the leadership in Tristan's Gate doesn't realize that. I'm honestly having difficulty processing what we just watched. It's...well...it's absurd and idiotic from a diplomatic perspective."

Cole looked to Painter's deputy, asking, "How many freighters do we have available right now?"

"There are nine in-system," he replied.

"Contact them right now, and inform them that I'm activating their reserve orders. I'm taking *Haven*'s battlegroup to Tristan's Gate, and I want freighters with me to offer the opportunity to depart the system for anyone who wishes to do so. People, unless someone talks me out of it, I'm going to sever any and all ties Beta Magellan has with Tristan's Gate. No trade, no tourism, nothing. As of this date, all Beta-Magellan-flagged ships will be forbidden from visiting Tristan's Gate, and all ships flagged in Tristan's Gate will be unwelcome in our space."

"Is this going to be a step toward invading the system?" Harlon's deputy asked.

Cole shook his head. "No. I do not expand our territory through conquest. Heh...well...except for Baldur, but I consider that to be a special case. Most systems won't have crime lords in control who also happen to be threatening us."

"Wouldn't that depend on how one defines 'crime lord?'" Garrett asked.

Chuckles and more than a few outright laughs erupted around the table, lessening the tension. Cole grinned and gave Garrett a surreptitious nod as thanks.

"In all seriousness, though," Cole continued, "we will not *start* the fight...ever. If Tristan's Gate thinks they have the wherewithal to conduct a war against us, let them try; we'll see if they get the point when I park a dreadnought in orbit around Tristan's Gate. Speaking of that, what's the status on the dreadnought in the shipyard?"

Sev's deputy swallowed as all faces turned to him, but he rallied, saying, "As of this morning, it's about forty percent complete. They just completed recycling the *Indomitable* last week, and all of that raw material is either stockpiled or being fed into the construction bay's fabricators."

Cole nodded. "Very well. Anything further? Does anyone disagree with severing all ties and contact with Tristan's Gate?"

"It's actually a rather restrained response," Garrett opined. "The government of Tristan's Gate seized a vessel flagged in Beta Magellan and jailed two people carrying formal letters of credence as ambassadors. Once word of this gets out, people will understand our response."

"All right then. Put out an advisory to all of our ships that as of fourteen-hundred-thirty hours today, no ship enjoying the protection of Beta Magellan can visit Tristan's Gate if they wish to continue enjoying said protection. If there's nothing further, we have a lot to do," Cole said as he stood, and everyone else stood with him.

———

Bridge, Battle-Carrier *Haven*
    Beta Magellan
    15 September 3003, 13:45 GST

The bridge seemed to hum with an uncommon level of urgency. Cole rather liked it; he just wished there was a different reason for it. The port hatch irised open to admit Brianna Vance and two marines; the marines didn't carry long guns, but they did wear sidearms. If Brianna was unsettled at being escorted to the bridge by armed marines, it didn't show as she almost marched up to the command chair and snapped to attention.

"Brianna Vance reporting as ordered, sir!"

Cole sighed, but it wasn't the time to revisit the matter of how he should be addressed, saying instead, "At ease, Brianna. I'm afraid the time has finally come where you have to choose. The new leaders of Tristan's Gate have seen fit to seize the courier ship and imprison Sev and Harlon. I do not care which side you choose, but you must declare your choice now: us or Tristan's Gate."

Brianna gaped at Cole, then shot a disbelieving look at Sasha. Sasha merely nodded.

"I...they...what were those fools thinking?" Brianna said, her eyes shooting wide as she processed what she'd said and where she'd said it.

Cole nodded. "That has been a recurring question, but it is immaterial to the moment. I can give you until we arrive in Tristan's Gate to make up your mind, but you will be restricted to your quarters. I should also tell you that what little systems access you had no longer exists."

"How long exactly do I have to decide?" Brianna asked.

"Once we leave Beta Magellan," Cole answered, "we'll arrive in Tristan's Gate in a little over a day."

"Thank you, sir," Brianna replied and pivoted toward the port hatch, where she was joined by her marine escort.

As soon as the port hatch irised closed, Cole said, "Comms, record for transmission, please."

"You're on, sir," the comms tech replied.

"System leaders of Tristan's Gate, on the off chance you are unaware who I am, my name is Bartholomew James Coleson. I am sending this message in response to your unwarranted and unprovoked seizure of my personnel and a diplomatic courier vessel earlier today. For clarification's sake, 'today' is September 15th.

"Please, consider this your formal notification that—in response to your egregious acts—Beta Magellan hereby severs any and all ties between our two systems. As of fourteen-thirty hours on the fifteenth of September, no ship flagged by Beta Magellan may enter your system and still enjoy our protection. Furthermore, I am resigning the reserve commission in Tristan's Gate SDF, and I feel confident you'll shortly receive an influx of similar resignations from the people aboard *Haven*.

"I anticipate that I will arrive in Tristan's Gate no later than the seventeenth. When I arrive—if Ambassadors Vance and Hanson are not aboard their consular vessel, unharmed and free to depart the system—I will use whatever level of force I deem necessary to secure the release of my people.

"In addition to the *Haven* battlegroup, I am bringing nine freighters outfitted for personnel transport. Any residents of Tristan's Gate who wish to apply for refugee status in Beta Magellan may request a place aboard one of these freighters for transport back to Gateway, where the application will be reviewed and processed.

"Thank you for your time and attention. Coleson out."

The comms tech soon announced, "Message ready, sir."

"Send it," Cole replied, standing up from the command chair. "Sasha, you have the conn; when all our ships report ready, take us out. I'll be in the flag briefing room conducting a press conference."

––––––––

That day, breaking news went out to all channels across Human space...or anyone who watched Human news services. Beta Magellan formally severed all ties in response to the egregious seizure of two accredited diplomats and their consular vessel. At the start of the press conference, Cole gave the reporters links to where they could download the letter of credence Cole had given Sev and Harlon, Sev and Harlon's data bursts, and the recording of his formal response to Tristan's Gate.

Within five hours of publication, the story overshot every other story in ratings across most systems.

CHAPTER TWENTY

System Periphery
   Tristan's Gate
   16 September 3003, 23:23 GST

Cole occupied the command chair on the bridge, and he looked at the tactical plot of the system. The quantum transponder of the courier vessel still indicated it was sitting at the spaceport where Sev and Harlon must've landed. He was not happy. The silver lining to this particular dark cloud, though, was that the courier vessel was the *only* Beta Magellan ship in-system...not counting *Haven*'s battlegroup of course. The port hatch irised open, drawing his attention, and he saw Brianna Vance enter the bridge.

"Sir," Brianna said as she approached, "I have prepared my letter of resignation for the Tristan's Gate SDF. Would you like to review it?"

Cole shook his head. "I'll arrange for an interview with Garrett once you've notified Tristan's Gate you no longer work for them."

"Aye, sir," Brianna replied.

When Brianna didn't budge, Cole lifted one eyebrow. "Is there anything else?"

"Sir, you should know that a message was waiting for me on the comms buoy," Brianna replied. "It contained signed orders from General Trumball, countersigned by the system president, directing me to attempt an assassination. To kill you, sir."

The two marines at the port hatch drew their sidearms, and the spacer at the tactical station produced a sidearm of his own. The Ghrexel at the helm swiveled to face Brianna's back.

Cole chuckled. "People have wanted me dead before, Brianna. Do you have any intention of acting on those orders?"

"No, sir," Brianna said. "I'm not a murderer."

Cole glanced around the bridge. The young Ghrexel whom Wixil had asked to serve in her place had swiveled the chair to face the command area; Cole could see her claws already extended. He took in the sidearm held by the spacer at Tactical and the two marines' drawn sidearms.

Cole returned his focus to Brianna and smiled, saying, "That's probably a wise life choice for you."

Cole watched Brianna notice the drawn sidearms and saw her become even more still than she had been. She barely seemed even to breathe.

"If you'd be so kind," Cole said, "please forward the message containing those orders to me, and if you'll excuse me, I have chastisement to deliver. Dismissed."

Brianna turned toward the port hatch and headed that way, moving very deliberately and with no sudden movements. She was fully aware every pair of eyes on the bridge—except Cole's—followed her...and not for a reason most eyes followed women.

"Okay, people," Cole said as the port hatch irised closed, "the show's over. Helm, prepare maneuvering orders for the battlegroup; take us to thirty light-minutes outside the traffic patterns of The Gate and Tristan's World at nine-tenths-light. Weaps, bring up the battlegroup TacNet; unless there's reason to do it sooner, I'll be calling the battlegroup to alert status when we're one light-hour out."

Two "Aye, sirs" came back to him.

Moments later, the spacer at Tactical announced, "TacNet is live, sir!"

Not even thirty seconds after that, the Ghrexel at the helm reported, "Maneuvering orders plotted, laid in, and uploaded to TacNet, sir!"

Cole nodded. "Thank you kindly. Helm, engage."

The Ghrexel's fingers flew over the console, and Cole saw the battlegroup start moving in the tactical plot.

Turning toward the port recess, Cole now said, "Flight Ops, my compliments to the CAG; please inform her I'd like two squadrons and two assault shuttles prepped for launch. Marine Ops, my compliments to Lieutenant Colonel Devereaux; please ask her to begin preparations for a forceful extraction of our people as soon as Srexx locates them."

The two spacers returned "Aye, sir" almost in unison.

————

A little over nine hours later, the battlegroup reached the one-light-hour demarcation. No SDF ships had even attempted to challenge them during their transit of the system, but it made sense, really; none of the SDF ships could catch them to challenge them. Instead, what looked to be the entire fleet of the System Defense Force occupied a position of challenge about thirty light-minutes out from the near-station and near-planet traffic patterns.

Cole sighed as he looked at the tactical plot. He'd hoped they'd be more sensible about this. "Weaps, bring the battlegroup to alert status."

The status lights around the bridge shifted from a pleasant green to amber that would flash for thirty seconds before settling to steady. Read-outs appeared on the tactical plot, indicating all shield layers were charging. Cole specifically did not want the charging of weapons to be included as part of the alert status protocol; to his mind, it was too provocative, and Cole had yet to encounter a situation where having weapons ready during an alert made any difference.

"All decks report secured for alert status," Jenkins announced, having taken over the comms station.

"Helm, prepare maneuvering orders for the battlegroup; take us in at one-quarter-light, same course."

Moments later, the Ghrexel at the helm reported, "Maneuvering orders plotted, laid in, and uploaded to TacNet."

"Thank you, helm; go."

At the relatively sedate velocity of one-quarter-light, it would take the battlegroup about two hours to close with the SDF line.

"Okay, people," Cole said, pitching his voice so everyone on the bridge would hear, "we have some time. Feel free to order food or drinks. Take a short walk. But I want everyone back at their stations no later than seventy minutes from now."

Most of the watch-standers accessed the galley's delivery menu and ordered breakfast. Cole did as well.

The seventy minutes came and went with no change in the SDF's deployment. The ships had not moved or lit off their drives for more than station-keeping thrust.

"Haskell," Cole began, "what can you tell me about those ships?"

The senior sensor tech grinned. "What do you want to know, Cap? The flag officer's breakfast menu? Access to their version of our TacNet?"

Cole almost sighed. "Let me guess. They haven't changed their encryption keys yet?"

"Oh, no," Haskell countered. "They did that within minutes of seizing Mr. Vance and Colonel Hanson. From what I've seen, though, Srexx has been using the courier vessel as a remote proxy; he's been browsing their planetary datanet since before we left Beta Magellan. The notations I'm seeing indicate Srexx updated our database with their new encryption key about ten minutes after they rolled it out."

Cole blinked. "Ten minutes?"

"I apologize, Cole," the overhead speakers broadcast Srexx's voice. "So much of my focus was on monitoring the transport and incarceration of Mr. Vance and Colonel Hanson that I failed to notice the SDF had instituted a new encryption algorithm. Once I became aware of the new encryption, however, I cracked it within ninety seconds."

Almost every person on the bridge shared Cole's grin.

"That's more like it," Cole remarked. "I was afraid you might be slipping in your old age."

"But Cole…I do not age."

Several people around the bridge chuckled as Cole grinned.

"Ah," Srexx continued. "This was another joke, was it not?"

"Yeah, buddy. I was messing with you."

"And this is what friends do?"

Cole nodded. "Yes. Good friends sometimes joke around and prank each other."

"Very well. As I consider you a good friend, I shall research this behavior and attempt to participate. Thank you for alerting me to it."

A small portion of Cole's mind wanted to whimper, *Oh, shit*, but the more he considered it, he wanted to see what kind of pranks Srexx would devise. He smiled, saying, "I look forward to it, Srexx."

"Cap," Haskell began, "the SDF ships are charging…ah…belay that. The SDF ships' reactors have just shut down. They're all on emergency power."

Cole swiveled to look at the sensors station, asking, "Did we do that?"

"No, Cole," Srexx replied. "We did not. According to the logs aboard the SDF ships, each chief engineer implemented a manual override when the captains ordered the ships to battle-stations."

Cole swiveled back to the tactical plot in time to see a veritable cloud of tiny dots erupt around the SDF fleet.

"Cap, we're being hailed," Jenkins announced.

"Put it on," Cole replied.

"Hello. This is Commander Garth Carruthers, and I am the former senior-most chief engineer of the SDF fleet. My associates and I have locked out the reactor controls aboard the SDF ships and tendered our resignations to Tristan's Gate, as we cannot support the conduct that led to the present situation. I have been asked to request asylum in Beta Magellan for those of us in life pods, as well as our families on Tristan's World."

"Jenkins, open a channel, please, and be sure we transmit in the clear," Cole said.

Not even five seconds later, the overhead speakers chirped, and Jenkins replied, "You're on, Cap."

"Commander Carruthers," Cole began, "this is Bartholomew James Coleson. First off, I want to thank you for saving your fellow spacers' lives; if the SDF had fired on us, we would have responded. I grant your request for asylum, pending the standard immigration evaluation all refugees must pass for full citizenship in Beta Magellan; if any of your people prefer not to pursue full citizenship, we will assist them in relocating to a place of their choice at no cost to them. I ask that you and your associates put as much space between your life pods and the SDF ships as possible; we will slow so that you can board one of the freighters. Coleson out." Once the overhead speakers chirped to indicate a closed channel, Cole swiveled to face Jenkins. "My compliments to the senior captain among the freighters, Jenkins; ask him to start a head-count so we don't overbook our carrying capacity. Oh...and ask him to be sure we do not leave with any of the life pods. They're property of Tristan's Gate, and no matter what else we may be, we are *not* thieves."

"Aye, Cap," Jenkins replied.

Cole swiveled back to face forward. "Helm, alter our maneuvering plan, please; we need to slow to intercept the life pods."

———

Slowing to take the life pods' occupants aboard freighters added forty minutes to their transit. As soon as the last life pod was dropped back into space deactivated and ready for recovery, the Beta Magellan ships ramped their engines back up to one-quarter-light and resumed their approach.

Cole had just stepped out of the head shared by his office and his day-cabin when the overhead speakers in the day-cabin broadcast Srexx's voice.

"Cole?"

"Yeah, buddy?"

"I have some information that might cause Sasha and her family emotional distress."

Cole felt like sighing. "What is it?"

"I have considerable correspondence between Nathyn Thyrray and upper-tier individuals within the Coalition and Coalition agents within Tristan's Gate in which Nathyn has successfully negotiated a deal to become the system governor in exchange for delivering Tristan's Gate to the Coalition. It appears he worked behind the scenes on several of the recently elected officials' campaigns, and he seemed to be rather influential in getting them elected. In a number of circumstances, he used his familial relationship with the Vance clan to secure groups' or influential people's support for his chosen candidates."

"Well...damn," Cole replied, this time heaving a heavy sigh. "That's not going to go over well."

"My probabilities support your conclusion, Cole," Srexx agreed. "I also have confirmation that Nathyn used his chosen candidates to advance an agenda of increased independence and self-sufficiency for Tristan's Gate, and it was this agenda that garnered them the most votes. My calculations indicate a very high chance that the people of Tristan's Gate will feel betrayed—possibly even defrauded—if you choose to publicize this information."

"Talk about a mess," Cole said. "What's the quantum comms lag to Beta Magellan right now?"

"At our current position, fifteen seconds, Cole...and I calculate you would want to know that the crews of the SDF ships are working to remove the engineers' lock-outs on the reactor controls. It is possible they will be combat-capable within an hour."

"Okay. Can you do anything to hamper their efforts?"

"Yes, Cole."

"Please, do so. It looks like we're going to be here a little longer than I thought."

CHAPTER TWENTY-ONE

Battle-Carrier *Haven*
    Orbiting Tristan's World
    Tristan's Gate
    17 September 3003, 17:55 GST

Cole sat at the desk in his office, accessing the comms function of his workstation. He selected Painter's deputy from his contact list and keyed the command to initiate a call. Twenty seconds later (plus or minus), a hologram appeared above Cole's desk.

"Yes, sir?" Painter's deputy asked.

"Select our best pilot and one of the couriers," Cole said. "Find Paol and his wife, and inform them that I'd like them to arrive in Tristan's Gate tomorrow. Assure them that their family is safe and that no one's in danger of dying; I need their input on a situation, and it would be better for them to be here than try to conference them in...even with a fifteen-second delay."

Soon, the deputy nodded. "Yes, sir. Do you need anything else?"

Cole turned the situation over in his mind for several moments before he answered. "No, thank you. But tell the pilot I am ordering him to max the hyperdrive for the trip here."

"Roger that, sir."

"Thank you," Cole replied. "Cole out."

The hologram blinked out of existence, and Cole leaned back against his seat. The situation was even trickier than he first thought at Srexx's revelation. The SDF were holding Carl and Lindsay Vance and Jed Hanson under guard in the Vance residence, down on Tristan's World. Technically, it was a violation of their civil rights, as the government had not issued an arrest warrant or a detention order for them; the government hadn't even issued any paperwork for the arrest of Sev and Harlon. At first, Cole thought it was an oversight, simply a matter of Nathyn's pet politicians moving faster than the formalities. When he had voiced this to Srexx, the AI countered with a different possibility: as Sev and Harlon were (a) individuals who enjoyed dual citizenship in both Beta Magellan *and* Tristan's Gate and (b) carried letters of credence as full ambassadors from a foreign star system, any arrest warrants or detention orders involving Sev and Harlon would have to pass through the system's High Court, where the justices were appointed to life terms and with whom Nathyn had no influence.

That piece of information put the whole situation in a completely different light, and Cole wondered how many of the SDF personnel actually realized just how legally exposed they were right now. President Harker's order to seize Cole's ambassadors and the courier vessel were illegal, and to make Cole's job even easier, the idiot had put the orders in writing. If Cole were being fully honest, he had to admit a certain pleasure in seeing that General 'Tree-Up-Her-Ass' Trumball had counter-signed the orders; a small, petty part of his personality that he tried to keep away from the public would very much enjoy watching the consequences of those orders come home to roost.

Within minutes of *Haven* and her associated ships entering orbit, a veritable flood of applications for refugee berths bombarded *Haven*'s comms node. Cole made sure Mattias Stone's family had a place along with the families of the former SDF engineers. After that, he referred all such messages to the senior freighter captain to be filled on a first-come-first-served basis. Every berth aboard all nine freighters was claimed within two hours.

Then, the messages from people who owned their own ships started arriving. It didn't take long at all for Srexx to ferret out the ads for berths aboard those ships and the shocking prices the owners were charging, and Cole informed the owners that no price gougers or opportunists would be welcome in Beta Magellan. If they wanted to relocate, fine. If they wanted to offer their ships' extra space to other people wanting to relocate, fine. But Cole drew the line at the owners charging people or families their life savings for transport to Beta Magellan. Cole was all for people making a profit...as long as it was responsible, clean and green profit.

When one of the ship owners called out Cole on the apparent hypocrisy of his statement, considering the impressive sum residing in Cole's accounts, Cole merely smiled and offered to show the man the records proving he'd paid for every piece of infrastructure in Beta Magellan and its associated systems—every house, every street, every orbital station, every hospital, library, or school...every single improvement—all by himself. Cole also pointed out that the citizens of Beta Magellan enjoyed the lowest tax rates in known space. Oddly enough, the ship owner declined Cole's offer.

Cole sighed and pushed himself to his feet. He couldn't put it off any longer. It was time to call the system leadership and ask about his people. It was a foregone conclusion in Cole's mind that he had come for his associates, but he didn't relish the idea of conflict with Tristan's Gate. It wasn't that long ago that he *defended* these people.

Cole entered the bridge, and the duty officer almost leapt out of the command chair, announcing, "Captain on deck!"

"I have the conn," Cole said as he approached the command chair and settled into it.

"Sir," the spacer at Marine Ops began, "may I ask a question?"

Cole nodded. "Sure. Ask away."

"A bunch of us are wondering why they haven't fired on us yet. I mean, every station and planet has defensive capabilities, right?"

Cole chuckled. "Well, you would think. Beta Magellan certainly does. But no...the Gate has no weapons beyond basic emplacements, and the planet has some ground-to-space missiles but nothing with enough punch to threaten us. Historically, the agreements between Tristan's Gate and the Commonwealth served as a deterrent against those who might be interested in moving against the system, and the SDF has always been sufficient as a police force and able to handle the few pirates who decided to try their luck."

"Huh...that's weird," the spacer replied. "Do you think it'll stay that way after this, sir?"

Cole shrugged. "In the long run, as long as they don't harass our people, I don't see the happenings in Tristan's Gate as being any of my business."

The spacer nodded his agreement and remained silent.

Cole shifted his attention to the comms station, saying, "Comms, if you please, hail the system leadership."

"Aye, sir," the comms tech answered.

Moments later, the main viewscreen activated to display a young man in a suit, and the speakers chirped, indicating an active call.

"Hello. I'm Lucius Brown, Undersecretary for Foreign Affairs," the young man onscreen said.

Cole nodded. "Greetings. I am Bartholomew James Coleson, and I've come for my people: Sevrin Vance and Harlon Hanson. Furthermore, Mattias Stone has requested asylum in Beta Magellan, and I have granted his request. You have one standard hour to return them to the location from which they were taken, or I'll save you the trouble and retrieve them myself."

"Yes," Undersecretary Brown replied. "I quite understand, but you see, I'm not empowered to negotiate—"

"Mr. Brown," Cole interrupted, "did anything I just said sound like part of a negotiation to you?"

"Well...no, sir, but I have no authority to grant any requests. They just told me to answer the call."

Cole sighed. "Right then, so you're wasting my time."

"I...I wouldn't say that, sir."

"You're not empowered to release my people, as you yourself just stated. If you're not wasting my time, just what *are* you doing?"

"Talking with you?"

It was a grievous breach of etiquette, and Cole knew—*knew*—he shouldn't do it. But he couldn't help himself. He closed the call with no further discourse, effectively hanging up on the poor soul.

"Srexx, do you have a location on our people and Mattias Stone?" Cole asked.

"Of course, Cole. I have maintained near-real-time awareness of their location and status since I learned of their situation."

"Would you please relay that information to Lieutenant Colonel Devereaux?"

"I did so while en route to the system, Cole."

Cole smiled. "Thank you much, Srexx. Forgive me, but I need to call a marine."

"Of course, Cole.

Swiveling toward the port recess, Cole said, "Marine Ops, my compliments to the colonel, if you please, and ask her to call when she has a moment."

"Aye, sir," the private first class replied.

Moments later, the overhead speakers chirped and broadcast, "Devereaux to Bridge."

"Bridge, Cole here."

"You asked me to call, sir?"

"I did indeed, Colonel," Cole replied, grinning. "Are you set to retrieve our people?"

"We have two assault shuttles loaded and waiting, and the recovery teams have been briefed on the plan. We're just waiting for the 'go' order, sir."

Cole nodded, even though the colonel couldn't see it. "Very well. Let me coordinate with the CAG—"

"Forgive the interruption, sir, but she's here with me. I'm in Pre-Flight; we were considering flight plans."

"Hey, Cap," Emily said over the comms channel.

Cole chuckled. "Hey, CAG. Are you ready to launch a recovery effort?"

"Yes, sir," Emily replied. "Two full squadrons await your order."

"Very good. One last question, ladies; if I ask you to divert one assault shuttle to retrieve the Vances and Jed Hanson, will that be a problem?"

"No," Emily answered.

"Not at all, sir," the lieutenant colonel said.

Cole nodded, even though they couldn't see it. "Very well. Since the system leadership seems reluctant to discuss the matter, I don't see as we have any other choice. Go. The battlegroup will provide overwatch."

"Aye, sir! Launching now," Emily said. "Pre-flight out."

The speakers chirped, indicating the closed call.

Cole heaved a sigh. "Sound battle-stations. Comms, signal the battlegroup to deploy for overwatch; we'll coordinate via TacNet. Helm, as soon as the Air Boss signals a clear flight deck, put us in our overwatch position as well."

Klaxons blared throughout the ship as the status lights shifted from solid amber to flashing red.

"Comms," Cole said, "record a message for broadcast."

Not even five seconds later, the comms tech replied, "You're on, sir."

"People of Tristan's Gate," Cole began, "I am Bartholomew James Coleson of Beta Magellan. As I hope you've become aware, the system leadership chose to seize two of our people whom I sent to your system as accredited ambassadors, and the former Defense Minister Mattias Stone, on the fifteenth of September. Upon my arrival, the leadership refuses to discuss the matter, which leaves only one recourse: retrieving our people ourselves. Even now, *Haven* is launching fighters and assault shuttles under orders to carry out this retrieval, and I send this message to assure you that we mean no harm to the citizens of Tristan's Gate, despite the conduct of the system government. As long as our small craft and marines are not fired upon, we will not initiate hostilities. Thank you for your time and cooperation. Coleson out."

Seconds later, the comms tech said, "Ready to transmit, sir."

"Flood the system," Cole replied, "every channel and frequency."

"Aye, sir, flooding the system."

"Srexx," Cole said, "I think the courier vessel has served its purpose. Can you pilot it?"

"Of course, Cole."

Cole nodded. "If you would please, send it home."

"And what of the individuals working to access the ship?"

"Do what you need to do to make sure they're aware it's taking off," Cole advised, "and give them ample time to reach a safe distance. As long as you do that, anyone who hasn't reached a safe distance is not our problem."

"Yes, Cole."

"Missile launch!" the spacer at the tactical station announced. "We have multiple surface-to-air launches!"

"Let the missiles reach a safe altitude, and then have the closest ship use their point defense to destroy them. Do you have a location on the launchers?"

"Orders sent via TacNet," the spacer replied, "and yes, sir. We have a very accurate location on the launchers."

"What is our risk for collateral damage?" Cole asked.

"None, sir. Those launchers are on the side of a hill out in the boonies. The closest residence is over a hundred miles away."

Cole nodded. "Very well, detail the nearest ship with bombardment platforms to eliminate the launch site."

A few minutes later, the spacer announced, "The launch site is now a crater, sir."

"Comms," Cole said, "patch me through to the Vance residence, please."

Mere seconds later, the comms tech replied, "Sir, there seems to be some tightly targeted jamming at that location. I can punch through it, but there's a good chance they'd hear the call in Zurich."

Cole didn't want to alert the people watching the Vances and Jed Hanson to what was happening, even though it was unlikely they *didn't* know Cole had come for his people.

"Hold on that, then," Cole said. "If you would please, contact Pre-Flight and ask the CAG and colonel to divert one squadron and assault shuttle to secure the Vance residence and offer our hospitality."

"Aye, sir."

The minutes passed in silence, and the more minutes that passed, the more Cole itched to be piloting one of the assault shuttles. He knew his place was on the bridge. He understood that. But it galled him that he wasn't out there with his people, leading from the front.

"Sir," the spacer at Flight Ops spoke at long last, "Assault Shuttle One reports landing at the detention facility; the squadron has shifted to area patrol."

"The marines have entered the facility, sir," the PFC at Marine Ops reported. "They report light resistance."

"Sir, Assault Shuttle Two has landed at the Vance residence," the spacer at Flight Ops announced.

The minutes continued to pass.

After what seemed like an eternity to Cole, the spacer at Flight Ops said, "Assault Shuttle One reports all parties back aboard, and they are lifting off. Mr. Vance, Colonel Hanson, and Mr. Stone appear to be unharmed. And now, Assault Shuttle Two reports lift-off with three passengers."

"The marines report no casualties among our people, sir," the PFC at Marine Ops reported, "but they also report leaving several facility guards and SDF personnel unconscious under heavy stun."

"Okay," Cole said, forcing himself not to show any of the relief he felt. "As soon as they clear the atmosphere, stand down from battle-stations."

Soon, the retrieval teams cleared the planet's atmosphere, and shortly after that, everyone was aboard. However, that only solved one of Cole's problems. As soon as Paol and Mira arrived, he'd break the news about Nathyn.

CHAPTER TWENTY-TWO

Battle-Carrier *Haven*
   Orbiting Tristan's World
   Tristan's Gate
   19 September 3003, 08:35 GST

Cole stood outside the hatch to the bridge briefing room. He was not looking forward to what was going to happen when he walked inside.

Paol and Mira Thyrray had arrived late last night, and Cole had arranged quarters for them to sleep off the urgent travel. Mira's parents, Carl and Lindsey Vance, spent the night in the flag officer's quarters, resting up from their period of home confinement. Jed Hanson spent the night in the captain's quarters and had already begged Cole on three separate occasions for a tour.

   Forty minutes ago, Cole had asked Sasha to gather her sister, her parents, and her grandparents in the bridge briefing room for a meeting at zero-eight-thirty.

. . .

Put your big boy pants on and get in there, Cole thought to himself. Heaving one last sigh, Cole stepped close enough for the hatch sensor to detect him, and it irised open. He entered the briefing room to the sounds of an impromptu family reunion, but the conversations faded as everyone turned to look his way.

Cole nodded and walked to his seat at the head of the table.

"Apologies for being late," Cole said as he eased into his chair. "So... I have some information I feel duty-bound to provide you, and once you've processed it, you can decide how we should best proceed."

"You make it sound like someone's dying," Paol remarked. "What's going on?"

"Srexx," Cole said, "would you please present the data you reported to me that led to this meeting?"

"Of course, Cole," Srexx replied via the overhead speakers. "The short summary of the data is that Nathyn Thyrray is conspiring with Coalition agents to secure Tristan's Gate for the Coalition through a non-violent coup masquerading as a normal election cycle."

Everyone at the table gaped and turned to Cole. Cole held up his hand to stave off any interruptions.

"If you will direct your attention to the hologram, I am currently displaying communications in which Nathyn negotiated with the Coalition agents via an encrypted message application. Once you've read those, please inform me, and we'll proceed to the next piece of evidence."

Cole noticed Paol and Mira looked rather pale, as did Sasha, Talia, and Lindsey Vance. Carl, on the other hand, just looked angry.

The presentation progressed until Srexx displayed the communications Nathyn had between the people from whom he'd obtained support for his candidates. A string of messages caught Carl's eyes, and his nostrils flared as his hands clenched the table in a white-knuckle grip.

"He used *my name*? My own grandson implicated *me* in this treason?"

"Dad," Mira interjected, "please, don't call it treason."

"Why not?" Carl shot back. "That's what this is."

"Treason's a capital crime, Dad," Mira replied. "Do you want your grandson executed?"

Carl slowly turned to face his daughter. "Mira, I understand; he's your son and you love him, but he has betrayed *everything* the Vances and Hansons and all the other families of Tristan's Gate have worked for across centuries. I have half a mind to kill him myself; I am certainly disowning him. Be angry at me if you want, but I refuse to countenance these actions. He used our family name, Mira. Look at those messages! Half the people who supported or endorsed these candidates only did so because Nathyn implied that I supported them, too."

"Maybe he was manipulated," Mira countered, her voice soft, almost a whimper.

"Forgive me," Srexx said, "but the data does not support that conclusion. Nathyn initiated contact with the Coalition agents. He apparently recognized them from the time your family was in the Commonwealth."

Mira broke out in tears, and she leaned against Paol, putting an arm around him as she placed her head on his left shoulder.

"Cole, I'm sorry," Paol said, "but I think we're going to need some time."

Cole nodded. "Srexx, put up all the data you have, and then, let's give them some privacy."

"Yes, Cole."

Cole stepped outside the briefing room and headed for his office when a thought occurred to him.

"Srexx," Cole began, "what happened to the SDF ships?"

"They are still thirty light-minutes away on minimal power," Srexx replied. "They have yet to defeat the encryption I placed on the engineering controls. I ensured life support is fully powered along with the Attitude Control System, which permits them to maintain position. They have signaled for tugs several times, but the tug operators seem reticent to risk our wrath...at least according to the replies they sent the SDF."

Cole chuckled. "I'll bet they're a bit peeved."

"Data suggests such a statement is what you would term an under-statement. General Trumball has been placed on medical stand-down for stress-related heart complications; current records indicate she is sedated in the infirmary aboard the SDF flagship."

"Ouch," Cole vocalized, grimacing. "I never liked her, but I don't wish her ill."

"I understand, Cole, but the likelihood of no hostilities if we permit them to bring their reactors back online is vanishingly remote."

Cole sighed. "I know, buddy. I know. I just wish things could've turned out differently, that's all."

———

Hours later, Cole was working through some reports on the battle-group when the hatch irised open. Cole looked up and smiled upon seeing Sasha.

"How's everyone holding up?" Cole asked.

Sasha walked across the compartment and almost flopped into one of the two guest chairs. She shook her head, saying, "Not well. Grandma eventually stopped crying, and she and Dad are holding Mom. She's not handling this well at all."

"How about you and your sister?"

Sasha shrugged. "Tallie's a little shell-shocked; she always looked up to Nathyn. I haven't really spoken with him since the blow-up before we went to Centauri, so I was kind of out of touch. Yeah...I wish he hadn't done this, but what's done is done. All that's left now is to clean it up. Dad and Grandpa are asking for you. Given what you survived in Centauri, they'd like your thoughts on the best response."

Cole nodded as he stood. "All right then. Let's go talk this out."

Cole led Sasha back to the briefing room, where everyone discussed multiple options. Mira never got past trying to get Nathyn out of the situation, but Carl refused to protect him from the storm that was coming. In the end, they settled on a plan, and Carl asked Cole to prepare everything.

———

Theater Four
    Recreation Deck, Battle-Carrier *Haven*
    Tristan's Gate
    19 September 3003, 19:00 GST

Theater Four was the venue that possessed an actual stage for plays, musical performances, and the like. The stage was currently configured for a speech, with a podium placed front and center, and a line of chairs stretched out across the stage a few feet behind the podium. The venue could seat almost two thousand people, but there wasn't even a tenth of that number present. Everyone in the audience was a journalist, with every network in Tristan's Gate and quite a few interstellar networks represented.

At nineteen-fifteen hours, Carl Vance and Cole led Lindsey, Paol, Mira, Sasha, and Talia out onto the stage. Carl and Cole walked to the podium; everyone else took a seat.

Cole approached the podium first, Carl standing at his side.

"Ladies and gentlemen," Cole began, "I'd like to thank you for taking the time to shuttle up to *Haven* this evening. Mr. Vance has a statement he'd like to deliver uninterrupted, so please hold your questions until he's finished. At the end of the conference, my people will provide data crystals with all the information discussed here today. Mr. Vance?"

Cole stepped aside for Carl and took the empty seat beside Sasha.

"I'd like to thank Cole—that is, Mr. Coleson—for his hospitality these past couple of days and his continued friendship with my family. What I am about to discuss would not have been discovered as soon as it was, were it not for his people," Carl said, starting his prepared remarks. "Ladies and gentlemen, I am here today to inform the public that a fraud has been committed against the people of Tristan's Gate, and I regret to say that my family's reputation was crucial to the fraud's success. I have in my possession irrefutable evidence that my grandson Nathyn Thyrray conspired with Coalition agents to elect a group of people whose sole purpose in office is to ensure a peaceful, quiet transfer of power from our established government to the Coalition.

"I deeply regret my grandson's conduct, and I wish to make it known now that I neither had knowledge of nor gave support to his actions in this matter. I apologize that I did not learn of it in time to prevent the use of my family's name and reputation, and I stand ready to offer my support to any reasonable initiative intended to rectify the situation. Now, ask your questions, please."

Carl's statement took at most two minutes to deliver. The assembled journalists asked questions for over five hours.

———

By noon the next day, the evidence of Nathyn's actions and intentions had spread throughout the system. The citizens of Tristan's Gate demanded a new set of elections after a public vote of No Confidence reported ninety-two-point-seven percent of voting adults in the system had no confidence in the present government. Fortunately, the public did not hold the Vances responsible for Nathyn's actions; in fact, the Vance clan enjoyed an upswing in popular favor and support...both for Carl's prompt disclosure of the situation and in sympathy over how Nathyn must've hurt his family.

Nathyn attempted to commandeer a runabout and flee the system, but at the request of the provisional system president, Cole dispatched a frigate to chase down the runabout and bring it—and Nathyn—back to The Gate. When the frigate delivered the runabout to its dock, system police were waiting at the airlock with a warrant for Nathyn's arrest on a charge of treason. Nathyn's Coalition agents had already been arrested on charges of espionage.

The provisional system president even went so far as to publicly rescind the orders for the seizure of Sev Vance and Harlon Hanson, offering a public apology for the actions of his predecessor and sending orders to the SDF to stand down from a hostile posture toward *Haven* and her battlegroup.

As soon as the SDF acknowledged those orders, Srexx decrypted the engineering systems of the ships so the SDF could bring their reactors back online. He also notified Cole in private of a message sent to the SDF flagship under seal: General Trumball had the choice of resignation or facing charges for her complicity in the whole affair.

With nothing left to accomplish in Tristan's Gate, Cole ordered the battlegroup back to Beta Magellan.

CHAPTER TWENTY-THREE

Conference Room, Citadel Station
  Beta Magellan
  5 October 3003, 10:07 GST

Cole looked up from his tablet when the hatch irised open and smiled as Painter led the group into the conference room. He stood and walked over to her, extending his hand. Painter returned the handshake and gave him a mock glare for a moment.

"You could've warned a girl she was an ambassador," Painter said.

"Why?" Sev asked from behind her.

"Yeah," Harlon said. "He didn't warn us...and *we* ended up spending time in a cell."

Painter grimaced. "I'm sorry you had to go through that, but if it makes you feel any better, you made the news in Zurich."

"I'm pretty sure they made the news everywhere," Paol said, stepping around the traffic jam at the hatch to find a seat. "It's not often star system officials arrest and detain accredited diplomats."

Cole shifted his attention back to Painter. "Welcome home. You did an excellent job in Zurich."

"Thank you, sir," Painter said as she moved to a seat at the conference table.

Returning to his seat, Cole watched the rest of his group enter the conference room and find seats. Sasha, Sev, Harlon, Sato, Paol, and Painter looked at him. Just then, the hatch irised open once more to admit Garrett and Mattias Stone. Cole looked to Garrett and quirked an eyebrow in a questioning expression.

Garrett nodded. "He passed."

Cole smiled. "Mr. Stone—"

"Please, call me Mattias. Every time I hear 'Mr. Stone,' I start looking for my father."

"Mattias, then," Cole resumed, "have you given any thought to your future prospects? Do you want to return to Tristan's Gate?"

Stone sat beside Painter, and Garrett assumed his normal spot at the opposite end of the table from Cole.

"No, I really haven't," Stone replied. "I do know that I have no interest in returning to Tristan's Gate, and my family is of the same mind. Don't get me wrong; Tristan's Gate *wants* me back. So far, they've sent a total of fifteen apologies outright begging me to come back...to my old job, even. But we'd been discussing a possible move to Beta Magellan for a while, and since we're here, why leave? We just hope there's something for us to do."

Cole grinned. "Oh, I think you'll find your talents well utilized. The system has slightly over a million-and-a-half people, and there are still about one-point-five jobs for every person. It's a buyer's market."

"Oh, well then," Stone said. "I guess it's just a matter of finding something that suits me."

"Did you like being Defense Minister in Tristan's Gate?" Paol asked.

"I did," Stone answered. "I felt like I was contributing."

"Want the job?" Cole asked.

Stone blinked. "Excuse me?"

"I need a defense minister. Until you arrived, my two best candidates for the spot also happen to excel as fleet commanders. I'm not saying they couldn't have done the job, just that they're far better suited to line command. Fair warning, you'll have to build the

Ministry of Defense yourself; it's a little bit of a ghost town right now."

Stone broke out into a huge smile. "I'd love to be your defense minister."

"You're hired. Okay. There are more 'minister' titles in the works, but the guy who's going to be my foreign minister still hasn't finished Beta Magellan's constitution yet," Cole said, adding a sidelong look at Paol. "Sev, can you arrange for Mattias to have a tour of our system infrastructure? I'm thinking the shipyards, especially, and our system forts."

Sev nodded and turned to Stone. "See me after the meeting, and we'll set something up."

Stone smiled and nodded.

Cole continued, saying, "Okay, people, we have five systems who have asked for our help. Where are we in being able to liberate those systems and hold them from the Coalition?"

"If matters have calmed over at Baldur," Sato said, "we could recall a few of those system pickets. We sent nine system pickets with you, and if we scale back just to two—one for Baldur and another for Midas —we'd have seven system pickets."

"May I ask a question?" Stone interjected.

"Of course," Cole replied.

"What constitutes a system picket?"

"Four cruisers, eight destroyers, and sixteen frigates," Cole replied, "but there are twelve line frigates and four scout frigates. We based the system pickets on *Haven*'s battlegroup."

Stone nodded. "So, these system pickets are utilizing *Haven*'s technology base?"

Cole nodded.

Stone took a deep breath and slowly released it. "Does anyone realize you have the most powerful fleet in known space?"

"My people and I work very hard," Garrett said, "to see that others don't realize it."

"This operation to liberate these systems will kind of be our unveiling party, though," Sasha opined. "I don't see how we could hide the ships we use."

"True," Garrett agreed. "At that point, it becomes a matter of keeping people guessing on just how many we have."

Cole chuckled. "You won't even be able to do that once we start rolling out home fleets for all these systems."

Garrett nodded. "Yes, but there's nothing to be done about that."

"What constitutes a home fleet?" Stone asked.

"Well," Cole replied, "right now, we're looking at a dreadnought, four battle-carriers, sixteen cruisers, thirty-two destroyers, and sixty-four line frigates...but that's a little up in the air at the moment. We're still building our first dreadnought."

Mattias's expression made him look just a little shell-shocked.

"Okay. I'll issue a recall order for seven of the system pickets, pending an okay from Scarlett. I haven't really heard anything from her outside of basic reports, so I don't really have a good feel for how things are going over there. Oh...that reminds me. Painter, let's allocate five mining ships and ten freighters to Midas; I want them to ramp up production to give us an additional revenue stream. I don't mind footing the bill for Beta Magellan, but if those five systems are serious about founding a federation, I'm not paying for that, beyond some initial setup-type stuff. Sev, how many scout frigates do we have available?"

"Available?" Sev repeated. "None, but they're very easy to build. What's on your mind?"

"I think we need to start doing comprehensive surveys of all the unaligned and unclaimed systems in the area. I realize Midas is probably a lucky strike, but there's no reason not to check for additional systems with a similar resource mix. Get with Painter and work up survey expeditions, and be sure to load them up with system claims buoys."

"Once the recalled system pickets arrive," Sato said, "we should begin reconnaissance flights through those systems. We need better intelligence than we have, and we also need to make the freedom fighters aware that they need to be ready."

Cole nodded. "That's an excellent idea. We'll meet with those four emissaries and find out if there are any recognition codes or some such our scout ships can use without alerting the Coalition forces to what we're saying."

"I would also suggest taking Admiral Trask as overall fleet commander," Sato added. "While you are coming along very nicely, you will need to focus on the system *Haven* is liberating. An actual flag officer and staff can oversee and coordinate the operation as a whole without distracting you."

"Good thought," Cole replied. "Thank you. I'll add that to my list, too. Okay. Anything else at this precise moment?" When no one offered anything, Cole nodded once and stood. "Very well, then. Let's do this. Paol, schedule a meeting with the emissaries."

That said, Cole led the group out of the conference room.

Conference Room, Babylon Station
Gateway
6 October 3003, 09:45 GST

Cole entered the conference room to find Paol and the emissaries already waiting. A marine followed Cole into the room, with another assuming station just outside the hatch.

"Thank you for seeing us on such short notice," Cole said as he picked a seat. "I have some news you may enjoy. We're close to having what we need to liberate and hold your systems from the Coalition. Within the next few days, we'll begin reconnaissance flights through the systems to get accurate information on what we're facing, and as soon as we've developed an ops plan, we'll proceed."

The emissaries shared looks among one another, all smiling.

"That is very good news indeed," the emissary from Oriolis said, apparently taking the lead for her associates once again.

"So," Cole continued, "what we need to talk about now is what's necessary to prepare your people for us liberating the systems. When we first discussed this, you mentioned having everything in hand, except for space superiority."

The emissaries nodded.

"That's correct," the Oriolis emissary replied. "We've been doing what we can to keep our people updated on the status in a general way. We don't communicate specific details or anything that would endanger the mission or our people, but we make periodic posts on boards they follow with code words."

Cole nodded. "What are the chances those code words have been compromised? I'm thinking of the fifth emissary who's still enjoying a cell in my brig on *Haven*."

"All our code word matrices are system-specific," one of the men explained. "Sure...she could've compromised the code word matrix for her system, but that doesn't affect any of ours. We were very, very careful to ensure that none of the code word matrices overlapped even a little long before she came on the scene."

Cole leaned back against his seat, nodding. "Excellent. As we get closer to the actual event, I'll meet with you again."

"Captain," Oriolis's emissary interjected, "we would like to accompany the ships that liberate our systems when the time comes. It would be good if we could return to our homes and help with the aftermath of the Coalition's occupation."

"I won't say 'no' out of hand," Cole answered, "but I won't say 'yes,' either. Let me think it over and discuss it with my people. I'll have an answer for you the next time we speak."

"Fair consideration is all we ask."

Cole nodded once and stood, the others standing with him. He shook hands with each emissary before turning and leading the way out of the conference room.

CHAPTER TWENTY-FOUR

Conference Room, Babylon Station
Gateway
30 October 3003, 08:47 GST

Cole entered the conference room with Paol just behind him and he smiled at seeing Yeleth and Wixil waiting for him. Wixil erupted in a huge grin and almost leaped across the room.

"Hi, Cole!" She exclaimed midair.

Cole caught her in his arms with a mild *oof* and returned her smile, saying, "Hi, Wixil. I'm glad you and your mom are back."

"I'm glad we're back too," Wixil said, purring. "Mom let me pilot the courier, but I missed *Haven* and everyone here."

Cole released Wixil, who dropped to the floor. He noticed she was now almost as tall as her mom. "Wixil, I think you've grown since I saw you last."

"I have, thank you."

Cole ruffled the fur atop her head between her ears and smiled. He approached Yeleth and nodded his greetings, saying, "Yeleth, welcome back. We've missed you. Sasha and your deputy especially, since they've worked together on your regular duties."

"It is good to be home, Cole," Yeleth replied. "May I introduce Viskha of Clan Ghrexel? The Clans of Myxtraal have named her ambassador to Beta Magellan."

"Viskha," Cole said, turning to her, "welcome to Gateway. How have you been since Tristan's Gate's ISA office?"

Now, Viskha gave a little purr of her own before she said, "I didn't know if you'd remember me. I have been well."

"Viskha, I'd like to present Paol Thyrray. He advises me on matters of state and will be my foreign minister as soon as he finishes writing the constitution for Beta Magellan."

Viskha nodded her greetings. "Well met, Paol Thyrray."

"Likewise," Paol replied.

"Well," Cole said, "shall we sit and discuss matters?"

"Red has also returned from his people," Yeleth said. "We met in the docks. He should be here shortly."

Cole nodded. "Well, in that case, does anyone mind if I call a few more people over from *Haven* and set up a conference call with Beta Magellan?"

No one minded, so Cole arranged a conference call with Sev, Painter, and Sato while Sasha, Harlon, Emily, and Garrett came over to Babylon from *Haven*. Red arrived at the conference room just about the same time as Sasha and the others from *Haven*, and everyone took a few moments to welcome Red and make sure everyone was introduced to everyone else. Soon enough, though, they settled and got down to serious business.

"In terms of my mission to my people," Red reported, "I expressed our concerns and left the copies of our data, but they were largely unmoved. I'm not certain my people have faced a serious threat in several generations, so they did not have the level of concern about the Coalition that we do."

"The Clans have a very similar outlook," Viskha said, "but we recognize the need to be aware of what happens with our neighbors before it spills over to us. That is why they decided to direct the first ambassador out of our space and to send me here."

"Well, it's my goal to see to it that the Coalition doesn't spill over anywhere," Cole replied. "Five systems want to found a federation with Beta Magellan at the center and leading it, and while I'm not wild about the idea, everyone whose opinion I trust loves it."

"Founding a federation to act as a counterbalance to the Coalition is an excellent idea," Viskha replied. "Why are you not enthused about it?"

Cole shrugged. "I wanted to build up Beta Magellan and make it a safe haven for anyone who wanted a place to live. I never planned to be a freedom fighter or a statesman or a leader on the galactic scale."

"We do not always have a choice in our path through this life," Viskha said, "and it is how we face and rise to the unexpected that demonstrates our caliber. From what little I've seen and know, you— Bartholomew James Coleson—are of better caliber than many."

A round of "Hear, hear" circled the table and the conference call, and Cole felt his face and ears heat. He didn't do all he did for self-aggrandizement. He didn't do it to be recognized or cheered. He did it because it needed to be done.

"Thank you for your thoughts, Viskha," Cole said. "Please forgive me for not having an area set aside for embassies. To be quite honest, we're not really to that point yet, but we'll get you some quarters, and I'll speak with Captain Vasquez about some space we can set aside for you until we figure out what we're doing."

Viskha nodded. "That is acceptable."

"Okay," Cole resumed. "Where are we with scouting those five systems?"

"Do you want me to leave?" Viskha asked. "Most would say it wasn't appropriate for me to sit in on your war council."

Cole shook his head and made a dismissive gesture. "Nah. I'm a very open and transparent kind of guy. You're welcome to sit through this conversation unless you want to leave."

Viskha chose to stay.

"We've had scout frigates in those systems under full stealth for ten days now," Sato answered from Beta Magellan. "There is no indication they've been detected. We've not attempted any high-resolution scans of the planets, but I'm confident we know all there is to know about those systems outside of the planets themselves."

"I've spoken with Admiral Trask," Cole replied, "and he's agreeable to acting as overall operations commander on this. Have the two of you put your figurative heads together to develop the ops plan yet?"

"We have a rough strategy," Sato admitted, "but we wanted to discuss which contingent will go to Epsilon Anubis. Since their emissary turned out to be a plant by the Coalition, we don't really have any way to contact the resistance there."

Cole chuckled. "I'll take Epsilon Anubis. Plan on *Haven* and her battlegroup going there."

"Very well. When do you want to launch the operation?" Sato asked.

"These five systems...they're not all border systems, are they?" Cole asked.

"No," Sasha answered. "The systems make up more of an L-shape or possibly a C-shape than...say...a line along the border. Oriolis is two jumps in from Epsilon Anubis, which *is* a border system and directly connected to Iota Anubis—also a border system. Spark is one jump anti-spinward from Oriolis."

Cole sighed. "Well, so much for my excellent idea of forming up on the jump gate and coming through in one massive transit."

Everyone exchanged looks around the table, with Sasha finally voicing what they were all thinking, "I—we—thought multi-ship transits weren't possible once you passed a certain size. That's what CIE has always said, anyway."

Cole grinned. "Yeah...there's a lot they don't tell people. The jump gates are rated to transit a combined mass of the *Haven* battlegroup, and that's *with* a safety margin."

Multiple pairs of eyes around the table—both physical and holographic—widened.

"Admiral Sato, my compliments to Admiral Trask if you please," Cole continued. "Work with him to establish a timeline of when each group needs to depart Gateway and on what setting to run their hyperdrives to allow for a simultaneous arrival in the target systems. Once you have that information, we'll set the date for the op. Anything else right this second?"

No one spoke up, so Cole nodded and stood. "Thank you, everyone."

————

Cole's Day-Cabin, Battle-Carrier *Haven*
    Gateway System
    30 October 3003, 22:57 GST

The 'Incoming Call' alert dragged Cole out of what had been a very peaceful, enjoyable sleep. The screen beside his bed showed the identity of the caller, and Cole took a moment to force away his immediate grumpy response before selecting the 'Audio Only' option.

"Cole here."

"Sir, please forgive the call, but we thought you'd want to know," the bridge's officer of the watch said. "The scout frigates reported picking up chatter that the Coalition is sending an invasion fleet to Tristan's Gate."

Cole pursed his lips and mentally growled several words that his mother would not have appreciated. A heavy sigh his only outward reaction, Cole replied, "Yeah, you did the right thing. Does this chatter give any indication as to when the fleet left or will arrive in Tristan's Gate?"

"Possibly as early as tomorrow, sir, but as late as next week. The chatter isn't really specific; it wasn't copies of operational orders or anything like that."

Cole scowled. A part of him really wanted just to let them twist in the wind. After the most recent stunt...but that had been dealt with, and the interim government offered a complete and public apology. The incident had been dealt with to such a degree, in fact, that Mira would have to go to a prison planet if she ever wanted to see her son again. That, at least, hadn't been too bad of an outcome; the jury voted that Nathyn should face life without parole instead of the death penalty for his actions. So, did the Coalition decide to try the invasion route, banking on Cole leaving Tristan's Gate to fend for themselves? If that was their guiding thought, they were in for an education; even leaving aside the formal public apology, there were still a lot of people in Tristan's Gate that Cole considered to be friends.

"Okay. Fine. Issue emergency recall orders for any personnel on Babylon. Send orders to the battlegroup to meet *Haven* in Tristan's Gate at best possible speed, since they didn't follow us here. Once we have everyone back aboard, set course for Tristan's Gate, and take us to max on the hyperdrive."

"Aye, sir," the bridge watch officer replied.

"Thank you. Cole out." The screen blanked as the call ended, and Cole rolled back to lay flat on the bed, staring up at the ceiling.

"As many times as I've bailed them out, they ought to join that federation those emissaries want me to form. At least then, they'd be entitled to a home fleet."

CHAPTER TWENTY-FIVE

Battle-Carrier *Haven*
Tristan's Gate
2 November 3003, 07:35 GST

Haven and her battlegroup decelerated toward The Gate. The system leadership was already waiting to take their call.

"What is it with these guys and November?" Cole muttered, sitting in the command chair.

"Sir?" Sasha asked from where she stood near Cole's right elbow.

"The first battle here was in November, too," Cole elaborated. "I was just wondering what it is about November that makes it so invasion-friendly for Tristan's Gate."

Sasha looked like she was fighting a grin. "I'm not sure there are any specifically invasion-friendly months, sir. I think it's just how these things work out."

"They're here, Cap," Haskell at Sensors announced. "Coalition ships just arrived through the Dante jump gate."

Cole chuckled, a compromise against an outright laugh. "Well, at least they're predictable. What's the comms lag with The Gate, Jenkins?"

"We're down to about twenty minutes, Cap," the senior comms officer for the ship answered.

Cole wanted to scowl. Twenty minutes of transmission lag was no way to hold a conversation.

"Very well," Cole replied. "Send a message to the SDF and system leadership that the Coalition fleet has arrived. Haskell, if you please, relay the ship types and numbers to Jenkins for inclusion in that message."

"Aye, Cap," both officers said, almost in unison.

"While we're waiting on their reply," Cole said, "put the ship types and numbers up on the tactical plot, please."

The hologram appeared in the center of the bridge, centered on the Coalition fleet. The top-right corner, where the shields and armor read-outs normally were, held a list of ship types and the number of each. Cole's eyes settled on the very first entry.

"Wow...a dreadnought? I'm impressed. Two battleships. Four cruisers. Eight destroyers, and an obscene amount of frigates. Really? Why would they bring so many frigates?"

The data blurred just then, and when it settled down, the frigate count was less than half of what it had been, but the type list had a new entry: troop transports.

"Ah, okay," Cole said. "That explains it. Those troop transports won't be well armed, but they still qualify as military targets."

"What are you thinking, sir?" Sasha asked.

Cole leaned back against the command chair and rubbed his jaw. "Well, honestly, I'm thinking we send the frigates and fighters after their frigates and troop transports. We—that is, *Haven*—will take the battleships and dreadnought."

"Spearhead?"

"No, I don't think so. That's my go-to, because our shields and armor are so much better against everything we've faced. This time, though, I think we're going to stand off and pound them awhile with missiles and torpedoes. Once we fire ourselves dry, we'll move into energy range. Emily's been wanting to try the bombers in a missile defense role, so this will give her that chance."

Sasha grinned. "They won't be expecting the change in tactics."

"Heh...I'll bet they weren't expecting us to be here at all," Cole agreed. He stood and approached the tactical plot. Reaching out, he zoomed out the plot to see more of the area around the fleet. "Huh... they're still hovering around the jump gate."

Cole took a half step back and tapped the tip of his nose with his right index finger as he stared at the plot.

Sasha walked up to stand beside him, asking, "You have your thinking cap on, sir. May I ask what you're considering?"

"Whether we want to force an engagement or not."

"How so?" Sasha returned.

"Well, I can shut down every outgoing jump gate in the system. The thing is, I don't know if we want to let them run to fight again another day. That's a good-size fleet. It would have to be a blow to the Coalition—even if just a little one—if we took it out of service."

Sasha turned, fully facing Cole as she asked, "Isn't it best to avoid a fight?"

"Yeah...in one respect, it is," Cole answered, "but we're going to be fighting these people, either way. Shouldn't we whittle away their ships where we can?"

"May I have a word, sir?" Sasha asked.

"Office?"

Sasha nodded once.

"Mazzi, you have the conn," Cole said as he turned toward the port hatch. "Ring if we get work."

Cole led Sasha into his office.

"So," he began, "what's on your mind?"

"If they're of a mind to turn around and leave, I say we let them," Sasha said. "I would never get too outspoken on the bridge, you know that, but I just don't see what having a battle here and now serves...aside from killing people and scrapping ships. Do we really need to rush into that?"

Cole sighed and nodded. "You're right, and I honestly agree. Besides, there's no guarantee they wouldn't have rebuilt any losses we give them today by the time we get to a formal war. I am not looking forward to that war, Sasha. It's going to be a mess of epic proportions."

"Wars usually are," Sasha replied.

"Anything else?"

Sasha shook her head.

"Right, then."

Cole stood and headed back to the bridge.

As he walked through the port hatch, Cole asked, "Haskell, how long would it take for light from where we are to reach the Coalition ships?"

Haskell did some quick calculations and answered, "Not quite eleven hours, Cap."

"Have they moved at all yet?"

"No, sir."

"Okay," Cole said. "Launch a quantum comms buoy to take up a position near The Gate, and put a standing order in the log to notify me immediately if they move. I have other things I could be doing."

————

At eighteen-hundred hours that evening, the bridge called Cole. The Coalition fleet was moving.

Cole entered the bridge and smiled at seeing the tactical plot already up. He walked to it, ignoring the "Captain on the bridge," and looked at the data. The Coalition ships were forming up for transit through the Dante jump gate.

"I guess they really did think we wouldn't be here," Cole said, as much to himself as anyone else. Cole turned and walked to the command chair, taking the seat. "Comms, hail the system leadership through the comms buoy, please."

Moments later, the overhead speakers chirped, and the main

viewscreen displayed a group of people arrayed out behind the interim system president.

"Yes, Mr. Coleson?" the president asked.

"Well, it seems the invasion has been averted for a time," Cole reported. "They're forming up to leave through the Dante gate."

Cole saw everyone with the system president visibly relax.

"Mr. Coleson," the system president replied, "words cannot express the debt owed to you by the people of Tristan's Gate. That you would still defend us after how your people were treated...well, I don't know many people who would do that."

Cole grinned. "Mr. President, you publicly and formally apologized for your predecessor's conduct. Your legal system has arrested, tried, and convicted the people involved for any crimes they committed. As far as I'm concerned, it's all in the past."

The president shared a look among those around him before speaking, "We have been discussing a matter we would like to bring to you, sir. The SDF is inadequate to defend against invasions, and honestly, it was never intended for that. Would you be willing to enter into negotiations for the stationing of a task force, here in Tristan's Gate?"

"What are we talking?" Cole asked. "Are you thinking something like the home fleets the Solar Republic members enjoy, or were you thinking a couple frigates and a courier?"

"We...ah...well, we hadn't gone that far in our discussions," the president replied. "We wanted to ask if you were interested in the idea, before we did any major planning or theorizing."

Cole nodded. "I can understand that. Honestly, the best thing to do is fire off a message to Paol Thyrray. He and his people handle that sort of thing for me."

"Very well," the president replied. "I can honestly say that we're very grateful you're open to discussing it. Thank you again for your defense of the system."

"You're welcome. I'll leave the comms buoy here for the time being. Its power source is good for a few hundred years at least, but I highly recommend that no one tampers with it. In the event that anyone does, the buoy will self-destruct in a rather spectacular manner."

"Oh, no, Mr. Coleson," the system president was quick to counter, "we would never presume to tamper with any of your property."

Well, at least some lessons can be learned, Cole thought as he forced his expression to remain bland and said, "All right then. That comms buoy will greatly reduce the time involved in communicating with Paol. Is there anything else, Mr. President?"

"No, I don't think so."

Cole nodded once more. "Very well. Best wishes to you and yours. We'll be heading out of the system now. Cole out."

As soon as the viewscreen deactivated and the speakers chirped, Cole ordered the battlegroup to return to Beta Magellan. They took it slow on their way to the system periphery, just in case the Coalition fleet decided to come back. After loitering for an extra day out at the periphery, the battlegroup engaged their hyperdrives and vanished from Tristan's Gate.

———

The preparations to liberate the five systems increased in tempo until they took on the feeling of running downhill. Cole recalled ten freighters—the nine that carried 'refugees' to Gateway from Tristan's Gate and one more—to Beta Magellan and sent them through the shipyard for temporary conversion to troop transports; it was faster than building the troop transports from scratch. Yes, the emissaries said their people would handle anything on the inhabited worlds, but Cole always liked to be prepared. Besides, every system had at least one station in it, and Cole wasn't going to leave the Coalition in charge of those stations.

The recruiting and training effort that had been going on for months was showing quality returns; there were sufficient marine recruits ready for service that Cole—after consulting Harlon— promoted several of *Haven*'s marines to fill out the leadership cadre throughout all troop ships. One promotion left Harlon close to spitting mad: Cole made him a general and 'promoted' him to overall strategic command of all Beta Magellan marines. One-star to start, but as the marines grew both Cole and Harlon knew Harlon was in for more stars on his shoulders. From what Cole could glean from the muttered snarls as Harlon left Cole's office, the former colonel in command of *Haven*'s marines never wanted to be a general. For that matter, Lieutenant Colonel Shandra Devereaux—Harlon's executive officer—seemed a little shocked when Cole dropped 'full colonel' and operational command of *Haven*'s marine contingent on her, too.

Admiral Trask and his staff seemed to settle in well aboard *Haven*. He was just as awed by the flag officer's official quarters as Cole was by the captain's quarters, and like Cole, he promptly took up residence in the flag-officer's day-cabin just across the corridor from the port hatch to the flag bridge. With *Haven* returned from Tristan's Gate, Admiral Trask included the battle-carrier in the simulation wargames he'd been running the op fleet through in preparation for the simultaneous liberations.

As their preparations neared completion, Cole sent a courier to Babylon Station in Gateway to retrieve the emissaries. He had decided they could accompany the task forces assigned to their respective systems after chatting with the task force commanders and ensuring the commanders understood the emissaries did not enjoy diplomatic status. When the courier returned, the fleet awaited it on the periphery of Beta Magellan. The courier moved between the task force command ships for the four systems from which they had emissaries: Oriolis, Spark, Eta Anubis, and Iota Anubis.

Cole made sure Trask understood that he had full operational command and that Cole would command *Haven* and its battlegroup. He didn't want Trask feeling weird about giving his 'boss' orders during combat.

Trask and Cole held one last fleet command conference, during which Trask outlined the staggered departure times for everyone to arrive in their target systems on the same day (and hopefully close to the same time). When Trask and Cole finished relaying the information they had to convey, Trask started the operation clock and ordered the first task force to engage its hyperdrives. Within two days, the entire fleet had vanished from Beta Magellan.

CHAPTER TWENTY-SIX

Epsilon Anubis System
   15 November 3003, 07:15 GST

Cole leaned back against the command chair and looked at the tactical plot. It was centered on the Coalition forces in the system, and the light from the arrival of *Haven*'s battlegroup hadn't yet reached the Coalition fleet or the inhabited world, Epsilon Anubis VI.

Sasha approached the command chair and stood at Cole's right elbow. Cole looked up and nodded in greeting, adding a smile as well.

"Well, there they are," Cole said. "What do you think?"

"They outnumber us," Sasha replied and turned to look at Haskell. "What's the count up to?"

"Four battleships, about twenty cruisers, thirty-six destroyers, seventeen frigates, and upwards of fifty corvettes. There's a little wobble in the numbers yet, because part of the fleet is occluded by the planet, the station, and the asteroid field."

"Corvettes? Really?" Cole asked, swiveling the command chair to direct an incredulous expression toward Haskell at Sensors.

Haskell nodded. "Yes, indeed, Cap. They have between forty and sixty corvettes. Once we get closer, we'll be able to refine the numbers."

"Well, the fighters are good for the corvettes," Cole said, swiveling back to look at the plot, "and we're almost on parity with their frigates. Our scout frigates don't have quite the weaponry the line frigates do, but I'm not worried about them taking on a Coalition frigate. Heh... one of our troop transports could probably take out one of their frigates."

"We only have four cruisers in the battlegroup, though," Sasha countered, "and eight destroyers."

Cole took a deep breath and released it as a heavy sigh. "Yeah... we're going to have to wade in with those...help clear the field a bit. When was our scout's last update? I don't remember seeing this force mix in the sensor logs they sent."

"Last night or early evening yesterday," Sasha replied.

"Huh...if I would've known about these ships, I would've added a system picket or two to the battlegroup. What are the sensor feeds from the other task forces showing?"

Sasha grinned. "You'd have to ask Admiral Trask. I don't have access to them."

Cole gave Sasha a mock frown. "Well, they're here, so we'll have to deal with them. Might as well get the party started. Mazzi, bring up the battlegroup TacNet, if you please. Wixil, please prepare maneuvering orders for the battlegroup; take us in at one-third-light."

Moments later, Mazzi reported, "TacNet online, sir!"

Not even five seconds after Mazzi, Wixil announced, "Maneuvering plan uploaded to TacNet, Cole!"

"What's our time to reach the planet?" Cole asked.

"A little over twenty-six hours and thirty minutes, Cole," Wixil replied.

"How are we passing the asteroid belt?"

"We're looping under it," Wixil answered. "I've noticed Humans seem to prefer going over things like asteroid fields."

"Fair enough," Cole said. "Let's go."

———

Around the halfway mark into the system, Cole walked onto the bridge and asked the spacer at the comms station to record for transmission as he sat in the command chair.

"You're live, sir," the tech announced.

"Greetings to the people of Epsilon Anubis. I am Bartholomew James Coleson. We are here in response to an appeal from the people of Epsilon Anubis VI, and we will be liberating this system from the abuses of the Coalition. We are currently thirteen hours out from the planet. Any ships that choose to flee will be permitted to do so. All surrenders will be accepted. Take the next six hours and decide whether or not you want to throw away your life for a government that cares nothing for you. Coleson out."

"Ready to transmit, sir," the comms tech said about forty seconds later.

Cole nodded. "Send it...no encryption across all channels and frequencies."

"Aye, sir."

Cole stood and looked to the officer of the watch, saying, "The bridge is yours."

Not quite four-and-a-half hours later, Cole's message reached the Coalition fleet...and the planet. All across Epsilon Anubis VI, the people erupted in cheers and began preparing to throw the Coalition off their world. A group of Coalition frigates tried to flee, and their own battleships promptly opened fire, wiping the frigates out of existence. Faced with that kind of fate, the remaining ships followed orders when the flag officer ordered the fleet out to meet *Haven*'s battlegroup.

————

At just a little over ninety minutes to contact, Cole examined the tactical plot as he finalized his opening formations in his mind. Their bombers had already been outfitted for missile defense, and the fighters were prepped and ready to launch.

"Centi-cred for your thoughts," Sasha said as she approached.

"This is going to be a fight," Cole replied. "Our frigates and fighters can handle their frigates and corvettes. The rest of our ships will engage their counterparts, and we'll start at the destroyers and work our way up to the battleships. I would say we just go straight for the battleships, but there are simply too many ships. We've got to whittle them down, or I'm afraid the battlegroup will get swamped."

Sasha nodded. "Good thoughts. I'm not sure even we could stand up to thirty-six destroyers pounding on our shields. Our cruisers are good, but I don't know if they're five-to-one good."

Cole frowned. "Okay. We need to salvage as many of these ships as we can...as intact and whole as possible. We'll take 'em back to Beta Magellan, repair them to full functionality, and conduct wargames to quantify just how many cruisers one of ours can take...and under what circumstances. We need to know that."

"Also good thoughts," Sasha agreed.

———

Forty minutes later, Cole nodded from his perch in the command chair and said, "Sound battle-stations, please."

The status lights on the bridge started flashing red as klaxons blared throughout the ship. He probably should've brought the ship to alert status first, but the ship and its crew would be ready long before they reached contact range.

"All ships report ready, Cap," Jenkins said.

"Very well," Cole replied. "Mazzi, are they within our powered missile range?"

"Yes, sir."

"Okay," Cole replied, nodding. "Program a fire plan. Let's take out as many of those corvettes, frigates, and destroyers as we can with missiles and torpedoes. Once we close to energy range, we'll shift to 'Spearhead.'"

"Aye, sir," Mazzi answered. Not quite five minutes later, she reported, "Fire plan ready and uploaded to TacNet."

"Fire."

One-hundred-three missiles and seventeen torpedoes erupted from *Haven*'s launchers, joining the more than seven hundred missiles and twenty torpedoes launched from the rest of the battlegroup.

"First launch complete," Mazzi said. "Flight time...six minutes and change."

"Wixil, slow us down to two-tenths-light," Cole said. "Let's give the missile and torpedo crews more time to work."

"Yes, Cole!"

"All ships report fully reloaded," Mazzi announced. "Locked onto second target group."

"Fire."

Another barrage of over eight hundred missiles and thirty-seven torpedoes erupted from the battlegroup.

"How many volleys can we manage, before we lose some birds to local control?" Cole asked.

"I can augment the ship's computer to assist with fire control, Cole," the bridge speakers broadcast Srexx's voice. "If the battlegroup could manage to launch all missiles and torpedoes, we would have the fire control links to manage them."

Cole nodded. "Fair enough. Thanks, Srexx."

"Reloaded and shifted to third target group, sir!"

Cole pointed in the air with his right index finger as he waved that hand, saying, "Fire."

When the battlegroup had five barrages in play, Cole held off launching number six. He wanted to see how effective his fire plan was as the first barrage arrived on target before he committed more to the plan.

The eight remaining frigates each caught a torpedo and simply vanished into expanding clouds of debris. The missiles took out forty of the corvettes as the remaining torpedoes bored in on the destroyers; of the twenty-nine torpedoes, twenty reached their targets, and those twenty destroyers ceased being combat-capable. In some cases, destroyers outright ceased to exist at all, as their fusion reactors burst into massive orgies of thermonuclear savagery.

By this point, the second barrage closed on its targets, ripping through the remaining sixteen destroyers and ten corvettes and leaving them to join the expanding clouds of debris trailing behind the Coalition fleet.

The third barrage encountered much more resistance. With seventeen cruisers receiving only forty missiles and two torpedoes per cruiser, plus the cruisers' much heavier point-defense batteries and the battleships joining in missile defense now, the third barrage didn't take any of the cruisers out of the fight. Damage them? Yes. In a couple cases, the torpedoes heavily damaged their target cruisers, but all of the cruisers remained combat-capable.

Then, Mazzi slowed the fourth barrage so that it would arrive on target with the fifth barrage. A little over sixteen hundred missiles and seventy-four torpedoes reduced four cruisers to expanding clouds of debris and turned the rest into drifting hulks.

Cole leaned back in the command chair and took in the destruction shown by the tactical plot.

"I don't understand it," Cole admitted. "Don't they have electronic warfare or something...anything to help defend against our missile attacks? This is worse than shooting fish in a barrel."

"To answer your question, Cole," Srexx replied, "yes, they do. However, the sensors aboard our ships are sufficiently advanced that I am able to eliminate the effectiveness of their electronic warfare. If they were even close to on par with us technologically, I calculate this battle would've been far more costly in both lives and ships."

Cole nodded. "We just have to be diligent in not becoming overconfident or warmongers. I do not want to subjugate the galaxy."

"Understood, Cole," Srexx replied. "I shall make note of that."

Cole watched the tactical plot, expecting the battleships to turn. There was still enough distance that they could deny Cole a complete victory. But no. The battleships continued their approach.

"Mazzi, prepare a fire plan. I want to launch five barrages and control their velocities so that all five reach their targets at the same time."

"Aye, sir," Mazzi replied. A little less than ninety seconds later, she announced, "Fire plan ready, sir!"

"Implement it," Cole said.

Not quite thirty minutes later, the four battleships—all that remained of the Coalition forces in Epsilon Anubis—became drifting hulks. Not even the combined destructive power of over four thousand missiles and one-hundred-eighty-five torpedoes could reduce those massive ships to expanding clouds of atoms, but those battleships would never fight again.

Cole looked at the system's new debris field on the tactical plot and fought to hold in his sigh, as he thought, *What a waste...all this destruction didn't need to happen.*

———

In the end, Cole's concerns over having to board the station were unfounded. When news of the Coalition fleet's destruction reached the planet and station, the station's commander offered Cole an unconditional surrender. Cole accepted.

The resistance forces all across Epsilon Anubis VI responded to Cole's message that he now controlled the system and surged out of hiding. The battle to free the planet began.

CHAPTER TWENTY-SEVEN

Epsilon Anubis VI
    Epsilon Anubis System
    30 November 3003, 09:47 GST

Cole, Sasha, Yeleth, Garrett, Harlon, and Admiral Trask sat around the conference table in the bridge briefing room. They directed their attention to a woman just on the cusp of middle age; she served as the liaison between Cole's people and the resistance on the planet below.

"The fighting is settling into siege tactics," the resistance liaison said. "We control all the food production, and they control most of the cities and governmental facilities. Well, perhaps it's a bit of an exaggeration to say they control the cities. A lot of their forces are concentrated in the cities, and they're beginning to learn just how unsuccessful they were at disarming the population."

"What do you need from us?" Cole asked.

The liaison shrugged. "That's difficult to answer right now. Your medical support is phenomenal. We don't have the facilities or the supplies to do more than battlefield triage, and between the field hospitals you've established and bringing the worst cases up to one of the ships...well...you've saved a lot of lives. I would say 'on both sides,' but it's funny how Coalition soldiers ask to join the resistance after their own commanders order them shot to keep them from being captured."

"I wonder if they'd be so eager to order their own people shot if they were on the receiving end," Admiral Trask mused.

The liaison shrugged again. "There's no way to know. Most of the officer corps are now true believers...for whatever reason." A momentary silence descended on the table before the liaison turned to Cole. "We've been in contact with Iota Anubis and Eta Anubis. They told us what happened with the emissary we sent to you, and we apologize for that. What became of her?"

Cole looked to Garrett and gave him a questioning expression.

"She's cooling her heels in a cell," Garrett answered. "We built a high-security prison on an asteroid in Gateway. So far, it only has one resident, but it's there if we need it."

"I suppose it's too much to ask that she's being tortured," the liaison almost muttered. "She would've ended a lot of lives if you hadn't discovered her, and I can't really say I have much sympathy for her."

"That would defeat the purpose of incarcerating her," Garrett replied. "She couldn't expose her contacts in the Coalition if she weren't in a condition to speak."

"She's talking?" the liaison gasped.

Garrett grinned. "After a fashion. We gave her a comms terminal. She refused to use it for the longest time, even after we assured her the terminal wasn't monitored. But a week or two before we finalized this op, she started sending messages back home."

The liaison frowned. "But if the terminal isn't monitored...?"

"Just because we don't monitor the terminal," Garrett answered, "doesn't mean we have no way of knowing where her messages go. Several are going home; she's been communicating with her mother and sisters a lot. But...every so often, a message or two go to a system that is otherwise uninhabited. We've flagged that system, and we'll get around to sending a scouting force once we've secured these systems."

"About that," the liaison said, turning to Cole. "The liaisons from Eta and Iota told us about their request that you establish a federation."

Cole nodded. "And your thoughts?"

The liaison let go a self-deprecating scoff. "We need it. Only a delusional fool would think we could stand on our own against the Coalition. What we don't understand, though, is what you get out of it. It's obvious that you don't need us. Why are you even open to discussing the idea of a federation?"

"That's an interesting question," Cole replied, leaning back against his seat. "You see...the first time they brought up the idea, I wanted no part of it. Up to that point, my goal was to build up and revitalize Beta Magellan. That was as far as my focus—or perhaps interest—extended. Then, the more reports about what it was like inside Coalition space came in, the more I realized someone had to do something, and given the Coalition's resources, it was unlikely that even the Solar Republic would be able to corral them. That left us. I'm not looking forward to it, and quite frankly, I wish it were not necessary. But wishing doesn't do all that much."

"The resistance leaders have discussed it," the liaison said, "and we want in. What will it take?"

Cole chuckled. "Beta Magellan doesn't even have a constitution yet, that I'm aware. Let's get your systems settled and safe, and then, we'll figure out something. I'm not really a fan of 'pay to play' governments, so at this point, I'm thinking a system joins if its people want to join. I'm sure we'll need to have some form of review process, but that's all in the future right now. Admiral Trask, status update from your side, please?"

"As you know, we lost two destroyers and five frigates across all engagements but with minimal casualties. I have read through the after-action reports, and I believe that Srexx was a deciding factor in our overwhelming success."

Chuckles went around the table.

"He usually is," Cole remarked.

Trask nodded, continuing, "At this juncture, we control the five target systems, and I recommend requesting a destroyer and five frigates from Beta Magellan to restore our combat losses. Further, I think we should release the freighters from troop transport duties and begin using them to deliver supplies...both medical and war materiel. We're the only system capable of being truly self-sufficient in regards to our extended mission of supporting the resistance, and that's only if we bring in mining crews to deliver feedstock to *Haven*'s recyclers and fabricators. Once we start getting freighters in-system, we can ferry supplies down to the planet using cargo shuttles with fighter escort." Trask frowned. "The other systems won't have the option of fighter escorts for their shuttles, so I'll recommend they use assault shuttles instead. Sir, we really need more battle-carriers if we're going to be conducting similar operations in the future."

Cole just nodded. "We need more of everything, Admiral. Most of the ships you brought to Gateway are still being recycled. That will help, but yes, we need ongoing construction and recruitment plans. Actually, what I need is for you, Admiral Sato, and Defense Minister Stone to sit down and work up a table of organization with force and staffing levels, so we have some target numbers."

"There is one matter," the liaison interjected, "I was asked to mention, but I've been reluctant to do so."

"We'll circle back around to your reluctance," Cole assured her, "but what's the matter?"

"The Coalition forces on the planet are being coordinated from a bunker in a northern mountain range. It's the most heavily defended site on the planet, and we've been unable to breach it. As long as they maintain that facility, the fighting on the planet could drag out for months, if not years."

When the liaison's voice faded and she looked down at the table-top, Cole waited. He gave her a few minutes before he spoke, "I'm guessing the resistance leaders would like us to attack the bunker?"

The liaison nodded. "Yes. I'm sorry, but it galls me that we have to ask for help to take back our own planet. We should be better than that."

Cole offered what he hoped was a reassuring smile. "Everyone needs help from time to time."

"Not you."

"Me most of all," Cole replied. "Everyone you see at this table helps me on a daily basis. Srexx helps me. The people aboard this ship help me. The people who have chosen to become citizens of Beta Magellan help me. I could not do what I do or accomplish everything I've accomplished if I were totally on my own. Prior to finding this ship, my life goal was to buy a planet and disappear; that's the most I aspired to, and I was going to use stolen funds to do it. Accepting my birthright and inheritance just allowed me to fund what these people need me to be. Now, I need to know two things: one, where is the bunker, and two, do you need it to remain intact?"

Later that day, *Haven* shifted orbit and moved to a position directly above the bunker. Cole occupied the command chair on the bridge, and the liaison stood a meter or so off his left elbow.

"Comms, record for transmission, please," Cole requested.

"You're live, sir," the spacer at Comms reported.

"May I have your attention, please? My name is Bartholomew James Coleson, and I am in orbit over your position right now, preparing a bombardment plan that will convert your bunker to a crater...or possibly a mountain lake, once the snow melts. I would much prefer that you surrender and walk out of the bunker before I level the mountain range, and I'm giving you one opportunity to do so. You have two hours from the receipt of this message before I begin our bombardment. Please, evacuate the bunker and surrender. I personally guarantee the safety of anyone who surrenders. Coleson out."

About one minute later, the comms tech announced, "Ready to transmit, sir."

Cole nodded once. "Send it."

. . .

Two hours later, Cole entered the bridge and waved off the 'Captain on the bridge' announcement. He walked to the command chair and sat. Turning to Sensors, he asked, "Any movement down there?"

"No, sir," the spacer at Sensors answered.

"Have we confirmed that they received and viewed the message?" Cole asked.

"Yes, Cole," Srexx answered via the overhead speakers. "I have accessed the bunker's logs and can show you the various timestamps where multiple people viewed your message in its entirety."

Cole took a deep breath and released it as a heavy sigh. "Well, they had their chance. Weaps, if you please, sound battle-stations – bombardment."

The bridge status lights started flashing the angry red associated with battle-stations as klaxons blared throughout the ship. Within minutes, the Alpha shift bridge crew replaced the Gamma shift, assuming their duty stations, and Cole knew that Sasha was already in Auxiliary Control.

"All decks report secured for battle-stations – bombardment," Jenkins announced from the comms station.

"Thank you, Jenkins," Cole acknowledged, then grinned. "My compliments to the first officer, if you please, Jenkins; signal her that I offer her the opportunity to push the button."

Not even thirty seconds later, Jenkins converted a laugh to a cough, reporting, "Commander Thyrray declines the offer, Cap; she says one bombardment is enough for her."

"Mazzi," Cole began, "initiate bombardment."

"Aye, sir," Mazzi replied, her fingers flying across the weapons console. "Bombardment away."

Cole thought he might—*might*—have felt a slight shudder in the deck just before Mazzi reported, but he wasn't sure. The bombardment projectiles consisted of massive warheads built inside chassis capable of penetrating no less than seven-hundred-fifty meters into a planet's crust through the hardest materials in the Gyv'Rathi database. The bunker wasn't much more than thirty to forty meters at its deepest, but Cole wanted there to be no doubt the bunker had been excised.

"Bombardment complete, sir," Mazzi reported. "The fire mission was successful. We can't see it yet from the cloud of debris ejected into the atmosphere over the site, but sensors report a fresh crater that might just end up as a lake once it cools."

Cole nodded. "Thank you, Mazzi. Stand down from battle-stations, please."

CHAPTER TWENTY-EIGHT

En Route to Beta Magellan
   11 January 3004, 18:57 GST

Haven and her battlegroup powered through hyperspace at the eighty-percent cruising speed that was the preferred 'maximum' for routine travel. They left Epsilon Anubis once a system picket arrived to take their place and the Resistance held all but a few locations on the planet. Cole still ran freighters into the five systems carrying all manner of supplies and food, just to be as sure as possible that no one starved, but as soon as Epsilon Anubis no longer needed *Haven* and its battlegroup, Cole ordered their departure.

Cole and Sasha sat at a table in one of the dining halls on the mess deck. It hadn't escaped Cole's notice that every seat within two tables of them was vacant, and Cole appreciated the crew giving them their space. He had a difficult subject to broach.

"So, I invited you to dinner to discuss something that's been on my mind," Cole said, once the dishes were set aside.

Sasha smiled. "Oh? Should I be worried?"

Cole shrugged. "I don't think so. I wanted to discuss your career plans. I'm pretty sure everyone believes war with the Coalition is inevitable at this point, so no one will be surprised when we start promoting people. You've been my first officer since before we had a crew, so as far as I'm concerned, you can have your own ship whenever you say you want one. I'm going to ask Sev, Sato, Trask, and Mattias to design build plans and training plans so that we have crew ready for each ship as soon as they come out of the shipyard. I want every system we control or with whom we're allied to have at least a system picket. When we establish that federation, we'll work our way up to every member system having a home fleet. Heh...I should probably throw Harlon in that conversation, too, because all of our ship designs have an accommodation for embarked marines. But Harlon's not here, and I think he still wants to call me bad names for making him a general. So, where do you want your career to go?"

Sasha sighed. "I...don't know. I mean, when I joined the Aurelian Commonwealth Navy, I wanted what every young officer wants: to be a flag officer held in high esteem by her peers. But now? Is it bad that I don't really want to leave *Haven*?"

Cole shook his head. "Nope. Not bad at all. Yeleth has no interest in being anything other than Ship's Purser here; I've already had a conversation with her, and Wixil is still technically a minor...if my math is right. Akyra likes it right where she is, too. Mazzi, though, I'd like to see her move into a first officer slot somewhere. I don't want her to leave *Haven*, but if you don't want your own ship, there won't be a first officer vacancy here anytime soon."

Sasha frowned and looked down at the table.

"What?" Cole asked. "What is it you're not saying right now?"

Sasha took a deep breath and lifted her eyes to meet Cole's. "I feel a little bad that I don't want to become a captain in my own right. I feel like I'm blocking the way for people to move up."

Cole scoffed. "Nonsense, and I want to be very clear about something else. If you ever decide that you do want your own command, say so. I don't operate on that business of 'refuse once, and it'll never be offered again' crap."

"Thank you. I guess I'm just not ready to leave *Haven* yet."

Just then, a text overlay appeared in Cole's field of vision alerting him to an incoming call from the bridge. Cole accessed his implant and accepted the call, choosing to route it through the dining room speakers.

"Cole here," he answered.

"Sir, a message just came in from Captain Vasquez at Babylon, and...well...it's not good."

Every head in the dining hall that Cole could see turned to look their way.

Cole chuckled and said, "You might as well give me the overview."

"Yes, sir," the bridge watch officer replied. "Captain Vasquez says about twenty ships—a mix of freighters and star liners—just arrived in Gateway. Those ships report that they came from the Duchy of Musilar, because two months ago, the Coalition made a major push and crushed the Duchy's navy and defenses in all their systems. From what he gleaned in conversation with the spokeswoman for the group, it sounded like the Duke led what was left of his navy in a 'last stand' to give these ships time to leave the Musilar system."

Sasha and Cole shared a look before Cole said, "Thanks. Could you send that message to my queue? I'm on the mess deck right now."

"Of course, sir," the bridge watch officer answered. "Will there be anything else?"

"Work up a course change for the battlegroup; I should probably visit Babylon Station to meet these refugees. Thank you. Cole out." The overhead speakers chirped to indicate the call was ended, and Cole looked to Sasha. "Want to watch the full message with me?"

Sasha nodded. "I probably should."

Cole nodded and stood. He collected their dishes and utensils onto one tray and returned them to the used dinnerware area before walking out of the dining hall with Sasha at his side.

Entering the day-cabin on Deck Three, Cole led Sasha over to the sitting area. He accessed his message queue through his implant and

instructed the sole message there to play on the viewscreen. Captain
Vasquez appeared on the viewscreen, and the message began.

"Hello, sir," Vasquez said. "We've had a development. About twelve
hours ago, twenty ships arrived in Gateway via the rim-ward jump gate,
the one that connects us to that brown dwarf system containing just a
couple of rocky planetoids. The system picket went out to meet them,
and they're broadcasting Duchy of Musilar transponders. Apparently,
they're all that's left of the Duchy. Here, I'll include the message we
received from the ships and come back after it plays."

The image on the viewscreen faded to a young woman about Cole's
age, and Sasha gasped. Even through a video message, the young
woman's entire demeanor radiated sadness and tension.

"Pause," Cole instructed and turned to Sasha. "What is it? Do you
recognize her?"

Sasha nodded, her eyes a little wide. "That's the Duke's daughter.
She would've been Duchess when her father died."

"Well, that explains the last stand," Cole replied grimly. "Resume
playback."

"Please forgive our unannounced arrival in your system," the young
woman began. "The pickets in the previous systems allowed us through
and suggested we make our course for Gateway. This collection of
freighters and passenger liners is all that remains of the free Duchy of
Musilar, and we have come to beg asylum from Mister Coleson in the
hopes of pursuing citizenship in Beta Magellan or one of his other
systems. Two months ago, the Coalition began a massive incursion into
the Duchy's space, invading the systems with overwhelming force.
Troop transports followed. By the time the invasion fleet reached
Musilar, the Duke took what remained of the Duchy's navy out to give
as many people time to flee as he could. We don't have direct information on the Duke's fate, but we presume him and all his forces to be
lost." The young woman's jaw trembled during the last statement about
the Duke, and her dark eyes glistened with moisture. "We don't have
much, but whatever we have, we will gladly pay just to have a chance at
a safe place to live. We...we have nowhere else to go."

The image of the young woman faded out, replaced by Captain
Vasquez.

"Sir, I have provisionally granted them asylum, pending your review of the matter. I'm not sure what else we can do for them at this time, beyond the basic Humanitarian stuff we do for all refugees that come here. She hasn't said so in any of her communications, but I'm pretty sure the spokeswoman for this group is the Duke's daughter and sole heir. Thank you. Vasquez out."

The viewscreen faded to black, and Cole turned to Sasha, saying, "That's why there wasn't any Coalition response to us liberating those five systems. Their focus was on the Duchy of Musilar."

"It would seem so," Sasha agreed.

Cole fell silent as he stared at the decking.

"I recognize that expression, Cole," Sasha said. "You're thinking about taking a fleet out to the Duchy, aren't you?"

Cole tried to grin, but it didn't quite make it. "You know me so well. That's exactly what I want to do...but I also know we don't have the ships or infrastructure. The last thing I can afford to do is to start a war with the Coalition before we're ready, but this infuriates me, Sasha. You have no idea how much what the Coalition has done just simply infuriates me."

"I can imagine, Cole," Sasha softly replied.

"Computer," Cole said, "record a message for transmission; save it as 'Musilar Refugee Welcome.'"

"Ready," the ship's computer replied.

"Hello, I'm Bartholomew James Coleson. First off, allow me to express my sympathies for the loss of your homes. Captain Vasquez tells me he provisionally granted you asylum, and I'm removing the provisional status. All of you are welcome to pursue Beta Magellan citizenship. I am currently returning to Beta Magellan, but as soon as Captain Vasquez's message arrived—which included your message as well—I altered course for Gateway. I don't have an ETA at this moment, but I would like to speak with you at a time convenient for you once I arrive. Don't worry; Captain Vasquez and his people will take good care of you and yours. Coleson out."

"Message saved," the ship's computer reported.

"Computer, record a new message," Cole said without missing a beat, "and save it as 'Message to Captain Vasquez.'"

"Ready," the ship's computer responded.

"Captain Vasquez, thank you for alerting me to the arrival of the refugees. Your message caught us a few days out of Epsilon Anubis, and I've already ordered the battlegroup to alter course for Gateway. I'm not sure of our estimated arrival time at the moment, but I'm coming to speak with the refugee leadership. I imagine Garrett will want to interview several of the refugees himself, as well. I'm attaching a message I'd like forwarded to the refugee spokeswoman, please. See you when we make port. Cole out."

"Message saved," the ship's computer intoned.

"Computer, attach 'Musilar Refugee Welcome' message to 'Message to Captain Vasquez', and send it to Captain Vasquez at Babylon Station."

Moments later, the computer returned, "Message with attachment sent."

"Thank you, computer." Cole turned to Sasha. "I'm making the correct choice, right? In not charging off on a mission of liberation to Musilar?"

Sasha slowly nodded. "As much as I'd like to join you on that mission, yes, we can't do anything right now beyond welcome those refugees and give a safe home to any who want one with us and pass the interview."

Cole nodded and more collapsed than flopped into one of the nearby armchairs. "I hate this feeling of wanting to act—almost needing to act—and not being able to do so. It doesn't sit well with me."

"It never sits well with anyone, Cole," Sasha replied, "not that I've seen, anyway. But I should probably let you relax if you can." Sasha stood and walked to the hatch, which irised open for her. She stopped and turned back. "See you on the bridge in the morning."

Cole nodded. "See you in the morning."

CHAPTER TWENTY-NINE

Babylon Station
Gateway
15 January 3004, 09:18 GST

Cole and Sasha walked with Captain Vasquez through the spaces set aside for newly arrived refugees. Sorrow and loss permeated the space like an invisible fog; Cole could count on one hand the number of smiles he saw. He made a point of exchanging a few words of welcome and well wishes with each person who reacted to his presence, and as they neared the hatch once again, Cole stopped and looked back over the large compartment, then turned to Vasquez.

"Captain, whatever they need—clothes, food, toys or sweets for the children, *whatever* they need—see that they have it, and send me the bill. Don't take it out of the regular refugee funds. You don't have to make a big deal of it, but I want these people to feel warm, safe, and welcome."

Vasquez nodded once. "Yes, sir. I'll see to it myself."

Cole turned and approached the hatch, which irised open. Red the Igthon fell into step behind the trio as they moved down the corridor.

. . .

A ten-minute walk delivered them to the conference room where Cole would be meeting with the refugee leadership. Entering, Cole saw Garrett already occupying a chair, and the old friends exchanged nods.

Cole had just enough time to get comfortable when the conference room hatch opened to admit the woman Cole had seen in the message, leading two other people he didn't know. Cole stood, prompting the others seated to do so, and extended his hand.

"Hello. Please, call me Cole. This is my first officer, Sasha Thyrray, and my...well...foreign intelligence advisor, Garrett. I believe you know Captain Vasquez. The Igthon in the corner is Red; forgive me for not introducing him by his proper name, but he swears Humans can't speak it."

The young woman gave him a respectable handshake, saying, "Thank you. I'm Victoria Rainier, and yes, my father was the Duke. The gentleman on my left is Jameson Mayweather, and the lady on my right is Beth Liu."

"It's nice to meet you," Cole responded, "though the circumstances could be much better. Please, be seated."

Everyone sat (except for Red), and Cole leaned forward, resting his forearms on the edge of the table and interlacing his fingers.

"I have people seeing to your various needs," Cole said, "and I understand the infirmary is tending a number of wounded or ill."

Victoria returned a half-smile. "Thank you, but I don't know how we can pay—"

"'Pay' is not a word that has any place in this discussion," Cole countered. "You and your people have lost a lot, and you'll have what you need to get your feet under you. Beta Magellan alone has about one-point-five jobs per person at this point, and we have other systems in need of people as well."

Some of the tension left Victoria's shoulders, and she nodded. "I... thank you. We didn't have a lot of time to pack before we left...but so many other people didn't even have the opportunity to flee." Her expression was bleak.

"I understand," Cole replied. "We don't have the resources right now—mainly ships and people—but as soon as we do, we're taking the fight to the Coalition. If they're not stopped, they'll just keep invading systems and brutalizing people, and I for one refuse to stand for it. We're not ready, not *quite* yet, but we're building toward that goal."

"I daresay you'll have quite a few volunteers from my people when you put out the call," Victoria said. "I lost count of the people aboard our ships wanting to take the fight to the Coalition...which isn't all that easy to do when you have nothing but unarmed freighters and passenger liners."

Cole shrugged. "It would certainly make for a challenge, if nothing else. Among your group, are there any specific needs you know of, beyond the basics like food, clothing, shelter, and diversions for the children?"

"I don't believe so," Victoria answered. "I...I just do not have the words to thank you for the welcome and hospitality we've been given. We'd heard Beta Magellan was receptive to refugees, but 'receptive' can mean a great many things."

Cole tried offering a smile, but the childhood memory of a burning colony tinged the smile with sorrow. "I know very well what it's like to be cast adrift in an uncaring galaxy, and as long as I am alive, good people who think they have nowhere to go *will* have somewhere to go. Now...as your people pass the interview process, we'll set them up with a local family that will help them get accustomed to life in Beta Magellan, or wherever they choose to settle. Everyone you meet in Beta Magellan—with one or two possible exceptions—was a refugee once; they know very well what you've faced, and they'll help you and your people start over."

"What about Gateway?" Beth Liu asked. "Isn't everyone here a former refugee, too?"

"Not necessarily," Cole answered. "You see, Gateway is our public port, for lack of a better term. At the moment, Beta Magellan is a closed system, and only people who've passed our interview process are permitted there for the long term...except for a few specific and temporary cases. Beta Magellan is the refuge, you see. It is the place of ultimate safety where people can rebuild their lives until such time as they want to live somewhere else, if they ever decide to move. The system can support well into the multiple billions, population-wise, so there's no reason yet for anyone to feel crowded."

"But couldn't someone just blitz past the station and use the jump gate into Beta Magellan?" Mayweather asked.

Cole nodded. "Yes, that's true, but until that kind of thing becomes a problem, I won't start locking down the gate here in Gateway. Besides, the jump gate forts are rather impressive. Even if someone did blitz through the gate, they couldn't get outside the range of the fort in Beta Magellan before the fort could reduce them to atoms, assuming of course they refused to stop and explain themselves."

"I didn't realize it was possible to lock down a jump gate," Victoria remarked.

Cole offered a slight shrug. "It isn't for the general public, but I own the jump gates."

"You own..." Beth's voice trailed off as her lips formed an almost-perfect 'o.' "Coleson as in Coleson Interstellar Engineering?"

Cole nodded. "Yes, that's me."

For a few heartbeats, Beth looked like she might faint.

"Sorry," Victoria said, little more than a whisper as she put her arm around Beth.

Cole waved it off. "Don't worry about it. I get that reaction a lot, honestly. Do you have any questions or concerns?"

"I have more concerns than I can count, but you or your people are seeing to many of them," Victoria replied. "Questions, though...no, not at the moment."

"Okay, then. We've covered everything I wanted to discuss. If something arises, see Captain Vasquez for whatever you need. We'll get through the interviews as quickly as possible, so your people can get ground beneath them and sky over them again."

"Thank you again. You have no idea how much this means to us."

Cole stood, and everyone else did as well. Cole shook hands with Victoria once more and nodded, saying, "You're welcome, and if you need me, Captain Vasquez can contact me."

Captain Vasquez took the initiative to escort Victoria and her people out of the conference room. Cole waited long enough for them to get a few meters down the corridor, before he, Sasha, and Red returned to *Haven*.

————

Cole's Apartment
    Citadel Station
    Beta Magellan
    25 January 3004, 17:35 GST

The hatch chime announced the arrival of Cole's guest, and he took a deep breath to steady his nerves before he walked to the hatch. When he neared it, the hatch irised open to reveal Sasha. Like Cole, Sasha wore casual 'civvies,' and not the ship-suits they usually wore aboard *Haven*, and Cole smiled in greeting.

"Hi. Thanks for coming," Cole said as he invited Sasha inside.

Sasha stepped into Cole's apartment and walked with him over to the sitting area, where she accepted Cole's invitation to be comfortable.

"You said you wanted to discuss something that had been on your mind a few days?" Sasha asked as she leaned back against the sofa.

Cole nodded. He sat in an armchair facing her across a coffee table, and he leaned forward, resting his elbows on his knees. "Yes. Scarlett had a chat with me on the way to Baldur, and I probably should've done something about it by now. But there have been so many things happening, and to be honest, it was easier to push it to the back of my mind." For just the briefest of moments, Cole thought he saw Sasha's breath catch. "The thing is, seeing those refugees from the Duchy really drove home that we're never guaranteed tomorrow; you'd think I'd be better acquainted with that concept, but there we are. Sasha, forgive me; I feel like I'm rambling. I...I want to ask you out on a date. Are you okay with me asking you out?"

Sasha sat swiftly upright, her eyes going wide, and her left hand flew up to cover her mouth.

Uh oh, Cole thought as he fought to keep his expression bland. *This isn't going well. I should've kept my mouth shut, and for that matter so should have Scarlett!*

"What..." Sasha's voice started out almost as a whisper but she stopped and took a deep breath. "What about *Haven*? I mean...I'm the first officer, and you're the captain. What kind of image is that going to present, and what happens when more people start dating on the ship?"

Cole shrugged. "I'm not sure if you've noticed, but I've specifically refused to include any regulations against dating on the ship. We have regs against rape and sexual assault, of course, but nothing about two consenting people deciding they want to try for a relationship. You know what...you're right. Hang on a sec." Cole accessed his implant and initiated a call to Srexx, routing the call through the apartment's audio system. The speakers immediately chirped to indicate a connected call.

"Yes, Cole?" Srexx answered.

"Srexx, buddy, may I ask a favor of you?" Cole said.

"Of course, Cole."

"Please remind me tomorrow to make a clarification to the regulations for the fleet. If it isn't expressly spelled out somewhere, I want to add a regulation stating that romantic relationships aboard ships are one-hundred-percent permitted, with the provision that one or both parties will be transferred off the ship if their conduct or relationship affects performance in any way."

"I shall remind you of that tomorrow," Srexx said, "but I can inform you now that no such regulation exists in the current document you have posted as fleet-wide regulations."

"Thank you, Srexx; I appreciate your help. Cole out." The speakers chirped again and Cole turned his attention back to Sasha, saying, "Sasha, I don't want you feeling like you have to accept, and if I've crossed a line, please tell me. Think it over, and let me know. There's no time limit on the question. I just—"

"Yes," Sasha said, nearly blurting it out.

When no further clarification seemed forthcoming, Cole lifted his eyebrows as he asked, "May I ask 'yes' in what respect?"

Sasha blinked. Cole thought he noticed her cheeks blush a bit, but she rallied, saying, "Yes, I'd like that date."

Cole fought once more to keep his expression neutral, but a smile did escape his control. "You would?"

————

Twenty minutes and some nervous conversation (on both sides) later, Sasha left Cole's apartment with a dinner date planned for two evenings hence. She managed to keep her expression neutral until she reached her own apartment, whereupon she immediately called her sister and said they needed to talk.

"We need to talk?" Talia asked. "Everything okay, Soosh?"

"Yes," Sasha answered with a broad smile on her face. "Cole asked me on a date!"

Talia was working a shift on the hospital deck when she received an incoming call request from her sister. Not giving it a second thought, she accepted the call. Fewer than ninety seconds later, everyone in the ward turned to look when Talia erupted in an excited squeal and pumped her fist in the air.

CHAPTER THIRTY

Cole's Apartment
  Citadel Station
  Beta Magellan
  26 January 3004, 05:37 GST

Cole rubbed his eyes as he staggered to the hatch. Someone was ringing the hatch chime like there was no tomorrow. As he neared his destination, Cole heaved a huge yawn and was barely finishing it when the sensors detected him and opened the hatch. Garrett stood in the corridor.

"Garrett," Cole said, "you're my oldest friend, but what in all the stars could've possessed you to ring my hatch chime at this hour?"

"The Duke of Musilar is still alive."

Cole blinked, instantly fully awake, and almost pulled Garrett into his apartment. "He is? You're sure?"

"The Coalition has publicized the Duke's upcoming execution, and I have people in the prison where he's being held," Garrett explained as they sat. "They smuggled out DNA confirmation that the person being held for execution is indeed the Duke."

"When's the execution?"

Garrett grimaced. "That's the problem...eight days."

Cole accessed his implant and called Srexx, routing the call through the apartment's audio system.

"Yes, Cole?" Srexx answered.

"The Musilar system," Cole said. "How soon could we be there at maximum on the hyperdrive?"

"One moment..." After no more than three seconds of silence, Srexx continued, "Three days, eighteen hours, and...well...the remainder is so small that it is not relevant for your answer."

Cole turned back to Garrett. "You are absolutely certain the execution isn't for eight days?"

Garrett nodded. "Yes. The new governor in the system is planning a big show in the former capital. The Duke, his admiral, and several others are all scheduled for execution at the same time. They want as many people to see it as possible; they're wanting it to be a demoralizing event. Help drive home that the Duchy is no more."

"Not if I can help it," Cole replied, almost a growl. "Srexx, if you please, issue an emergency recall of all personnel for the battlegroup and the two system pickets we brought back from those five systems."

"Yes, Cole."

"Garrett, get anything you need for the trip," Cole said as he almost jogged to his sleeping quarters.

"I'm ready to go," Garrett said as he waited on Cole to change out of his sleeping clothes.

Cole hopped out of his sleeping quarters in his boxer-briefs, in the process of pulling on his pants. A shirt hung across one shoulder.

"My, my," Garrett remarked. "Imagine if Sasha could see you now."

Cole stopped, almost mid-hop with his right leg lifted to slide into his pants. "Not funny, Garrett. Really not funny."

"Oh, don't be a fuss-budget. Everyone has been waiting to see if you'd ever figure out that she has a serious thing for you."

Cole finished donning his pants and pulled on his shirt, then started hunting for his shoes. "Well, make it known that I don't care who ribs me about it, but the first person to say anything flippant about Sasha won't appreciate my response...not one bit."

"Everyone will think you'll blackball them if you leave it like that," Garrett remarked.

Cole grabbed his shoes and flopped on the sofa beside Garrett and started pulling them on and tying them. "Heh...fine. You can let it be known that I'm not so far removed from Jax Theedlow that I won't take someone down to the flight deck and kick his ass from the bow to the stern if he says anything nasty about Sasha, and you've seen me fight, Garrett."

"Yes," Garrett replied. "Yes, I have. And if the offender is a woman?"

Cole finished tying his shoes and stood. "You ready?"

Garrett stood as well and nodded. "Let's go."

Cole led the way to the hatch, saying, "If the speaker of the rude comment is a woman...well...I'll just offer the use of my flight deck to Sasha."

Bridge Briefing Room, *Haven*
Beta Magellan
26 January 3004, 07:45 GST

Cole, Sasha, Emily, Harlon, Yeleth, Red, and Garrett occupied their usual places around the table. Joining them were Admiral Trask (also seated at the table) and Admiral Sato, Painter, Sev, Paol, and Mattias Stone via holo-call.

"Apologies for the early morning, people," Cole said, "but Garrett woke me up with news I feel we have to act on. The Duke of Musilar is alive, as are a number of his closest advisors and officers. They are scheduled for execution in eight days, and we can be there in three days and eighteen hours. I'm advocating we go get them. Right, then. So, someone talk me out of this, or I'm giving the departure order."

"Could this be some kind of elaborate trap, after the drubbing we gave them in those five systems?" Admiral Trask asked.

"Good question," Garrett said, "and no, I don't believe it is. At least not in the sense that the Duke and his people won't actually be executed if we don't show up. What Cole has never actively mentioned is that I am—for all intents and purposes—his Head of Intelligence. I have a rather impressive network of informants and dead-drops, and one of those informants works in the prison where the Duke and his people are incarcerated. The person smuggled out multi-factor, biometric verification that the person awaiting execution is indeed the Duke of Musilar. I have confirmation on the identities of the others as well. Now, full disclosure...the Coalition has a considerable fleet presence in Musilar as well."

Garrett tapped a few commands into the conference table, and a hologram appeared above the table's center. It was the system scan for Musilar as of three days before.

"That..." Admiral Trask said "...is a lot of ships. Two dreadnoughts, eight battleships, nineteen cruisers, twenty-five destroyers, and fifty-six frigates." Trask turned to look at Cole. "What are you planning to take in there?"

"*Haven*'s battlegroup," Cole answered, "and the two system pickets that followed us home after our most recent op."

Trask turned back to the hologram, his expression thoughtful. Then, he brought his attention back to Cole, saying, "Okay. That could work."

"What kind of information do you have on the prison facility?" Harlon asked.

Garrett just leaned back against his seat. "I have floorplans with guard posts highlighted."

"Want to help me plan an extraction by force?" Harlon asked.

Garrett smiled. "Love to."

Cole surveyed by sight everyone around the table. "Okay. If no one is going to say this is a bad idea, we need to get moving. We'll send a scout frigate ahead of us to recon the system under full stealth, but unless something's radically different than what that system scan shows, I'm planning on blitzing into the system close enough to launch the extraction teams and then blast away at every ship in range until the teams return. Thoughts?"

"We'll refine that a bit over the next couple of days," Trask said, "but as a framework, it's not too bad."

Cole nodded. "Okay, then. Let's get going. Thank you, everyone."

Everyone stood up from the table, except Cole. As the others filed out of the briefing room, Cole said, "Sasha, a word please?"

Sasha resumed her seat.

Once the hatch closed with Cole and Sasha the only people still in the briefing room, Cole said, "I hope we can still continue with our dinner plans, as long as you don't mind having dinner aboard the ship."

Sasha smiled. "I'm okay with that."

Cole sighed his relief. "Good. I was worried that if I rescheduled, you might think I was afraid of our date or something like that. Don't get me wrong; I am a little nervous about the date, but I'm glad I asked and glad you said 'yes.'"

Sasha sat in silence, holding eye contact with Cole for several seconds. Then she stood and took the few steps necessary to reach him. After one moment of appraisal, she leaned in and kissed him full on the lips. When she finally decided to give him a break, she inclined her head close to his left ear and whispered, "Don't worry, flyboy; you can run, but you can't hide."

Then she pulled back, gave him a wink, and left the briefing room.

CHAPTER THIRTY-ONE

System Periphery
    Musilar System
    30 January 3004, 13:05 GST

Cole stood with Admiral Trask. It was the first time he'd ever been inside the flag bridge, and the space was subtly different enough from Cole's bridge that he had a twitch between his shoulder blades. Trask's staff occupied various stations around the compartment.

The flag plot looked very similar to the tactical plot Cole was used to seeing. The core differences seemed to be more detailed ship vectors and different coloring for range increments, but Cole supposed the different coloring could have just been Trask's preference.

"That," Trask said, "is a lot more ships."

The current focus of the two officers was the mass of ships near Musilar's sole inhabited planet, Musilar Prime. Instead of the forces reported by Garrett's informant, there were now *five* dreadnoughts and fifteen more cruisers, bringing that total up to a whopping thirty-five.

Cole nodded. "Yeah...more ships arrived from somewhere." One specific ship-code drew Cole's attention. Cole reached up and zoomed in on the plot to get a better look at the ship. It was a dreadnought, by all appearances the same as the other four near Musilar Prime, but when Cole zoomed in, the ship's transponder data appeared in the space beside the ship-code. The ship's transponder squawked a ship name of *Coalition Alpha*. "Oh, holy crap."

"Holy crap, indeed," Trask remarked.

"Garrett has never been able to identify the capital for the Coalition," Cole said. "I want to get Srexx within easy comms range of that monster."

Trask heaved a deep breath and shook his head slowly, saying, "Cole, I understand this operation is important to you...and not just you, to so many other people as well. But the presence of those ships changes things. We were at near parity before, between the two system pickets and the battlegroup versus their ships. There is now an additional dreadnought and fifteen more cruisers. I'm no longer certain this is a fight we can walk away from, let alone win...certainly not using the blitz-in/blitz-out plan."

Cole frowned. "How soon until they see us?"

"Ah," Trask vocalized as he scanned the flag plot for their current distance, "I'd guess ten hours, plus or minus."

"If I may," Srexx interjected, "we are sixty-eight AUs from the near-planet space. It will take approximately nine-point-four-three hours for the light of our arrival to reach Musilar Prime."

"What if we blitz to what is our extreme missile range," Cole began, "and launch the extraction teams under full stealth? We wouldn't be in a position of overwatch, but we should be able to pull the fleet orbiting the planet out to meet us."

"Why would they care that we're out there?" Trask asked. "What would they gain from coming out to meet us? Every engagement they have forced with you has been an overwhelming, embarrassing defeat for them. Did they not decline battle in Tristan's Gate the last time?"

"Yes," Cole replied, "but they have us decisively outnumbered in capital ships and cruisers. Wouldn't they want to take the chance that they could kill me or capture some tech they could reverse-engineer?"

"What if that *Coalition Alpha* dreadnought high-tails it for a jump gate?" Trask countered.

"So, we position a scout frigate under full stealth to get close enough to act as a relay for Srexx," Cole replied. "Oh, that's a good idea. One sec..."

Cole accessed his implant and sent orders to one of the scout frigates in *Haven*'s battlegroup to go to full stealth immediately and maintain it until further notice.

"Sorry," Cole said. "I just ordered one of the scout frigates in the battlegroup to go to full stealth."

Trask merely nodded, still focused on the flag plot.

"We still don't have reliable data on just how many ships of an equivalent class one of our ships can defeat," the admiral said after a few more seconds, "and now is certainly not the time to try and find out. I still think we should pull back. Yes...the Duke's execution would be a huge morale victory for the Coalition and a major blow to whatever resistance remains, but I simply do not think we can survive attempting this against the Coalition forces currently in-system."

Cole nodded. "Okay. I'm going to take a walk and think on this."

———

Cole stood in the center of the unused Captain's Quarters on Deck One. Each bulkhead around him displayed silent live holos of the dining halls on the mess deck. He took in the laughing, boisterous ambiance of the dining halls, drinking in the sheer vibrancy of his people as he wrestled with the decision he faced.

Cole turned when the hatch behind him irised open, and he smiled when Sasha walked inside. She approached and stopped at his side.

"You've been off-comms for a while now," Sasha said. "No one could find you, but I appealed to Srexx. You have a few people worried."

Cole nodded his understanding of her statement but said nothing.

"So, care to tell a girl what's on your mind?"

"'But if these men do not die well, it will be a black matter for the king that led them to it,'" Cole answered.

"That sounded like a quote," Sasha commented.

Cole nodded again. "It's from a fifteen-hundred-year-old play, give or take on the fifteen-hundred years. The playwright is one of the most well-known figures in Human literature across the ages."

"Okay. So, what has you thinking about men not dying well? That's kind of sexist, by the way. Women are just as capable of not dying well, too, you know."

"Not back when the play was written," Cole replied. "It wasn't until the mid-2000's—somewhere between 2000 and 2050—that women started being accepted in actual combat units across most militaries, and the play was already centuries old by then."

"All right. You've dodged my question very well and for long enough. What has you contemplating people not dying well?"

Cole took a deep breath and heaved it out as a sigh. "There are five dreadnoughts and fifteen more cruisers in the system now. Trask thinks we should bug out like we were never here."

"And what do you think?"

"I think, if we bug out, one more person is going to lose a parent far sooner than they should. It's nothing I can put my finger on, but I know—not just think, *know*—we can pull this off. We can rescue the Duke and his people scheduled for execution. But at what cost? And is this cause just and good?"

All at once, Sasha knew the source of the doubt that plagued Cole. She knew it as certainly as she knew her own name.

"You've never lost anyone in combat, have you? You've never been in a situation where people under your command died because they were following your orders."

Cole shook his head. "No matter what I do, people who shouldn't are going to die."

"*Haven*," Sasha said, "turn off all visual feeds."

The holograms disappeared, and Sasha walked around to look Cole right in his eyes.

"Cole, you need to understand something, and you need to make it a part of you. The sooner, the better. People *will* die because of orders you give. You've been uncannily lucky so far, but it's not a question of 'if.'"

"It's a question of 'when.'"

Sasha nodded, continuing, "Exactly, and you can't be the captain and leader everyone needs you to be until you come to terms with that. Now, I'm not saying forget about them or that their deaths don't matter. I've lost people under my command, and I still remember their names…every single one. And yes…I have moments where I wonder if I did everything I could've done, and so will you. And you're going to make mistakes. You might as well accept that right now, too." Sasha heaved a sigh. "In the long run, there are just two things you can do: first, do everything you can to make sure the cause your people fight and die for is just, honorable, and good; second, do everything you can to ensure you never make the same mistake twice. So…you tell me this, Cole; is saving the lives of those nine people a good cause, a worthy cause?"

"It is to me," Cole answered.

"Then, where you lead, we will follow."

Cole saw the truth of her words in Sasha's expression. He held her gaze for quite some time before he nodded.

"Okay," Cole said at last. "Let's do this."

———

Admiral Trask led his chief of staff and tactical officer into the bridge briefing room and found Cole, Sasha, Harlon, Emily, Mazzi, and Garrett waiting. A hologram looking similar to the tactical or flag plots hovered above the conference table. When Trask didn't move after a brief moment, Cole invited him to sit with a gesture.

Trask stepped to the table and chose a seat, his officers following him. As he sat, he scanned the faces around the table and knew what he was about to hear.

"You want to go ahead with the op," Trask said, making it a statement instead of a question.

Cole nodded. "I can't shake the conclusion that it is the right thing to do. I understand everything you said on the flag bridge, Admiral; I truly do. But I believe the chance to extract the Duke and his people is worth the risks we'll have to take."

"And are you prepared for the casualties we'll probably take making the attempt?" Trask asked.

"No...probably not," Cole answered, "but I won't come apart on you during the op. That much, I can promise you."

Trask held Cole's gaze in silence for almost a full minute before he scanned the other faces arrayed around the conference table. After what seemed like an eternity, he nodded once and said, "Then let's plan this out."

Over the next few hours, they developed a strategy everyone in the briefing room believed offered the best chances for success. It was based on Cole's suggestion of blitzing into missile range and lobbing shots into the Coalition fleet to serve as a distraction for the fighters and assault shuttles being launched under full stealth. Once the assault shuttles were close enough, Srexx would use them as a relay to attack the planet's sensor grid. The stealthed scout frigate was already moving into a position where Srexx could use its quantum comms to hack *Coalition Alpha* for any information he could glean. The fighters escorting the assault shuttles would carry armaments for both air-to-air and air-to-surface engagements, and Emily would finally have the opportunity to use her bombers in a missile defense role.

"Oh," Cole said, "here's a thought."

Everyone turned to look at him.

"What if we arrange some of our ships in a hemisphere under full stealth? The Coalition forces wouldn't be able to see them, and they'd charge *Haven*. Once they were in the trap, the extended ships would drop stealth and attack the Coalition's flanks."

Trask's tactical officer quirked an eyebrow. "Battle of Cannae?"

Cole shrugged. "It's an idea."

"Under the proper circumstances," Trask replied, as he looked at the plot, "it could work. But I think we're going to have enough of a fight on our hands as it is."

Cole nodded. "Fair enough."

Trask broke into a grin. "I've always wanted to try it, too...just never found the right circumstances outside of a wargame."

"Oh, you tried it in a wargame?" Cole asked.

Trask nodded.

"Then we don't want to try it here," Cole countered. "We have to assume they have those records from the Commonwealth Navy."

"Ah, yes," Trask agreed. "I hadn't considered that. Perhaps Sato would've been a better flag officer for this mission."

Cole made a dismissive wave. "That ship has sailed. Let's do the best we can with what we have."

After a little more discussion, they concluded their formulations and distributed a maneuvering plan to the fleet. Moments later, the ships engaged their sublight engines, ramping up to ninety-seven-percent of light-speed. They'd need just a little over nine hours and twenty minutes to reach their extreme missile range.

CHAPTER THIRTY-TWO

Musilar System
30 January 3004, 22:37 GST

The fleet was at battle-stations. TacNet connected the tactical systems of the fleet. The extraction teams traveled to Musilar Prime, under max stealth. All of *Haven*'s bombers led the fleet, loaded for missile defense. The Coalition fleet was coming out to meet them, including *Coalition Alpha*. The stealthed scout frigate trailed the fleet, providing Srexx a relay through which to peruse the datanet of *Coalition Alpha*.

"The lead elements of the Coalition fleet are within missile range," Mazzi announced.

"Message from Admiral Trask," Jenkins at Comms reported. "He says, 'We go on your order.'"

Cole nodded. "Mazzi, missiles and torpedoes...fire."

One-hundred-three missiles and seventeen torpedoes from *Haven* soon became over two thousand missiles and fifty torpedoes, as the rest of the fleet launched. Cole watched the cloud of dots move toward the oncoming ships and waited.

"All launchers reloaded," Mazzi reported. "Next target group selected."

"Fire," Cole replied.

The cycle repeated until five barrages were in flight. Like Epsilon Anubis, Cole wanted to see what the effect was before he sent more. Cole was watching the tactical plot when a veritable fog of dots appeared around the Coalition fleet.

"Missile launch!" Mazzi announced. "Twelve thousand—repeat: one-two-zero-zero-zero—birds inbound! Flight time estimated at twenty minutes."

"Quantity is a quality all its own," Cole muttered as he watched the dots representing the Coalition missiles move beyond the Coalition lines on the tactical plot.

"Fleet-wide orders from the flag," Jenkins reported. "Coordinate missile defense through TacNet."

Cole chuckled. "Well, of course. That's half its purpose."

"Was that a reply, Cap?" Jenkins asked.

Cole swiveled and found the senior comms officer grinning unrepentantly. Cole gave him a mock glare and swiveled back to the tactical plot.

By now, their opening salvoes started eating into the Coalition fleet. Frigates and destroyers fell by the wayside, if they weren't destroyed outright, and their formation was starting to develop a concave depression on its forward edge.

"Jenkins, my compliments to Admiral Trask, if you please; ask him to signal the fleet for another five missile barrages, targeting the same area but ships deeper into the formation this time," Cole said.

Jenkins replied, "Aye, Cap! Reply from the admiral: I've never had my flag captain sign my paychecks before."

Cole laughed.

"Orders going out fleet-wide, Cap," Jenkins continued. "Five more missile barrages, same area targeted but ships deeper into the formation; *Haven* leads."

"Ready, sir," Mazzi reported.

"Fire," Cole said.

Cole's fleet cycled four more launches before the Coalition missiles reached interception range.

"Bombers launching interceptors," Flight Ops reported.

Cole watched the count of incoming missiles drop as the bomber-fired interceptors did their jobs. One of the Coalition missiles took a near-miss that damaged its guidance and target-acquisition platform; it curly-cued for several seconds before nose-diving onto one of the bombers. Both the damaged missile and the bomber vanished into a cloud of expanding particles.

"Bomber Bravo-Two down!" Flight Ops reported. "All remaining bombers reporting dry launchers."

"Bring them back for reloads," Cole said.

"Interceptors launching," Mazzi reported, and Cole watched the count of incoming missiles start dropping again. Then, she said, "Point-defense batteries firing."

It wasn't enough.

All along his fleet's line, missiles detonated against shields. Some ships took enough missiles that their forward shields failed. Cole zoomed in on the tactical plot, watching the icons for his ships flash amber. The icons remained a solid amber if the ship it represented took actual damage and not just against the shields, and several of the icons for his ships were solid amber now.

Cole looked at *Haven*'s stats in the upper-right corner of the tactical plot. Outer shield layer at seventy percent. Shield Layer Two at ninety percent. No physical damage, and only one bomber lost.

More dots appeared on the tactical plot around the Coalition fleet.

"Missile launch!" Mazzi announced. "Eight thousand—repeat: eight-zero-zero-zero—birds inbound. Flight time approximately fifteen minutes."

"Srexx," Cole said, "how are you and the computer aboard *Coalition Alpha* getting along?"

"Very well, Cole," Srexx replied via the bridge's overhead speakers. "Is there any specific data you prefer I prioritize?"

"Yes, please," Cole answered. "Get the navigation logs. I want to know where the Coalition capital is."

"I shall focus on that data at once," Srexx agreed.

"Thanks, buddy."

As the Coalition missiles closed in on Cole's fleet, Cole watched his fleet's missiles reach their targets. More Coalition ships flickered and dropped off the tactical plot, and the formation that had once been almost a globe now looked very much like a skull with vampire fangs. The tail of the last barrage chipped away at a couple of cruisers, and Cole was debating his next recommendation for targeting when the Coalition missiles arrived.

"Point-defense batteries firing!" Mazzi announced.

Cole glanced at the plot and watched missiles vanish in puffs of pixelation. Then, the icons for his ships started flickering as the remaining missiles pounded their targets. These Gyv'Rathi ships could take a beating, though, and still be combat-capable. Whether unlucky or just in the wrong place, one destroyer took the brunt of more than its fair share of missiles, and Cole watched its icon flicker between amber and red.

"The destroyer *Argyle* reports it is launching life pods," Jenkins reported.

Cole zoomed in on the destroyer icon flickering from amber to red and back, seeing it was indeed the *Argyle*. A cloud of dots already surrounded it, those dots moving to the next closest ships.

"Cap," Haskell said, "something's happening with the *Argyle*."

Cole watched the plot as the *Argyle*'s icon moved out of its position and headed for the Coalition fleet, ramping up speed.

"Cole," Srexx said, "I am uploading a command script to the helm console. That script needs to be distributed to the fleet and activated at once."

Cole's trust of Srexx was so absolute that he didn't even hesitate, saying, "Wixil, do it. Srexx, what does the script do?"

"It will protect you," Srexx replied. "The core aboard the *Argyle* is failing containment."

Cole frowned. Ship cores lost containment all the time. Why would...oh. Cole's ships used *singularity* cores.

"Are you saying we're about to have an unrestrained black hole in our immediate vicinity?" Cole asked.

"Yes," Srexx replied.

"I have the script ready to execute, Cole," Wixil reported. "It looks like it does something with the hyperdrive."

"It does," Srexx agreed. "The script will activate the hyperdrive without propulsive effect during the time the *Argyle*'s core fails containment, remaining thus until the core fully collapses. Normally, activating the hyperdrive this far into the gravity well of a star system would have deleterious effects, but—"

"Forgive me, Srexx," Cole interrupted. "Lecture later, please. Are those life pods safely aboard ships?"

"The cruiser *Leonidas* just picked up the last dozen, Cap," Haskell reported.

"Jenkins, fleet-wide comms, emergency priority: run Srexx's script now. Make sure our stealthed scout frigate is included. Wixil, do it."

Cole watched the icons of his ships partially fade out of the tactical plot; the *Argyle*'s data code reached the periphery of the Coalition formation just as its containment failed. Klaxons blared throughout the ship as the sensors reported a Class VIII singularity less than five light-minutes away; the massive singularity at the center of the Milky Way was only a Class V.

Cole zoomed in the tactical plot, centering it on the Coalition fleet. Several of the smaller ships—frigates and destroyers—simply no longer existed. The more damaged cruisers were already breaking apart, and the dreadnoughts appeared to be red-lining their engines just to maintain their position on the fringe of the event horizon. Cole watched in rapt fascination as the singularity's gravitational force ripped away the engines and pieces of the aft sections of the dreadnoughts...and vanished as suddenly as it had appeared.

"All helm functions restored," Wixil reported.

"Cap," Jenkins said, "in addition to the number of combat casualties, the survivors of the *Argyle* report that the captain personally piloted the ship into the Coalition formation. I also have casualty reports coming in from the rest of the fleet."

Cole nodded. "Make sure the admiral receives those. I'll review them once we retrieve our extraction teams. What's the status of the scout frigate that was trailing the Coalition fleet?"

Jenkins was silent for a few moments, Cole guessing he was scanning through incoming comms, "They report no damage, Cap. I don't think the Coalition ever knew they were there."

"And now, they're having problems powering life support, let alone sensors or weapons, so our scout frigate should be safe," Haskell interjected. "I regret the cost, but wow...what a weapon."

"Haskell..." Cole said.

"Yeah, Cap?"

"We're sitting on one just like it."

"Oh...yeah," Haskell replied, his voice far more subdued.

"Wixil, if you please, plot maneuvering orders for the battlegroup to approach Musilar Prime," Cole said. "Jenkins, my compliments to the admiral, please; ask him to have the remainder maintain overwatch while we move in to retrieve our extraction teams. Also, Jenkins, if you would, please have our stealthed scout frigate proceed with all haste to Musilar Prime to act as overwatch for the extraction teams until we arrive."

"Maneuvering orders ready, Cole," Wixil announced, "and distributed to the battlegroup."

"Fleet-wide orders from the flag," Jenkins reported. "*Haven* and her battlegroup will approach Musilar Prime to recover the extraction teams while the remainder of the fleet serves as overwatch and a reserve, and the scout frigate copies, reports it is moving."

"Engage, Wixil," Cole replied. "Let's go get our people."

CHAPTER THIRTY-THREE

Upper Atmosphere
Musilar Prime

Lieutenant Commander Jack Rodriquez was the pilot-in-command for Assault One, the assault shuttle carrying the first of two extraction teams to the target facility. If he were completely honest with himself, he felt a little antsy. This was the first op where the Captain wasn't hovering over their target like the Sword of Damocles, and he missed having the overwatch. After all, no one in their right mind would invite a reprisal bombardment from *Haven*; the video from Caledonia—almost five years old now—still circulated on the Galactic Datanet, getting new views by the day.

Oh, well...at least it was night on the side of the planet where their target was.

"Assault Elements, this is Alpha Leader," the wing commander for their escort spoke over their op channel. "Be advised: we have detected the presence of targeting radar and lidar. LZ may be hot."

Lt. Commander Rodriquez keyed his mic, saying, "Copy that,

Alpha Leader. May we ask you to handle any launch sites that announce themselves?"

"The CAG did order an air-to-surface payload for part of our load-out, Assault One," Alpha Leader replied. "I suppose we could launch a few if a hostile or two advertises themselves."

"We appreciate your sacrifice, Alpha Leader," Rodriquez replied and switched his mic from the open channel with their escort to the public address in the assault bay. "Good evening, ladies and gentlemen, this is your pilot speaking. Be advised that our escort has detected the presence of targeting radar and lidar. There may be hostiles at the LZ, so we ask that you keep your seat-backs in their upright and locked positions until we land, and prepare for a heavy welcome. Thank you for flying the unfriendly skies."

The assault shuttles and their escorts broke through the heavy cloud cover, finding themselves in the middle of a massive thunderstorm. If they had been restricted to the Mark I eyeball, visibility would've been—maybe—six inches, except when savage lightning bolts lit the sky like high noon.

"I wonder how the fleet is doing," Lieutenant Mack Bertram—the co-pilot—said.

Rodriquez shook his head. "That's not our problem right now. Fly the mission. Worry about them when we're back in black."

"Uh, Commander," Lt. Bertram replied, gesturing with his right hand, "it's pretty black around us right now."

No sooner had Lt. Bertram spoken than a bolt of lightning, five feet across if it was an inch, flashed right across the nose of the shuttle. The cockpit's flare filters kept the pilots' vision from being impaired, but it was still a startling experience.

"You were saying, Lieutenant?" Rodriquez asked.

"Roger that, sir," Bertram answered, his voice far more cowed. "Wait till we're back in black to worry about the fleet."

Rodriquez smiled at the young man's reversal as he minded his board.

· · ·

Minutes later, the target appeared on Assault One's sensor plot. Rodriquez switched his mic back over to the op channel and keyed it.

"Assault One to all elements, I have the target on my scope."

Rodriquez hadn't even released the mic yet when a flurry of dots erupted on the sensor plot, accompanied by the shrill squeal of the incoming missile warning.

"Missile launch!" Rodriquez announced into the op channel. "Multiple missiles inbound! Going evasive and launching interceptors."

Sweeping his fingers over the touch-sensitive controls, Rodriquez fired off half-a-dozen anti-missile interceptors and killed the shuttle's engines as he brought the nose down into a crash dive. Thank the stars the target facility was located in a hilly region and away from the cities.

The shrill squeal ended when the interceptors completed their work, and Rodriquez keyed the commands to bring the engines back online just as he noticed his co-pilot's hands getting a bit white-knuckled on the console. The engines engaged with no problems, and the assault shuttle leveled out a little over five kilometers above the deck.

"You all right over there, Lieutenant?"

"Y-yes, sir," Bertram answered. "I think so."

Rodriquez grinned. "Shit, son; that was nothing. Get the CAG to tell you the story of Oriolis VI sometime. The Captain's piloting makes mine look tame."

When Bertram slowly turned to stare at him with wide eyes, Rodriquez merely nodded, saying, "Yup. No joking."

Rodriquez directed his attention back to the op channel just in time to hear Alpha-Three report the final launch ending in a plume of smoke and a shower of debris. The up-side to the Surface-to-Air-Missile (SAM) launchers revealing themselves was that a couple of Alpha Wing were able to fly right over the target facility, their automated systems uploading high-res scans to the OpNet.

Rodriquez switched his mic over to the local channel, saying, "Pilot to ExCom."

"Go for Extraction Command," Colonel Deveraux—the new commanding officer of *Haven*'s embarked marines—replied.

"Alpha Wing uploaded high-res scans of the target to OpNet," Rodriquez said. "Thought you might like to know, ma'am."

"Good call, Pilot," Devereaux responded. "Appreciate it."

Rodriquez switched back to the op channel.

———

The two assault shuttles dropped into the courtyard of the military prison amid a hail of weapons fire from various emplacements as the escort wings settled into their air cover and superiority phase. Devereaux left two squads on each assault shuttle: one squad manning the assault shuttle's weapons and the second securing the shuttles. She personally led the primary extraction team.

The two extraction teams—Blue for primary, Gold for secondary—entered the facility and proceeded to their specific objectives. Gold Team's part of the plan involved destroying the on-site generators and feed lines from the local power grid and locking down all security stations. Blue Team was to take the shortest path from the courtyard to the cell block where their extraction targets were being held and evac them to Assault One.

Of all the adages passed down throughout Human history, few are more time and experience-tested than 'No plan survives contact with the enemy.'

———

The point marine on Gold Team turned the corner that should have revealed the facility's generators and walked right into what looked like a heavy weapons squad. That worthy didn't yelp in surprise (the first reaction that came to mind); he did, however, drop straight to the muddy grass, announcing over the team channel, "Contact front! Contact front!"

The firefight between the lead elements of Gold Team and the Coalition heavy weapons platoon was short-lived. The point marine saw to five of the enemy himself, taking three hits in the process, as his comrades moved up to engage.

Gold Team's commanding officer, Captain Shara Chakrabarti, arrived within seconds of the final Coalition soldier falling and took in the scene. She nodded and reached out to offer a commending shoulder tap to the point marine.

"Good job," Captain Chakrabarti said. "Excellent quick thinking. How's your armor?"

"Left arm holding at ninety percent, rear torso at eighty," the point marine replied.

Chakrabarti nodded. "Very well. Remember the regs; if any section of your armor drops below fifty percent, sound off and rotate to rear guard."

A lightning bolt lit the sky, and the facility lights around them flared to extreme brightness. Chakrabarti was just starting to shout, 'Run,' when the surge from the nearby lightning strike reached them. It sparked from the facility to the two closest armored marines, one of whom carried the explosives for the generators. The other carried the remote detonator.

Chakrabarti returned to awareness and pushed against the bone-deep throbbing ache across her entire body, forcing herself to stand. She saw her team arrayed around the blast point in an expanded form of the classic death flower, and she breathed a sigh of relief when she saw several of them start moving. Three of her team, though, would never move again, and one of them was the point marine she'd just commended.

At least one part of her objective was complete. The generators were little more than scrap.

———

"What do you mean it's empty?" Devereaux almost growled.

She hoped Gold Team was having a better time of it than they were. The facility's security force must've been holding some kind of drills, because Blue Team had engaged in a running firefight all the way to the target cell block, only to find the cell block devoid of occupants.

At least the facility's power was down now. The security force didn't seem equipped for blackout conditions.

"Colonel," the point marine almost hissed across the team's channel, "I don't have a stutter. Nobody's here, sir."

"Somebody find a...damn. They already cut the power. Nobody's searching the database now." Devereaux deactivated her mic and took a couple seconds to express her frustration in the most eloquent profanity she knew; fortunately, the armor was sound-proof. Then, she took a deep, calming breath and keyed her mic. "Okay. Fan out in fireteams. Search door to door, and sound off when you find them. Everyone have pictures and biometrics of our targets?"

Every member of Blue Team answered in the affirmative.

"All right. Go." Devereaux turned to her fireteam and gestured for them to head out.

Twenty minutes and six firefights with security forces later, one of the fireteams found the targets in the section of the facility used for solitary confinement.

"Assault One to ExCom," sounded over Deveraux's comms circuit.

"Go for ExCom," she replied.

"Don't mean to jiggle your elbow, Colonel," the pilot began, "but Beta Wing just reported a rather impressive convoy headed our way."

"Beta Wing will have to take out the convoy," Devereaux shot back. "We just found the targets and do not have a route out that's verified secure."

"Roger that, ExCom," the pilot replied. "Will advise Escort elements we need more time."

Devereaux didn't bother to respond. She turned to check the status of her people and the targets and saw the targets exiting their cells wearing the night-vision equipment Blue Team brought for them.

"We good?" Devereaux asked.

"One of the targets has a sprained ankle," a marine answered.

Devereaux fought the urge to growl. "Fine. Carry that one. There's a convoy on the way, and we really need to move."

. . .

Blue Team egressed the facility without further incident, and the torrential rain promptly soaked the targets to their skin. Gold Team was already back aboard Assault Two, casualties included.

Devereaux flopped into her seat and started strapping down once all of her people were secured, the assault shuttle shuddering through take-off around her. This certainly hadn't been the most auspicious start to her tenure as CO of *Haven*'s marines, but Devereaux was grateful the losses were as minimal as they had been.

CHAPTER THIRTY-FOUR

En Route to Gateway
  Cole's Day-Cabin, *Haven*
  1 February 3004, 16:23 GST

"Hey, Srexx?" Cole asked as he leaned back against the sofa.

"Yes, Cole?" Srexx replied via the overhead speakers.

"Did you manage to get anything from *Coalition Alpha?*"

"I managed to obtain a considerable amount of data from that dreadnought before it went into an emergency power state and ceased all functions beyond those of basic necessity. Before you ask, yes, the first data I obtained was the ship's navigation logs."

Cole smiled for the first time since leaving Musilar. "Excellent, buddy! Where's the Coalition capital?"

"It appears to be Carnelon, in the former Carnelian Bloc, but I shall copy these logs to Garrett for an independent analysis to confirm my findings."

Cole laid his head back against the sofa, smiling. "Well, that's a bit of a hike from Beta Magellan, but it's good to know."

"May I ask a question?" Srexx said after several moments of silence.

"Of course, buddy. Ask me anything."

"I find myself in a state I have never before experienced. Over the past couple of days, a small but non-zero percentage of my compute cycles has been accessing and scanning all available records of the people we lost in Musilar, specifically what information exists regarding who they were as people. Is this behavior aberrant?"

Cole sighed. "No, Srexx. I'd say it's one way you manifest sadness. The casualty list has been weighing on me, too. I can't help wondering if they felt the goal in Musilar was a worthy one."

"What criteria is used to evaluate whether our goal in Musilar was worthy?" Srexx asked.

"It's all subjective, Srexx," Cole replied. "I'm afraid there isn't a rubric somewhere for us to consult that will allow us to quantify how worthy a goal Musilar was."

"That...seems inefficient and imprecise."

Cole chuckled. "You have no idea, buddy. You really don't."

The hatch chime rang.

Cole didn't really feel like seeing anyone at the moment, but that moment had been extending since shortly after leaving Musilar and seeing the initial casualty lists. With a sigh, Cole pushed himself to his feet and ambled over to the hatch. When it opened, Cole found Sasha looking back at him.

He smiled and waved her inside, saying, "Hi. Please, come in."

Sasha nodded and stepped into Cole's day-cabin. Cole led her over to the sitting area and returned to the sofa. Sasha sat on the sofa with him.

"So, how have you been?" Sasha asked.

"I've been okay," Cole said, adding a shrug.

Sasha leaned her head toward her right shoulder just a bit and raised an eyebrow. "Sure you have. No one's seen you in two days. Only Srexx's word and the dispenser records have kept us from coming in here to make sure you're not dead."

Cole heaved a sigh. "Yeah. I guess I have been laying low the past couple days."

"It's time that stopped," Sasha said, her voice firm. "Come on. We're getting dinner."

"Srexx found the Coalition capital," Cole remarked as he allowed Sasha to pull him to his feet.

"Naturally," Sasha replied, pushing Cole toward the sleeping compartment that also held the shower. "If the data was on *Alpha*, Srexx could find it, but don't think you're going to distract me. Go shower."

The next day, Sasha came to Cole's office. She entered and sat in a chair across from Cole.

"Okay. People are responding to you. The mood on the ship is lifting, now that people have seen you out and about. So, we need to have a discussion. I don't know if you've thought about it, but we should probably have some medals and decorations."

Cole nodded. "You're right. Get Trask and Harlon, and ask Paol and Sato to conference in from Beta Magellan. We should have this worked out before we get back to Gateway."

Sasha stood. "Meet in the bridge briefing room?"

"Sounds good."

CHAPTER THIRTY-FIVE

Babylon Station
  Gateway
  8 February 3004, 15:57 GST

Victoria strode down the corridor, Beth and Jameson straining to keep up with her. Mr. Coleson had said it was urgent she meet him in the conference room as soon as possible but remained annoyingly vague about why. She'd left a grieving wife whose husband had just succumbed to his wounds, and if Cole's reason for summoning her wasn't more important than that, there would be some choice words exchanged. She didn't care how welcoming he'd been to her and her people. There were just some things a person shouldn't walk away from.

As she neared the hatch to the conference room, Victoria squared her shoulders, mentally preparing herself to scold Coleson for wasting her time. She slowed just enough for the hatch's sensors to register her presence, almost storming into the conference room as the hatch irised open...and stopped so suddenly that her closest confidants nearly ran over her.

No. It...it couldn't be. He was supposed to be dead.

A single tear escaped each eye and ran down Victoria's cheeks as she whispered, "Daddy?"

"Hi, Sweetheart," Thomas Rainier said, his own eyes bright with unshed tears.

Victoria crossed the intervening space in a blur and threw her arms around her father, clutching him tightly and releasing the torrent she felt within her. Beth and Jameson backed out of the conference room and took up positions on either side of the hatch, allowing father and daughter their privacy.

"I thought you were dead," Victoria whispered between sobs.

Thomas held his daughter just as tightly as she held him and kissed her forehead just like he did when she was little. "I know, Sweetheart. I thought I was, too."

After several moments, Victoria moved just far enough to look up to her father's eyes, asking, "What happened? How'd you get away?"

"I didn't," Thomas replied. "I was in a prison near the capital, scheduled for execution, when marines from Cole's ship came for me. I don't know how he found out I was still alive, but he brought a fleet all that way to pull us out and bring us here."

Victoria blinked. "He did?"

Thomas nodded. "He did."

Victoria pulled her father into a tight embrace again, her head against his shoulder.

———

"You did a good thing, Cole," Sasha said, as she and Cole watched a video monitor showing Thomas and Victoria leaving the conference room together, Thomas's arm around his daughter's shoulders.

"No, Sasha," Cole countered. "We all did a good thing. There was no way I could've pulled that off by myself, and I need to be sure the fleet knows that. I just wish the cost hadn't been so high." After several seconds of silence, Cole nodded and said. "Okay. Let's go. Our work here is done."

"She's going to want to thank you," Sasha remarked.

Cole shrugged. "Seeing them walk down the corridor together was thanks enough. Besides...I'd like to have dinner with you again."

"I like the sound of that," Sasha replied, grinning.

CHAPTER THIRTY-SIX

Babylon Station
Gateway
12 February 3004, 09:00 GST

It was the largest space aboard Babylon Station. When Cole had requested it be added to the design plans, several of Sev's team—including Sev—wondered why Cole would want such a large open space. No one wondered now.

People filled the space, sitting in neat rows for the most part. Each person had at least one family member with them, and in the very front row, a person sat with two children, a fourteen-year-old girl and her twelve-year-old brother.

At the front of the space, a small stage with a podium stood. On the left side of the podium (from the audience's perspective), there stood a table holding several scrolls secured by red ribbons and an array of small cases. At the appointed time, Cole stepped through the hatch and walked down the center aisle. Like every other spacer present, he wore his regular ship-board attire. He could've donned a suit tailored specifically for him that cost more than most people made in six months, but that wouldn't have been appropriate to Cole. It wouldn't have felt right.

The low-level chatter faded as Cole stepped up to the podium. He looked out over the assembled people and nodded once in welcome and greeting. Then, he began his prepared remarks.

"Thank you for being here today. We have assembled to inaugurate our own system of awards and decorations, and I will start by sharing with you a little about Commander Zara Khouri.

"Zara Khouri was one of our first citizens; a single mother of two children, she came to us from Iota Ceti. She loved space and starships, testing high for the aptitudes necessary to excel in ship-board placements, and she was first in line when I put out the call for crew aboard *Haven*. As our fleet expanded, Zara transferred to other postings, always striving to conquer the next challenge. She beamed with barely contained joy when I offered her a promotion to full Commander and her first command, the destroyer *Argyle*.

"Commander Zara Khouri conducted herself as the finest example of what it means to be both a person and a citizen in all facets of her life. She loved her career. She discussed and debated major policy issues facing our society, offering her opinion and thoughts in respectful, reasoned discourse, and there's no doubt in my mind that her first thoughts after waking up and her last thoughts before going to sleep were of her two children, each and every day. I would have much preferred to present this citation to Commander Khouri in person, and we must never allow ourselves to forget the sacrifice she made."

Cole paused and cleared his throat, then continued, "Attention on deck."

Every spacer and marine present snapped to attention. The civilians present rose to their feet alongside them.

"'For conspicuous gallantry, honor, and bravery while serving in combat as Commanding Officer of the destroyer *Argyle* on 30 January 3004. When faced with a failing ship that threatened the entire fleet, Commander Khouri chose to sacrifice her own life to give her fellow spacers the best possible chance at survival...all while dealing a critical blow to the enemy fleet. The sole person aboard, and with an engine core progressing toward containment failure, she piloted the ship as close to the Coalition ships as possible in the time available. Commander Khouri's actions dealt a considerable blow to the enemy fleet, ending the engagement and preventing further loss of life. At this time, I hereby name Commander Zara Khouri as the first recipient of our Medal of Honor and ask Lieutenant Commander Martin DeBlasio to present this citation and medal to Aliya Khouri."

Commander Khouri's first officer stepped forward, and Cole handed him a rolled scroll secured by a red ribbon and a case. He pivoted and walked in a measured cadence to the front row where Commander Khouri's children sat, extending the scroll and medal case to her daughter and oldest child. When Aliya accepted the items, he pivoted and stepped to an empty seat among the ranks of his former ship-mates.

Cole retrieved the next scroll and case, starting the next citation.

CHAPTER THIRTY-SEVEN

Babylon Station
  Gateway
  5 March 3004, 09:00 GST

At the appointed time, six delegates filed into the conference room. Each person represented a different system: Oriolis, Spark, Eta Anubis, Epsilon Anubis, Iota Anubis...and Tristan's Gate. Cole was already waiting on them. The delegates' identities and loyalties were previously confirmed through Kiksalik-assisted interviews.

"Welcome," Cole said, as he stood and shook hands with each delegate in turn. "I have received your letters of credence for this summit, and I accept them." The six delegates took seats around the table.

"The first topic we'd like to discuss," the delegate from Oriolis immediately stated, "is technology transfer upon formally establishing the federation."

Cole allowed himself a small smile, saying, "Yes, I thought that might come up. The answer is no." Every delegate bristled. "Beta Magellan will release specific technologies, in such fields as medicine and food production, but we will not—*I* will not—release any technologies that could even be tangentially related to weapons or drive systems."

"You would have us be *that* dependent upon Beta Magellan?" the delegate from Eta Anubis asked, almost a growl.

Cole shrugged. "You already are. You simply don't realize it...or perhaps refuse to admit it. The fact of the matter is, I have trust issues, and I do not believe that the wholesale release of the technology represented by *Haven* and its databases is a wise path to follow."

"Suppose we say there will be no federation without that tech?" the delegate from Spark asked. "What then?"

Cole laughed. "Then there's no federation. Your people came to me. The federation was never my idea, and you and your new system governments need to remember that. Your systems need Beta Magellan far, far more than Beta Magellan needs any of you, and people who believe I will allow the federation—if it ever exists at this point—to dictate terms to Beta Magellan aren't just mistaken. They're utter fools."

The delegates from the five liberated systems stared at Cole, and Cole felt a twinge of surprise that their jaws hadn't dropped. The delegate from Tristan's Gate—one Geralt Hanson, the former system president—simply sat back and enjoyed his associates' collective discomfort.

When no one spoke after several seconds, Cole scanned the faces looking back at him and asked, "So, would you like to take a break to regroup and write home for instructions?"

———

Cole entered the temporary quarters he'd been assigned aboard Babylon Station and flopped into a chair. The delegates had chosen to 'write home,' as Cole put it, and he wasn't looking forward to the delay. Heh...if it drew out too long, he'd just go back to Beta Magellan and let them wait until he gave enough of a hoot to come back. It wasn't like they could do it without him. Cole grinned at the thought. Well, they could, he supposed, but the Coalition would move back in within weeks—maybe even days—of Cole pulling his forces out of those systems. The true kicker was that those systems' delegates knew that, too.

Cole's implant alerted him to an incoming call from Sasha, and he smiled. That had been going very well the past few weeks, and he was glad he'd asked her on that first date. Accepting the call, Cole routed it through the overhead speakers.

"Hey, Sasha," Cole said.

"Hey yourself," Sasha replied. "Did the talks break for an early lunch or something?"

"Heh, not so much...no."

Cole could almost hear the groan as Sasha said, "Oh, Cole...what happened?"

"They went straight to demanding we share all our technology with them, and when I refused, they threatened to walk away from the talks and not found the federation. I laughed and said, 'Go ahead. It wasn't my idea anyway.' Well, there were more words than that, but that's the gist of it. I almost offered to pull our ships out of their systems, but I thought that might be going a little too far. They are supposedly writing home to see how their governments want to proceed."

"I don't blame you for refusing to share all the technology Srexx gave us," Sasha replied. "Some of that stuff is wicked scary."

"Tell me about it," Cole agreed. "I found schematics for a planet-buster bomb in Srexx's archives the other day. Almost scared my hair white when I realized what I was looking at. Can you imagine what the Coalition would do with something like that?"

"Nothing good, I'm sure. So...since the talks have kind of stalled, you free for lunch?"

Cole grinned, suspecting he knew what Sasha's plans for dessert were given the tone of her voice. "I do believe I have some availability in my schedule, yes."

"Great! When you're ready for lunch, just come on by. We'll order in." Sasha's voice was almost a purr now.

———

The next morning, the delegates sent messages saying they had received replies from their respective governments and were ready to resume talks. The messages struck Cole as a bit snippy, and while he realized one should never apply emotional content to plain text, he also didn't feel the same urgency about the whole federation idea that everyone else did. So, he thanked them for the update and left it at that.

That afternoon, Cole and Sasha were touring the new arboretum on Babylon Station when Sasha asked, "So, how long are you going to let them twist in the wind?"

Cole shrugged. "Not really sure. I know all of you said it was a good idea, but I'm really not seeing the benefit to Beta Magellan in all of it. I see only obligations and downsides. I mean, sure...we need to stop the Coalition, and this region of the galaxy does need stability. But I'm not all that convinced yet that Beta Magellan needs to be a formal part of it. I should tell them to form their own federation, and we'll be here if they get their shorts caught in a shredder."

Sasha snickered. "You realize any federation they form on their own would have zero credibility, right? They don't have the resources to protect themselves; why should anyone else expect them to protect others?"

"Not our issue," Cole countered. "I do not want us getting drawn into being who everyone runs to when they have a problem. Galactic threats, sure...we'll step in and help defend everyone, and I do see the Coalition as a galactic threat, at least a threat to Humanity. But I refuse to allow everyone else to drag us down to their level."

"Okay," Sasha said. "What happens when we encounter something we can't defeat alone?"

Cole sighed. "Then we'll have a problem. If we can't defeat whatever it is by ourselves, none of the systems that want to leech off us would make any difference. Heh...I wouldn't be surprised if they turned tail and ran at the first opportunity."

"Don't you think you're being a little harsh?"

"Nope. I truly believe that we are fundamentally on our own, 'we' being the people who've chosen to become citizens of Beta Magellan and its other systems. Sure, they'll nod and smile and act like they're assisting with our agenda...as long as they get what they want out of it. But none of them are our people, Sasha. None of them have stood up and said they want to be a part of what we're building."

Sasha stopped walking, prompting Cole to do likewise. She moved to stand directly in front of him and looked him in the eyes as she asked, "Haven't they, though? They came to you and said they wanted to join a federation with Beta Magellan—and you—at its head."

"And what was their first negotiating point? How soon they could get our technology..."

Sasha pursed her lips to keep from frowning. Cole had a point, even though she didn't want to admit it. Maybe it was just being raised as a daughter of one of the founding families of the Aurelian Commonwealth, but Sasha truly believed forming a new federation was the best course of action. She just didn't see a way to bring Cole around to her way of thinking.

Cole offered Sasha a slight smile and pulled her into his arms, holding her tight.

"It's okay," he said. "I get it. You're a Thyrray of Aurelius. I'm sure you are certain down to your bone marrow that a federation is the way to go. That's okay, too. It just so happens that I don't agree with you on that point. Are you okay with that?"

Sasha turned the question over in her mind, and the answer she found startled her. She wasn't going to give up her ideals, but at the same time, it was okay that Cole didn't agree with her. Besides, with the right words and enough time, she might even be able to convince him she was right.

"Yes," Sasha answered, leaning back just enough to look up at him.

Cole grinned and leaned in for a kiss.

———

The next morning, March 7th, Cole found himself once again in the conference room waiting on the delegates to arrive. They weren't late —yet—but he'd give them fifteen minutes past the scheduled meeting time, and then, he was gone...both from the conference room and Gateway. There was too much to do in Beta Magellan to waste his time with these people.

At five minutes to spare before being officially late, the hatch irised open, and Geralt Hanson led his associates inside. Cole stood and shook hands with everyone again, and they all assumed their seats.

"So, where are we?" Cole asked once everyone was seated.

"Well, I for one do not—" the delegate from Spark began, his voice almost a growl.

Geralt Hanson clearing his throat stopped the man's tirade before it even wound up to get started. The delegate pursed his lips and looked down at the tabletop.

"My fellow delegates heard back from their respective systems," Geralt said, "and they came to me to discuss the matter, claiming that my past experience with you gives me an excellent insight into your goals and agenda."

Cole lifted one eyebrow as if to say, 'Oh, really?'

"Yes," Geralt replied, "utter ass-kissers, the lot of them, and unashamedly so, but they do have a very good appreciation for the balance of power now. Their governments all agree they have no leverage to create a more favorable negotiating field and asked me for my opinion. This is what I proposed."

————

All news agencies received an invitation to attend a landmark treaty signing on 15 April 3004. The signing would take place in the Grand Ballroom on Babylon Station, and the signatories were Beta Magellan, Tristan's Gate, Oriolis, Spark, Eta Anubis, Epsilon Anubis, and Iota Anubis.

The treaty founded the Haven Protectorate.

RATE THIS BOOK

Did you enjoy this story? If you did, please consider leaving a review.

Reviews are the lifeblood of visibility for independent authors, especially on the eBook retailers. The more reviews a book has, the more visible it will be on the retailers' sites.

I appreciate all reviews...good, bad, or indifferent.

If you would like to leave a review, visit this book's review page (http://kfplink.com/p2i).

AUTHOR'S NOTE

27 August 2019

First and foremost, thank you for reading...both the novel and these notes! I hope that you've enjoyed reading this story at least half as much as I've enjoyed writing it.

This was possibly the most difficult novel I've written yet, and I wish I knew why. I'd like to say that the trip to Alaska finally happening (first started discussing it back in August of 2018) had something to do with it, but I was already having difficulty writing it.

My original plan with these novels was to be writing Book 5, "Solar Eclipsed," in July and then have everything finished and be working on other projects while each book released each month between July and November.

I like to paraphrase a saying that had to have come out of a military organization at some point, "No plan survives contact with life."

I'm looking forward to continuing this series, and I haven't forgotten my Epic Fantasy, Histories of Drakmoor. I'll be working on its next volume, "Archmagister," as well.

Thanks for reading these notes, and I hope you enjoyed "Haven Ascendant!"

TYPOS

Typos and little slips in grammar are the bane of any author. Unfortunately, they are almost impossible to eradicate completely. I can show you many traditionally published books—twenty years old and more—that have a 'whoopsie' here and there.

That being said, if you find a typo or something that seems to be an error in grammar, please do not hesitate to contact me at typos@knightsfallpress.com.

I will periodically collate any emails and produce updated PDF and eBook files, and I'll make an announcement in my monthly newsletter when the updates have been published.

ACKNOWLEDGMENTS

There's an old saying: it takes a village to raise a child. I don't know if that's true or not, but it certainly seems true where publishing a novel is concerned. You would not be reading this were it not for contributions from several people.

The editor of this work, T. F. Poist, deserves far more than a simple 'thank you' for her efforts with this work. Her time, knowledge, and expertise improved this work beyond measure.

Did you like the cover? The background image was created by Jakub Skop (https://www.behance.net/JakubSkop).

I'm sure there are many who will see this next paragraph and think, "Goodness, he's acknowledging his parents and grandparents *again*?" My greatest regret is that I cannot hand my grandfather, Bob Miller, a paperback copy of my novels. So, yes...the Acknowledgements page of *every* book I publish will have the paragraph that follows. Consider yourselves forewarned.

Without my grandparents, Bob & Janice Miller, I honestly don't know where I'd be today; my grandfather taught me to read and love reading, and my grandmother taught me to develop and exercise my imagination. This novel (not to mention my life in general) certainly would not have happened without my parents, Vernon & Judy Kerns.

ADVANCE TEAM

Whether you use the term 'beta readers,' 'eARC group, 'advance team,' or something else, it's very nice to have a group of people who want to read an advance copy and tell you anything you and the editor missed... because that happens. And it happens with *every* book.

Anyone willing to help me make my books a better product deserve all the thanks I can give them, including recognition here.

Fletcher Hawkins
Rob Law
Marti Panikkar

THE NOVELS OF ROBERT M. KERNS

For a complete and accurate listing of all publications, both currently available and forthcoming, please visit Knightsfall Press.

Knightsfall Press - Books

https://knightsfall.press/books

SO...WHO'S THE AUTHOR?

Robert M. Kerns (or Rob if you ever meet him in person) is a geek, and he claims that label proudly. Most of his geekiness revolves around Information Technology (IT), having over fifteen years in the industry; within IT, he especially prefers Servers and Networks, and he often makes the claim that his residence has a better data infrastructure than some businesses.

Beyond IT, Rob enjoys Science Fiction and Fantasy of (almost) all stripes. He is a voracious reader, with his favorite books too numerous to list.

Rob has been writing for over 20 years, and *Awakening* is his debut novel.

Connect with Rob at knightsfall.press.

f   facebook.com/RobertMKerns
a   amazon.com/author/robertmkerns
BB bookbub.com/authors/robert-m-kerns